Were she and Austin on the course of true love, or was it all just lopsided wishful thinking? She would give anything to have the strength to ask Austin that question – straightforward and direct. Looking out at the dark, perturbed she stared at her reflection. Maybe last night was the answer to her question. Sighing she closed her eyes, maybe . . . maybe . . . maybe . . . so what if he never expressed the depth of his feelings for her. His inability to express his love, if that was indeed his feelings, did not diminish or negate the realness of her love for him. Besides, if he never said, "I love you", would she stop loving him?

As they pulled into the garage, she wondered of the outcome of others that made it their habit of loving without the guarantee of ever being loved in return.

Resting against Austin's chest, Sedona took in his scent. Every morning she tried to make it point to wake a few minutes before he stirred. In some ways, this early morning interlude was even more sensual than their lovemaking. She felt as if she truly had him to herself- no internal unspoken demons or distracting memories to fend. Somehow the quiet seemed to assuage, at least temporarily, all of the reminders of the tenacity of their relationship. Silently reminding herself not to get too used to things, she closed her eyes and willed him to sleep just a bit longer.

A LARK ON THE WING

PHYLLIS HAMILTON

Genesis Press Inc.

Indigo Love Stories

An imprint Genesis Press Publishing

Indigo Love Stories
c/o Genesis Press, Inc.
1213 Hwy 45 N, 2nd Floor
Columbus, MS 39705

A Lark On The Wing

ISBN: 1-58571-105-5
Manufactured in the United States of America

First Edition

Visit us at www.genesis-press.com
or call at 1-888-Indigo-1

Dedication

To My Muse

A very special thank-you to my husband, Jesse; children, Jesse and Whitney; dear friends, Sharletha and Cynthia; and the supportive expertise and friendship of my attorney, Kenny Kirby and Lester Taylor, Publicist.

I would like to acknowledge the following individuals for taking the time to respond to my many questions regarding the various technical aspects related to this novel. Master Chief Hospital Corpsman Terry A. Woodcock – United States Navy, you've helped to create within my characters realistic dimension. Marshalena Delaney – United States Coast Guard, thank you for giving me an understanding of the U.S. Coast Guard's 'Search and Rescue' procedure. Tommy Foster, thank you for your New Orleans footwork. And a sincere thanks to stained glass artists Linda Abbot, Mary Ann Celinder – IGGA, and Kenny Torres – Delphi Creativity Centers.

PROLOGUE

"Happy Birthday!"

The fifteen brightly shining candles dancing on top of the home-made cake caught him by surprise. "Chocolate," he laughed as he took a swipe of frosting, "You wrote my name on it and everything." Leaning down to give his mother a kiss, he whispered a thank you. "You must be feeling better today, maybe all of that medicine is finally starting to kick in."

"I wish that I could take the credit, but you're thanking the wrong person, baby. Stephanie baked the cake."

"Stephanie!" Turning to his sister, he lovingly pulled her into a bear hug. "So that's what you were doing back in the kitchen this morning. I thought that you were mixing together some type of flour paste or the other for one of your wacky projects.

"Good, that's what I wanted you to think. I even had dad fooled."

At the mention of their father, Austin released his sister, and his expression darkened, "So was he staggering in or stumbling out."

"In . . . he just left a little while ago though, mumbling something about needing to catch a ride into Houston with Mr. Bogey."

"I guess today is my birthday then." Helping to reposition his mother's pillows as she hacked out a particularly rough cough, he asked, "So did he at least poke his head in to see how you were doing?" From the disgusted edge in his voice, it was apparent that he already knew the answer.

His mother, looking far older than her 33 years, ran a tired hand through her thin hair. "Austin, don't be so hard on your father, give him a break. He's still finding all of this a bit hard to take. Give him time; some of us just aren't as strong as others, that's all. You mark my words, he'll get back right. I know your father, deep down under all that pain is a decent man. You just mark my words."

"A decent man? How can you keep defending him? You can count the number of times in the past two years that he's even asked about your . . ."

"Let's take a look at that cake that Stephanie worked so hard on and drop all of this ugly talk," his mother interrupted as she glanced over at her daughter.

Austin, reminded of his little sister's presence, refrained from going on about their ne'er-do-well father. What was the point anyway, he was who he was – a good for nothing, lousy drunk. No amount of wishing or talking was ever going to change those dismal facts. If his mother and sister needed wishful thinking to make it through the day, so be it, but he refused to go through life setting himself up for one disappointment after the other, he only dealt with the facts. And the fact of this matter was that he, Austin James, was the man of the house-had been for a very long time. In a manner far too mature for any fifteen year old, he turned towards his sister and playfully tickled her sides. "So, when do I get to taste a piece of that cake? It's not going to make me sick is it?"

"No, it's chocolate."

"It's chocolate?" he mimicked as if her statement said it all. "Well, since it's chocolate, and made by a chocolate pudding pie, then I know that it has *got* to be good."

Beaming from ear to ear, his sister reached underneath their mother's bed and brought out two brightly colored packages, "Before we cut your cake, Mommy and I have something for you."

At a loss for words, Austin slowly accepted the gifts. Despite the fact that it was his birthday, never in his wildest dreams did he expect a gift, and certainly not two. Between his after school grocery clerk job and the little money that his dad didn't drink away, there was barely enough to keep food on the table, pay the bills and to purchase what the state didn't pay of his mother's cancer medication. "Mom, you did get your pain medicine, didn't you? I wouldn't . . ."

"Shh! Don't worry about me; the nurse came by with this week's supply. So, I'm fine," she gave his arm a reassuring pat. "Go on and open up your gifts."

Carefully peeling back the tape, Austin took his time in folding away the layers of tissue paper. It wasn't that he was trying to tease his younger sister, he just seldom received gifts and wanted to savor the moment; plus he knew that Stephanie would want to keep the paper. She liked to fashion flowers and butterflies out of any paper item that was brightly colored; the whole apartment evidenced her handiwork.

"Open the smaller one first," whispered his sister as she stood on tiptoes, peering over his shoulder, looking first at the gift, and then at her brother's face, "It's from Mommy."

Handing Stephanie the tissue paper, Austin opened the box top lid of what used to be See's Chocolates-Assorted Variety. Even though the candy was long gone, what was inside was sweeter than any piece of chocolate that he had ever tasted. "Mom, you're giving me your book? This is the one that Aunt Penny gave you? I thought . . ."

"I want to give it to someone who will appreciate it. You enjoy Robert Browning about as much as I do. I read his poems to you while I carried you; I read them to you when you were a baby. It got so, that at bedtime, you would take out the book and beg me to read you some more. In fact you still do."

As he leafed through the worn pages of the book, stopping at the poems that were his favorites, those that he could recite from memory, it dawned on him why his mother was giving him one of her most cherished possessions. It was her way of telling him that her time with him and Stephanie was drawing to a close. Swallowing hard, he somehow found the courage to look over in her direction. As soon as they made eye contact, he knew that his suspicions were correct.

"Come on, open mine!" Directed his sister, oblivious to the heartbreaking message being shared between mother and son, "And this time, don't be so slow."

"Alright, alright," again handing the paper carefully to his sister. The gift this time sat in a shallow handkerchief box. Raising its lid, Austin let out a low whistle. "Wow, Steph, did you do this?"

Nodding proudly, Stephanie grinned from ear to ear as Austin carefully lifted up her present. His sister, who was by far the most creative member of the family, selected his favorite Browning poem, "The Year's at Spring", from the poetry book. She painstakingly copied the text onto artist's vellum onto which she water colored a beautiful background. For the finishing touch, she framed the artwork with a remnant of gold thread found in her mother's sewing basket.

The Year's at Spring

The year's at the spring
And day's at the morn;
Morning's at seven;
The hill-side's dew-pearled;
The lark's on the wing;
The snail's on the thorn:
God's in His heaven-
All's right with the world!
-Robert Browning

CHAPTER ONE

"For crying our loud, of all days for it to rain!" Thoroughly exasperated at both the weather and the course that her carefully planned day was taking, Sedona quickly changed lanes as she seized an opportunity to maneuver her convertible forward. One thing that could be said about New Orleans rush hour traffic, with or without the rain, was that its pace aptly matched the city's famous moniker, "The Big Easy." *C'mon girlfriend, keep your cool*, she admonished herself. *While everyone else is driving as if it's Sunday in the park, your blood pressure is spinning triple digits.* After riding the bumper of the car ahead of hers for several blocks, Sedona nudged into an opening and finally broke free of the pack. If luck was on her side, she could just make the traffic light that was preparing to change its green arrow to yellow. Ten good seconds that was all that she needed. Despite the fact that there were rail tracks crossing the intersection, she was determined to take it all of the way. Just as she floored the accelerator, a city utility truck positioned further down in the adjacent lane, decided that he too wanted to make the arrow and jumped ahead of her. *Okay, don't despair, if we both hurry, the arrow is still ours for the taking. Come on truck – no guts, no glory. Pick up speed . . . c'mon . . . make the turn . . . make . . . .* Never had she slammed on her brakes so hard.

"You . . . you . . . idiot! Why didn't you make the turn?"

The truck driver, thoroughly oblivious to the fact that he foiled her strategy, returned her scowl with a broad grin via his rear view mirror. Never had she wanted to wipe a smile off of a man's face so badly. Taking a deep breath, she momentarily closed her eyes to regain control of her temper. *Get a grip, Sedona. That man is not even thinking about you, and you're allowing yourself to go off the deep end. Where's your control? Control belongs to you . . . remember promise #4.* Good Lord, when was the last time that she pulled that one out? It seemed like another lifetime ago, seven years to be exact, when the therapist encouraged her to write a contract to herself centered on a set of promises. At the time, her first thought was that she was being handed a load of 'psycho-babble' manure. The only promises that she was interested in making were that she would never again be so feeble minded and desperate for love and affection to fall head over heels *in* love. In fact, she was determined that the next time that a man came knocking at her heart, the blinders would be off, her radar calibrated, and the 'precede with caution' flag up and waving high. Humph . . . she must have *inhaled* and *exhaled* at least a half a dozen times since then, and now here she was again, back to reciting promises about control.

Ding . . . ding . . . ding! *Control my ass, I don't believe it! A train, a freakin' train. It would have to be today of all days.* Helplessly watching the railroad-crossing gate descend, she angrily banged the steering wheel when the truck driver ahead of her, ignored the flashing red lights and raced across the tracks. *He has the courage to beat a train, but couldn't make a turn on yellow.* Exasperated, she brought back her head heavily against the seat as she took in the sluggish speed of the train. With no end in sight, it was obvious that she would be stuck waiting for a very long time. *The story of my life.*

Sedona, determined to make the best of her lot, turned off the dashboard clock – no point of blaring reminders, and reached for her favorite CD. Maybe a little Lou Rawls would help to 'de-stress', she reasoned. So, with attention shifted from the ambling train to the music carrel, she flipped through an eclectic collection of about twenty albums. After searching through the music several times, she felt her fuse re-ignite. *C'mon I just played the darn thing the other day.* Remembering that she had taken the CD into the house the evening before to play while she e-mailed her *friend*, Austin, she dropped her head back against the seat at the thought of him waiting for her at the airport. *Austin, baby, I'm sorry. I know that you must be indubitably fuming by now.* "Indubitably," repeated Sedona aloud. In fact, fuming would be putting it mildly. Austin had little patience for triflers – those who couldn't manage time, money, and/or emotions.

At the beginning, she assumed that Austin James' pragmatic take on life had to do more with his years as a physician in the Navy than anything else. But as she had gotten to know him, she had come to the conclusion that in all likelihood, he had stepped out of his mother's womb focused and ready to do battle with life. In fact, his layette probably included a wristwatch, day planner, and the map of his life with all of its various paths and side trips marked out and brightly highlighted. Austin was about as military as they came – punctual, efficient, forever practical and at times, infuriatingly self-possessed. He was one of those people who without much effort, were always prepared, always correct, always . . . well just always whatever they are supposed to be, should be, or aspiring to be at the time.

Ordinarily 'perfect' people irritated her, they tended to be not only smug in their certainty of having gotten 'it' right, but they were also a constant reminder of her own imperfections. Until her divorce seven years before, her life seemed to be comprised of nothing but 'perfect' people. Both her parents and ex-husband were long standing members of the 'perfect' set. But Austin, 'emotionally detached' though he was, seldom made her free-spirit style seem less than acceptable. In fact, his amused appreciation of her spontaneity and colorful expressions validated what her mother often referred to as her 'attitude'. On the prerequisite flip side though, despite his seeming acceptance, she was never quite sure as to how Austin interpreted their friendship or level of commitment. She had learned from her ex-husband to make no assumptions concerning how committed a man is to a relationship. Hell, usually it isn't even *'how'* committed, but *'if'* he's committed.

With the train's end still nowhere in sight, she passed the time by touching up her makeup. Between God blessing her with clear skin and good looks, and her mother teaching her how to properly care for and protect her face from the unrelenting sun, she needed very little to enhance her natural beauty. From the satiny nutmeg complexion given to her by her mother, to the thick coarse hair gifted by her dad, she was an attractive composite of all of the pluses that her gene pool had to offer. For years, the one gene that she used to wish that she could have waved aside with a "thank you, but no" was the low resonating timbre of her voice. Often mistaken over the phone as her mother's, growing up, she used to try to raise its pitch a notch of two by adding a bit of perkiness. As an adult though, having come to terms with the fact that despite her efforts to the contrary, she would always possess tones of her mother, she tried to view the similarities as positives, and in some cases, even as her strengths.

Soft and sexy, that was her aim for the evening. Usually, she allowed her natural bent for the practical to rule her style of dress, another trait inherited from her mother, but not tonight. With muted fuchsia as her palate, she dispensed with the classic clean lines that filled her closet, and instead wrapped her Nubian thighs, breasts, and hips in a sinfully sensuous silk. Not quite the way Austin last saw her, that's for sure.

As Lou Rawls seductively stated his case, ". . . Cause I know what you want, yes I know what you need," Sedona sang in agreement, "Let me be good to you. " Almost as if on cue, the train's caboose passed and the crossing gates lifted. Gunning across the tracks, Sedona turned the corner and broke free of the pack as her mind turned to her very first encounter with Dr. Austin James. Sight unseen, intuition told her that there was more to the career navy man than met the eye. Braking in response to the cars ahead, she smiled as she recalled the beginning of their long distance friendship. Two Christmas seasons before, as part of a handmade Christmas card design project for her high school art students, she requested from the USO, a list of names of servicemen who would be away from their families during the holidays. After divvying up the names, she decided to send one of her own creations to the Senior Medical Officer. Inside the card, she calligraphied two lines from a Robert Browning poem, *God's in His Heaven – All's Right with the World!* and included her address. To her surprise, he responded a few weeks later with the complete poem from which the phrase was taken, thus the beginning of their friendship.

Twelve months before, while Austin was in town for a naval conference at the Earnest J. Morial Convention Center, they finally met face to face. Sedona found that her instincts had been correct. She immediately felt comfortable with him – a true affinity. It was as if they had always known one another. Austin's manners were impeccable, almost charmingly old fashioned, and she found herself being flattered by his thoughtful attentiveness. He seemed to enjoy introducing her to the couple that he was visiting, along with the other friends he had in the New Orleans area. They even spent several evenings with the family of her best friend and ex-husband's cousin, Mazey Matteson.

The visit would have been perfect, except for one omission; he never kissed her, never made any kind of move that could have been construed as romantic passion. So, six months later, when it became apparent that he intended to demonstrate the same type of restraint when he invited her to spend Thanksgiving break out at his San Diego condominium, she decided that enough was enough, no more waiting with 'bated breath'. It was time to fan the ardor smoldering under his controlled facade. And fan she did, to the point of starting a fire so intense that her carefully planned Thanksgiving meal was relegated to little more than a late evening afterthought. Her panties still went wet at the memory of the warmth of his hands slipping under her blouse. Despite the fact that Austin made love to her as if it were their last time, the holiday failed to provide her with the assurance that she longed for-the assurance that he felt for her as she did for him. She longed to feel that finally she had garnered an immoveable spot in someone's heart.

It was only while at the airport, saying their goodbyes, did he hint at how deeply she had touched him. Momentarily closing her eyes, she could still feel the tender strength of his embrace and quaking heart. She even remembered when it was obvious that neither of them wanted to be the first to part, the overwhelming emotion that flooded her soul when she looked up and met his dark gaze. Searching his eyes, her heart stopped at their undeniable sadness. Reaching out, she reached up and gave him the gentleness of kisses. It was her way of telling him that he possessed her heart.

Austin, in spite of that wonderful emotional connection, did not respond in kind. Instead, he immediately shuttered her out. His detached response should not have surprised her; it was typical Austin. Still in all, it left her feeling hurt, rejected and then angry. Also, it seemed so out of character with the rest of his personality. From their conversations, and her observations of him with others, she had come to know him as being not only thoughtful, but also tender and gently loving. Refusing to accept that Austin might not be interested in their relationship developing into one of permanence, that perhaps her destined role in his life was just to be that of a friend – someone to share the weight of the world; Sedona instead chose to conclude that some awful hurt, perhaps a past relationship was holding his emotions captive. Besides, she wouldn't know what to make of things if he viewed her as simply a friend. In terms of a man relating to a woman, its ambiguity ranked right up there with the word 'commitment'. If there was any kind of romance involved, a man very seldom refers to the relationship as a 'friendship', and definitely not if they were also enjoying sex. A woman on the other hand, had no problem with calling the object of her romantic affection a friend. In fact quite often, the deeper the "friendship," the better and more meaningful the lovemaking is.

In this area of their 'friendship', the caution flags were furiously waving. No matter how a woman feels during the lovemaking, in the end, there is no redeeming value in one day waking up to the realization that you're little more than just salve to an ego. Through most of her marriage, Gary viewed and used her as such. Despite the fact that Austin's sensuality sent her into throes both in bed and over the phone line, this time around, she wanted to be something more; she wanted him to want her in the way that *she* needed to be wanted.

Austin's letters and e-mail, although frequent, offered very little indication as to whether or not he desired to see their relationship progress to one of permanent intimacy. Despite the fact that their phone conversations and correspondences were always lively and candid, and neither shied from sharing their opinions on whatever topic was being discussed – it was increasingly obvious that Austin kept an important part of himself hidden. True, everyone had a dark side and very few reveal all of their idiosyncrasies, but Austin's brooding manner was more than occasional. It was such a part of his makeup, that in her mind, she had begun to weave a sad, teary account of his past.

Letting out a self-deprecating chuckle, she cautioned herself not to fall into her usual trap of deluding herself into believing that somehow she held the magic potion to mend everyone's broken lives. She had spent all of her childhood and a good portion of her adult life trying to fulfill the definition of "good daughter" and "good friend". Somewhere in her youth she had embraced the notion that with a little extra effort she could make everything all right for those who were close to her, and maybe in the process, even get them to love her. It wasn't until after her marriage fell apart that she had slowly begun to realize that other's problems were rarely about her. Therefore, the only consolation she could offer was to make herself available as a shoulder to cry on, or a convenient object to blame. Unconsciously giving in to the wave of melancholy that had managed to depressed her spirit, she found herself reciting,

> *. . . Through the sad dark the slowly ebbing tide*
> *Breaks on a barren shore, unsatisfied.*
> *A strange wind flows . . . then silence, I am fain*
> *To turn to Loneliness, to take her hand,*
> *Cling to her, waiting, till the barren land*
> *Fills with the dreadful monotone of rain."*

Quite out of nowhere, it popped into her head. Easily relating to its mood and spirit, she had memorized the Katherine Mansfield poem years ago. Well, not today, she told herself. If God is smiling down on me, then today's rain is going to have got to bring along with it, a bit of pleasure.

Exiting off the freeway towards the airport entrance, Sedona suddenly realized that there was a much more immediate dilemma. She had no idea as to which gate or terminal Austin was scheduled to arrive.

CHAPTER TWO

"Sedona Tinney, please pick up the courtesy phone . . ." Austin James impatiently glanced at his watch as he listened to his message being announced over the airport's intercom. Debating whether or not to rent a car and leave, he anxiously wondered what could be keeping his errant friend. Even with his plane arriving thirty minutes late, he still found himself waiting close to some forty-five minutes. Considering the weather, the wait would not have been so irritating, but it was Sedona's idea to pick him up. In fact, when he telephoned the night before to inform her of his change in travel plans, she was the one that insisted on meeting him at the airport.

Originally, he had planned on paying Sedona and his ex-navy buddy, Charles DuPree, a visit at the end of his leave. The first half of his leave he had set aside for his sister, Stephanie, who still lived back in their hometown, Galveston, over on the Texas side of gulf. She was battling ovarian cancer, the same horrible disease that claimed their mother thirty years before. Other than Steph's husband, there was really no other family around, at least none that he claimed.

As he watched a large family send off a loved one with a barrage of tearful hugs and goodbyes, he absently wondered how it felt to be so loved by so many; to leave a place knowing that your presence would actually be missed. Every time he left for deployment and looked out at the sea of families tearfully waving their goodbyes, he was reminded that his absence made little difference to anyone except maybe to the paperboy and only to him because it meant one less customer. He could be gone six months or six days, no one would notice, much less care. Yup, a busy airport was the last place that he wanted to be.

Turning his back to the demonstrative family, he glanced at his watch, after the four-hour flight, he was tired. From the moment he boarded the plane in San Diego until they landed, his thoughts kept straying to childhood memories related to his sister and mother. It felt as if someone had purposely opened a floodgate and was making him swim. Typically, he wasn't one to reminisce. It wasn't a stroll that he relished. His mind wouldn't allow him to preferentially discriminate between the bad memories and those that were good.

Staring out of the wide expanse of window at the wet tarmac, Austin found himself thinking once again about his mother. Not sure whether it was the taxing plane preparing to lift off that prompted the memory, or suddenly wanting to feel loving arms about him, he found himself recalling how she would diligently save a dollar here, a few cents there for their grand vacation out west. Whenever he or Stephanie felt down after witnessing one of their father's alcoholic tirades, she would pull out the jar where she hid their vacation money and help them count out their savings. As they counted, she would recount a childhood trip that she had taken with her Aunt Penny. Being swept away in a daydream, no matter how unrealistic, always seemed to give the three of them a bit of hope that the future was going to be wonderful and bright. He learned the hard truth about dreams when they used the money jar to pay for her cremation – some trip. Dreams were just like promises and to a large extent, people – you better not pin your hopes on any of them because you'll only wind up hurt and disappointed.

Maybe that was why he impulsively decided to change his plans and give Stephanie and her husband the vacation of their dreams. Even though his sister insisted that the remission that she was experiencing was permanent, his medical training made him fear otherwise. So while her health was holding out, he treated them to three weeks of sailing in the Caribbean. Both she and her husband were expert seamen.

Touched by her brother's generous gift, she insisted that he too do something pleasurable; perhaps spend a week or two with Sedona. "Surprise her with a visit, take her somewhere fun, do something out of the ordinary and spontaneous for a change." Stephanie genuinely liked Sedona. She had a way about her that left you feeling warm, cared for and loved. His sister defined this quality as earthy; he called it sensual.

Stephanie had heard him speak of Sedona from time to time, but she didn't really get to know her until one day, while in Thailand on deployment, he mistakenly sent one the other's package containing US designer goods purchased for a song. Sedona, familiar with the fact that Stephanie was battling cancer, sent along with the box, one of her hand-painted baskets filled with aromatherapy and herbal bath items. From Sedona's loving gesture, a true friendship formed.

Glancing around the terminal, Austin softly chuckled. It seemed that Sedona had a natural knack for cheering up even the weariest of souls. While he could always count on the unexpected when he was with her, there was something about her that was almost serendipitous. He sensed it even before he physically met her. When he received her initial Christmas card, he was intrigued by the poem that she calligraphied, "The Year's at Spring," it was the same poem that his sister had framed for his 15th birthday. The name, Sedona, also could not be ignored. To him, it was more than just an uncanny coincidence that the Red Rocks his mother spoke of when she recalled her childhood memories were located in the northern Arizona city, Sedona. The rocks, many believe sit on an energy vortex. Taking a small snapshot of her from out of his wallet, he smiled as he wondered if she was aware of the whirlpool of emotions that she induced. All at once, he realized just how much he was looking forward to seeing his long-distanced lover. It had been a little more than six months since she had paid him a visit, and if memory served him correctly, she was late that time as well.

Intently studying the photograph, Austin remembered how pleasantly surprised he was when he first laid eyes on her. He could not have dreamed of a woman more pleasing to the eye – from her deep set warm brown eyes, kissable lips, curvaceous body, to her soft wavy shoulder length auburn hair that always managed to seductively caress the sides of her face. This charming package was all wrapped up in silky smooth nutmeg brown skin. Not only was Sedona beautiful, as evidenced in her witty and soul-reaching e-mail, but also her captivating personality was full of intelligence, sincerity, creativity, spirit and insight. Scanning the terminal for her face, it dawned on him just how difficult it was to become annoyed with a woman who was as personable as she was beautiful.

Pulling into a parking space, Sedona frantically emptied her oversized purse as she looked for the piece of paper that contained Austin's flight information. Racking her brain for any remembrance of the flight and gate number, all she could recall was the name of the airline that he had flown in on. Well aware of the lateness of the hour, she decided to give up the search and grabbed her wallet and car keys from the mess dumped on the seat. Crossing her fingers, she prayed that she wasn't parked too far from his gate. Silently cursing the downpour and wishing for an umbrella, she sloshed through the numerous puddles that had formed on the pavement.

The fat, heavy raindrops drenched her dress in a matter of seconds. Any other time she would have accepted the fickleness of the weather and just enjoyed the walk in the rain. But, this evening was the exception. She had put considerable effort into readying herself for Austin's arrival. In fact, after her last class was dismissed, she had impulsively bought a new dress with the sole intent of wowing the socks off of Lt. Commander Austin E. James, MC.

"Boo!"

Feeling a pair of cold damp hands on his shoulders, Austin swung around in his seat with a smile. "Sedona . . ." his voice broke off as he eyed his tardy friend. "Good Lord, what lake did you fall into?"

Laughing Sedona self-consciously smoothed her dress, "I guess I must look a sight, huh?"

Austin, quickly standing, let out a soft chuckle as he placed his hands on his waist and appraised the drenched woman. Despite the fact that he couldn't have found her any more beautiful, he teased, "That's putting it mildly. It didn't pay for you to get dressed this morning, did it? You look like you've just stepped out of the shower."

His unflattering comment, although good-natured, was the last thing she wanted to hear. She would have much preferred a little carnal heat, perhaps a kiss and hug that rang 'I missed you,' loud and clear, or at the very least, a 'hello darling'. As she bristled, she looked up at the towering figure. "Believe me, after a tiring day at work, a nice warm shower is where I would be right now; that is if I weren't instead playing taxi in a damn monsoon."

Taken aback by the sudden change in her manner, it was Austin's turn to bristle, "If memory serves correctly, you volunteered . . . or should I say, insisted on driving out here. You know, I didn't ask you to pick me up. In fact, I told you that it made far more sense for me to get a rental car here at the airport, instead of waiting until I get to the hotel. As it is, I've already wasted almost an hour."

Not liking the course their conversation was taking, but not quite knowing how to stop it, Sedona felt involuntary tears sting the back of her eye lids. With pride in tact, she hissed, "Well, excuse me! Since it wouldn't do for you to do anything that wasn't thoroughly pragmatic, it'll make more sense for me to head back home and leave you to your own devices."

Emotionless, Austin shrugged, surveyed her face and stuffed his hands in his pockets. Leaving was the last thing that he wanted her to do; but as far as he could tell, he hadn't said nor done anything to make her angry. In fact, if anyone had the right to be upset, it should've been him. Allowing his initial annoyance to resurface, Austin silently made it clear that Sedona could damn well do whatever she pleased because he wasn't going to beg her to stay.

Waiting for a response, or any move on his part that would indicate that he wanted her to remain, Sedona momentarily hesitated. After scrutinizing his unreadable expression, she realized that none was forthcoming, so she turned and quickly made her way through the terminal towards the exit. Still hoping that Austin would follow and stop her, Sedona crossed her fingers and briefly paused as the automatic doors opened to the pouring rain. Wiping away tears, she wondered how things could have gone so terribly wrong so quickly.

They hardly even had a chance to say little more than hello. In less than five minutes, her hopes for a romantic evening had been dashed. Surely this wasn't the end. Jumping into her car, she wondered how she could have so terribly misread what she thought they had between them.

With one last furtive glance towards the terminal, she turned the key in the ignition – not a sound. Once again she tried to start the engine, still nothing. Unable to turn on the overhead interior lights and radio, she realized that the car battery was as dead as a nail – which hardly made sense. She had been gone only for ten, maybe fifteen minutes at the most. Today was definitely not one of her better days. Angrily slamming the door shut, she once again braved the heavy rain and made her way through the terminal towards a security kiosk.

After explaining her plight, she was assured that a safety officer would jump-start her car, but she would have to wait a while. It seemed that she wasn't the only driver who was experiencing car trouble. Just as she was thanking the officer for his assistance, Sedona heard a familiar voice.

"Sedona, what's going on?"

Turning to meet Austin's black, magnetic eyes, Sedona still angry, but trying in vain to hold her tongue, hissed "So now he's moved to speak . . ."

Choosing to ignore the remark that he had just overheard, the officer directed Sedona to listen for her name over the airport's intercom and quickly left the couple to continue their conversation.

"What was that all about?" Austin innocently inquired.

Crossing her arms against her chest, she made a point of meeting his gaze. *Good Lord, just when I thought that this man couldn't be any more infuriating.* "What was what all about? My conversation with the police officer or my remark to you?"

With condescending amusement, Austin casually placed his hands in his pockets and answered, "Oh, I know why you made your little dig. I gather that you're angry with me over something that I've said or done. But we can talk about that in a minute, right now I'm more concerned with why you had to seek the assistance of a police officer?"

It was obvious that he hadn't a clue as to why she was really angry. It was so typically male that it took every ounce of willpower to keep from laughing. Deciding to give him the benefit of the doubt, Sedona reminded herself that this was possibly a second chance to still make the evening work. Adopting a conciliatory air, she answered, "It seems that my battery has gone dead. Maybe I left my lights on, I don't know." Softening her tone, she continued, "Um . . . I guess I was just a little too anxious to see you."

Recognizing her olive branch, Austin penetrating eyes warmed as he studied her face. "You know, I've been looking forward to seeing you every since we tied up two weeks ago." Smiling he added, "I thought you knew that."

No longer able to maintain her angry front, Austin's words were like a sweet balm. Beaming, she reached up to give him a kiss. "Austin, I . . . Achoo! Achoo!" Unable to control a barrage of sneezes, she began to noticeably shiver.

Quickly handing her his handkerchief, he realized that not only was she soaking wet, but cold as well. In a manner that was both attentive and loving, he draped the jacket that he had been carrying across her hunched shoulders. "Here take this, it's no wonder you're sneezing. Not only are you soaking wet, you're freezing. If you're not careful, you are going to find yourself in bed as my patient."

Gratefully snuggling into the deep folds of his jacket, Sedona remained silent as she enjoyed a warm rush imagining how it would feel to be under Austin's attentive care.

Oblivious of her thoughts, Austin suggested, "Since the rain isn't showing any signs of letting up, why don't we head on over to the coffee shop. While you warm up, we can sit, do some catching up and listen for your name over the intercom."

"Ok, but first I want to stop by the ladies room and try to make myself a bit more presentable."

Smiling down at her, Austin gave a wink and pointed across the terminal. "Don't be too long. I'll head across the way, over to the restaurant." Watching her retreating figure, it was obvious where his thoughts were heading.

Looking in the mirror, Sedona grimaced at her reflection. What was once a very flattering mid thigh turquoise sarong, now looked no better than an expensive silk washcloth. No wonder Austin couldn't help but laugh, she looked as if she had rolled right out of the gutter. Not only had the water spotted the dress, but also in some places, the fabric was almost transparent. Every inch clung to her frame as if it had melted. Desperate to fix herself up, she turned on an electric hand dryer and directed its nozzle first towards her dress, then her hair. The difference the effort made was negligible, not even a fresh application of lipstick helped.

Giving up, she reached for Austin's jacket and placed the cotton fabric up to her face. The warm sandalwood scent that still clung to its' fibers immediately conjured emotions so strong, that they literally left her weak in the knees. She couldn't wait until she had him alone. Even though he mentioned staying at a hotel instead of her place – some 'gobbledygook' about wanting her to know that his visit was about more than just the physical aspect of their relationship, Feminine intuition assured her that she could change his mind. That was the easy part. After all, despite his pragmatic mind, he was still a man. She knew all too well that his cool exterior was just a protective cover for simmering emotions – not to mention the practical point that he had had just spent six months out at sea. Austin James was just as warm blooded as the next man, this she knew for a fact. What she had to figure out was much harder. She had to get under his skin, in his head and capture his heart. A week or two of pleasure would be wonderful in the short run, but what she wanted was Austin, *in total.*

As she slipped an arm into a sleeve, the wallet which he had tucked into one of its' pockets, fell open and onto the floor. Hastily picking the items up, Sedona let out a laugh as she noticed the snapshot that she had mailed a year before while he was on deployment. She had sent it to him on impulse after an especially delightful telephone conversation during which he mentioned a craving for crawfish, a gulf coast favorite. Remembering their conversation, the following day, she had her best friend Mazey take a picture of her eating a heaping platter of the steamy bright red sea creatures, and sent it to him via e-mail. Not wanting to add insult to injury, she arranged for a dry iced order to be shipped to him, all the way to Yokosuka, Japan. From the worn edges of the photograph, it was obvious that he hadn't just shoved it into his wallet and forgotten about it. Though pleased, she was puzzled. If Austin cared enough to carry her photo around, why was he so willing to allow her to leave the airport without a backward glance. Frowning as she carefully replaced the wallet back in the jacket's pocket, she reminded herself to pay attention to all red flags.

CHAPTER THREE

Sedona, glancing over at her passenger, couldn't help but smile as she noticed how Austin's imposing six foot three inch frame filled her small convertible. He was every bit as handsome as she remembered. In fact, he seemed to have fared quite well during their separation. The gray in his freshly barbered hair was a bit more pronounced, but it's affect along with the well-groomed beard that he was fond of wearing when on furlough, was very striking. Austin James screamed masculinity, from his dark brown skin to his soothing unhurried baritone drawl.

Momentarily locking eyes, Austin slowly winked and teased, "Do you always pay so much attention to the road?"

"I'll have you to know that I'm a very cautious driver, and am quite capable of doing more than one thing at a time."

"Oh . . . so, other than driving, what were you doing just then?"

Not wanting to let him know that she was checking him out, she coyly smiled, "Trying to read your mind."

Returning her smile, Austin, with a twinkle in his eyes responded, "All you have to do is ask, and I'll tell you whatever you want to know."

Afraid of the answers she would get, Sedona artfully shifted the conversation to a safer topic. "Why are you staying at the Saint Louis instead of with the DuPrees?"

"Well, I had originally intended on staying with them, but with my change of plans being so last minute, I didn't want to impose. Besides, Charles mentioned that the "Jazz and Heritage Festival" was this weekend. So, I'm pretty certain that they are going to be busy enough at their restaurant without having to worry about me. And you know Loretta, no matter what you tell her, she'd climb to the moon if she thought that it would make you feel happier and more at home."

Having met Charles and Loretta DuPree during Austin's last visit, Sedona understood his concern. They were by far the happiest and friendliest couple that she had ever met. Their infectious warmth even flowed into their popular restaurant, "The Blue Fish." Which, along with its' wonderful Creole cuisine, was the reason that the eatery was considered by many to be a French Quarter dining "experience."

Chuckling Sedona asked, "I know Charles and Loretta, how did you ever get them to agree to you staying at a hotel? I'm surprised they weren't insulted. Charles loves you like a brother, and in Loretta's book you can do no wrong. She is so protective of you that I think that if I ever got on your bad side, she'd put a *gris gris* on me."

Austin, laughing out loud at his companion's dramatic choice of words, found it difficult to imagine his dear sweet friend casting a voodoo curse on anyone. Speaking to his companion in military fashion, he playfully remarked, "Tinney, you say the damnedest things."

Dismissing his comment, Sedona continued, "You know that I'm right. Loretta clucks over you like a mother hen . . . and you know how hard that is, you're a pretty big chick."

Not holding back his laughter, Austin's pleasant voice filled the automobile. "Well, thanks a lot. Don't worry about Loretta though; she's going to get her chance to cluck. They made me promise to come by for meals and to stay with them for a few days."

Pleased to hear that Austin was going to be in town for a while,

Sedona debated whether or not to ask about his sister's well being. The night before, he had briefly explained Stephanie's condition and his change of travel plans over the phone. But she had noticed that at the airport coffee shop, when she had tried to bring the matter up, he quickly changed the subject. Deciding not to risk bringing down his upbeat mood, she discussed the jazz festival's all-star line-up and suggested that they attend the seven-day outdoor music event together.

As she pulled up outside the elegant Saint Louis, Sedona noticed that Austin made no comment one way or the other on her suggestion that they attend the festival. So warning herself to play it cool, she resisted the temptation of asking if he wanted her to accompanied him into the hotel. Prepared to simply wave a casual goodbye and leave, she was pleased when upon removing his luggage from the trunk, he suggested that they spend the evening together.

"I thought that perhaps after I get settled in my room, we could go over to the restaurant. Loretta would kill me if I didn't bring you over for dinner."

Smiling with what she hoped was nonchalance, she accepted his invitation and walked with him through the old world appointed lobby towards the large throng that had formed at the front desk. "Wow, look at the crowd, I wonder what's . . ."

Austin, glancing at his watch interrupted, "Either there's a convention in town or they're here because of the jazz . . ."

". . . festival," completed Sedona. You're probably right, it's a good thing that you have a reservation, or else you might've found yourself either sleeping in your rental car or on the DuPree's sofa."

Frowning, Austin glanced at his watch once again. "That still may be the case, I was certain that I would be here on time, so I didn't bother to guarantee my reservation." Pursing his lips, he prepared himself, "Oh well, I better go get the bad news." After speaking to a desk clerk, Austin's fears were confirmed. It seemed that not only had the hotel given his room to someone else, but along with all of the better hotels in the area, had overbooked as well. Outwardly unfazed, Austin returned to Sedona and humorously remarked, "Well, by default it looks like it'll be the sofa tonight, and a rental car won't be available until tomorrow evening."

Placing a hand on his arm, Sedona full of apologetic concern sighed, "Oh Austin, I'm sorry. This whole fiasco is all of my fault. If I hadn't been so late picking you up, then . . ."

"Nonsense, I've traveled enough to have known better. I've just had so much on my mind lately, I'm not thinking straight. I'm usually, how did you put it . . . much more pragmatic."

Fully aware that he was making a reference to the snipe that she had made during their earlier conversation at the airport, Sedona, without missing a beat patronizingly patted his hand. "I know you are honey, but don't be so hard on yourself. Try to remember that not even you are perfect."

By the twinkle in his dark eyes she could tell that he found her comment amusing. She appreciated the fact that he was willing to laugh at himself, many people didn't quite know how to take her sense of humor, but it was obvious that Austin rather enjoyed it.

As if reading her mind, Austin remarked, "Tinney, I hope that you realize that the only reason you're getting away with saying the things that you do is because you're so damn cute."

Despite the fact that she was caught off guard by his rare compliment, Sedona quickly sassed, "And here I thought that you were being nice to me because I'm your set of wheels for tonight."

Momentarily caught up in Sedona's easy humor and inviting beauty, Austin impulsively reached over and smoothed a wayward lock of hair from her face. It was the type of gesture that from any other person, she wouldn't have given a second thought. But from Austin, it was very uncharacteristic. And from the abrupt manner, in which he placed his hand in his pocket, she realized that it he was just as caught off guard by his actions.

Breaking the awkward silence, she asked, "Since there's no room at the *inn*, what do you want to do now?"

Reaching for his cell phone, he shrugged, "I guess I should warn Charles and Loretta that I'm on my way. It wouldn't do to just show up."

"No it wouldn't . . . but why don't you call from my place." Anticipating the ever-logical Austin to point out that the "Blue Fish" was right up the street, Sedona hurriedly explained. "I know that it doesn't make much sense to leave the Quarter to go over to where I'm at, but I really do need to change."

Eyeing Sedona's rumpled dress and mussed hair, he laughingly agreed, "I guess you do look . . ." Remembering how quickly he had gotten into hot water the last time he commented on her appearance, he quickly corrected himself. ". . . great, but if you insist, that's fine with me."

The distance between the French Quarter and the pricey neighborhood where her 134 years old town home sat was relatively short. Ordinarily, on a high school teacher's salary, the home would have been completely out of her price range. But thanks to a little foresight, her ex-husband's desperate eagerness for marital freedom and her divorce lawyer's finesse, the lovely digs were hers free and clear.

It saddened her that Gary still assumed that the only reason she so tenaciously held on to the charming house was because she had been advised that the property was a guaranteed investment. Despite the fact that she had spent the bulk of their ten year marriage, as well as her salary, lovingly restoring the house to its' former charm, he refused to believe that she sincerely viewed the elegant Victorian structure as being home – her retreat from the rest of the world.

One of the things that first attracted her to the neighborhood was its convenient proximity to the vibrancy of the French Quarter. When the weather was clear and the traffic flowed, it took little more than fifteen minutes – twenty at the most, to reach it from the heart of the city. However, this evening proved to be quite different. By the time they had left the hotel, the rain had turned into a torrential downpour, bringing traffic to a snail's pace.

When they finally arrived, Sedona's nerves were understandably frayed. Along with having to maneuver through flooded streets and negotiate around stalled vehicles, it seemed as if every lunatic in town had chosen the evening to take a drive. Adding to her level of stress was Austin, her stoic passenger, who mutely clutched the passenger armrest the entire trip. Even though he had not verbally criticized her driving ability, she could tell from his silent preoccupation with the needle on the speedometer and her use of the accelerator and brake, that he had serious concerns regarding her ability to handle a moving motor vehicle.

Sedona, dropping her keys into the handbag that was laying on the seat behind her, quickly stepped out into the garage, slammed shut the car door, and walked over to where her travel wearied passenger was unfurling his long legs. Reading the expression written on his face, she fully expected him to drop to his knees and kiss the ground.

Noticing her perturbedly scrutinizing his face, Austin quietly closed his door, "What are you staring at so hard? Has my hair turned completely gray yet?"

With a raised brow, Sedona folded her arms across her chest and matched his tone. "No, your hair is fine. I'm just trying to understand why a forty-two year old man who has braved battle and the rough high seas is so . . . so old womanish when it comes to taking a simple car ride."

"A death ride would be a more apt description," Austin dryly corrected, "Do you realize that in the span of 35 minutes you cut off two drivers, ran a red light, changed radio stations no less than fifteen times, all which I might add, while talking non stop."

"When I went through that last intersection, the light was still yellow. Something you would have noticed that if you weren't so busy keeping track of the number of times I touched the radio dial."

Leaning against the car, Austin let out an amused smirk that only served to further fuel her fire.

"You know, the only reason why I rattled on like a Chatty-Cathy was because you were making me nervous sitting there like some . . . some pillar of salt."

Once again charmed by his lady friend's penchant for the dramatics, Austin stifled a chuckle. "Sedona, someone had to watch the road, you were switching radio stations like a mad woman. What were you searching for anyway?"

"I wasn't searching for anything. Do you know how frustrating it is to carry on a conversation with someone who is bent on giving only one word answers?"

Unable to resist one last jibe, Austin quickly shaking his head glanced her way and answered, "No, I haven't had that pleasure . . . especially not today."

Sedona, well aware that Austin was referring to her, felt the corners of her mouth tug. Doing her best to try to hide the uncontrollable smile that had formed on her lips, she walked to the rear of the car. "Well . . . Mr. Funnyman; even you can't argue with the fact that I got us here in one piece, safe and sound."

Walking over to where she stood, Austin gently laughed, "Well . . . I guess it pays for one to say their prayers."

Just as she was about to comment, a bolt of lightening struck right outside the garage causing the lights to first flicker, then go completely out. When they came back on, Sedona found that she had unconsciously inched herself towards Austin. Patting the hand that she had inadvertently laid on his shoulder, he suggested that they collect their things from the car and head inside. Agreeing, she tried to open first the driver's door, then the passenger's side, but to her dismay she quickly realized that they both were locked.

Austin, as he unsuccessfully made the same attempt, checked the windows for even a fraction of space to finagle a wire or clothes hanger. Seeing none, he inquired if she had a second set of keys hidden away somewhere.

Again trying the door handles as if she could will them to open, Sedona answered, "My only extra set is upstairs in my bedroom. Usually I'm quite careful."

"You mean you don't keep a set with neighbors or hidden somewhere in a . . . a flower pot or urn?"

"I don't own an urn." Frantically thinking aloud she placed her hands on her hips, "Now, Mazey has the keys to the house, but she's out "antiquing" this weekend so that's no good, but . . ." Staring intently at Austin, "If you're game, the bathroom window upstairs is unlock."

"If I'm game? I know that you're not suggesting that I shimmy up the drainpipe. It's pouring rain."

"That's the only way I see it. The front, back and garage doors are dead bolted, and the windows are all locked."

"Why can't we just break out a first floor window?"

"No! Most of the glass in this home are the original panes and it would be heartbreaking if I was forced to break any of them simply because I was careless."

"Well . . . why we don't call a locksmith, I got my cell phone right here."

"We could, glancing at her watch, but on a night like this, it will take hours."

Sighing Austin wanted to wait no more than Sedona. He was beginning to feel not only tired, but hungry as well. "Do you at least have a ladder?"

"Yes I have a ladder, but it'll only reach a part of the way up." Thinking she continued, "But you could hoist me up. There's a window sill I can boost myself up onto."

Not liking the idea, Austin once again mentioned his reservations, "That sounds very dangerous to me. What if you fall?"

"Psst! I won't fall; you won't let me. Besides, there's a tree right where we'll put the ladder – we can use it for balance. Come on; let's give it a try. I'm sure it'll work."

Half convinced, Austin took down the ladder and they walked to the side of the house. "You still want to do this?"

"Positive."

With her dress already clinging to her skin, Sedona climbed the ladder, closely followed by Austin. Just as he was preparing to lift her up to the sill, a bolt of lightening flashed across the sky. As a natural reaction, Sedona quickly stepped down a rung and braced herself against his hard chest. Instinctively putting his arms protectively around her, Austin looked deep into her eyes. Despite the cool rain, she felt quite warm. Swallowing hard, Austin leaned against a tree limb, repositioned his footing and huskily asked, "Do we go on?"

Nodding, Sedona allowed herself to be effortlessly hoisted up towards the window. Grasping hold of the sill, she quickly shoved open the window and deftly crawled in. Looking out, she smiled down and waved, "Told you we could do it . . . I'll go down and let you in through the garage."

Shaking his head, he folded the ladder and walked back to the car. Inside the garage he was met by Sedona, triumphantly smiling. Opening the convertible with her spare key, she eyed her companion who was now drenched, "It looks like both of us are going to need to shower and change."

Removing a stray leaf from Sedona's hair, Austin responded, "Knowing you as I do, I'm sure that you getting some perverse delight out of the fact that . . .

"That now you too look like you've fallen into a lake?" Sedona impishly offered. "Yeah, I am."

CHAPTER FOUR

Pausing to listen to Austin move about the guest bedroom, Sedona leaned against the adjoining wall and closed her eyes. Used to the usual pin drop stillness of her house, she found his presence very comforting. Concentrating on the sound of his movements, she toyed with the idea of slipping into his room wrapped only in her terry cloth towel. How he ever managed such cool, calm and collectiveness, she'll never know. Any other pair of lovers who had been separated for six months would have been all over the other before they even made it to the car. Not Austin, a kiss and a hug when she joined him in the café at the airport were the best that he could muster. If he were any other man, she would assume that he was playing some sort of mind game. As she crossed her arms, she reminded herself that Austin was about as average as a celibate Martian. Even if her dinner attire consisted solely of a thong bikini, a see through brassiere, and spike high heel shoes, Austin would still insist that they spend the evening with Loretta and Charles.

Startled at the sound of his bedroom door suddenly opening, her heart caught in her throat. For a brief second she wondered if their thoughts had finally wandered down the same path. Listening at her door with the romance writer's bated breath, she irritatingly stuck out her tongue as she heard his footsteps retreat down the stairs.

Well Mr. James, I'm not going to allow you to escape my snare so easily. Tossing aside the ankle length skirt she had initially planned on wearing, Sedona opened her closet and replaced it with a flirty mini. After a quick perusal through a dresser drawer, she donned a delicate low cut cropped hand crocheted pink sweater. Shaking her hair free from its loose topknot, she deftly framed her soft auburn waves around her face.

Critically assessing her oval face in the mirror, she reached for her makeup and applied a bit of eye shadow and blush, and a touch of lipstick, followed by a quick dusting of face powder. Satisfied at the reflection staring back, she took a deep breath and rubbed the palms of her hands against the fabric of her skirt. *Not bad for a thirty-seven year old woman.* Walking that fine line between looking flirtatiously sexy and seductively sensual, she debated whether or not to reveal a bit of her breast's soft curves by unfastening the top two buttons of her sweater.

Sedona, well aware of the benefits of occasionally playing the role of a coquette, hastily slipped off her sweater and rifled through her lingerie chest until she found an intricately laced bra in almost the exact shade of rose as her sweater. With a mischievous smile, she refastened the sweater's buttons leaving the top two undone, but not before spraying the floral scent of a favorite cologne across her hair and shoulders. When dealing with Austin, she had to solicit help wherever she could find it. So, halfway out the door, she reached for the bottle a second time and applied a bit of fragrance to the pulse points between her breasts and inner thighs; after all, a little wishful thinking never harmed anyone.

Quietly sitting on the bottom step, Sedona was offered an opportunity to observe Austin unnoticed. He was sitting on the window seat that looked out onto the side garden listening to the soothing sounds emanating from her small wooden 'rain box'. The small metal balls softly pinging against the set of chimes that sat at the bottom of the box, blended surreally with the sound of the rain still falling outside. Sedona noticed not for the first time that he appeared tired and worn. Even though she had never seen him look so vulnerable, he still exuded a sexy uncontrived virility that left little doubt that although he was worn out, he was still was very much in control. Not sure whether or not it was the way that the brightness of his crisp white shirt burnished the rich brown tone of his skin to a warm glow that caused her to almost taste the sandalwood cologne that he was fond of wearing, or, whether or not it was the way his garment's military crease coursed along the taut muscles in his legs and arms and across his broad shoulders. It was impossible to say. The appeal of Austin James was a combination of all of those things and many other intangible traits that were difficult to express, but impossible to overlook.

Once again, her eyes rested upon the faint worry lines that creased his temple and added to his brooding dark expression. How she wished that she could take him into her arms and kiss away all of the buried pain. Surprising both herself and Austin, she heard her voice offer, "Why don't you stay here tonight?"

Brought out of his reverie, Austin met her gaze with an unreadable dark expression.

Before he had a chance to object, she hurried, "I mean . . . come on, it's not as if this is our first time together, plus if you think about it, it makes the most sense. The rain doesn't show any signs of letting up, so it'll take us forever to drive back down to the Quarter. Then we'll have to find a place to park and walk through God knows how much water. Besides . . ." she continued as she joined him on the window seat, "You look just plain ol' dog tired."

Thoughtfully surveying her face, he was struck by the genuine sincerity of her offer. Everything about her was so soft, comforting and easy. Her inner peace at that moment was so palatable that it took everything he had to refrain from reaching over and laying his head on her breasts. Keeping his thoughts to himself, he offered a slow smile, "So, I look not just tired, but dog tired huh?"

. "So what do you say?"

"Thank you."

As their eyes held, she knew before ever feeling his lips brush against hers, that he was going to kiss her. *Finally*, she silently screamed. Pressing her hands against his chest, she was surprised and more than a little disappointed when he did not offer the kiss that she expected . . . wanted, but abruptly stood and gave her hand a pat. "I'll stay only on one condition, you allow me to scare something up for supper?"

"Okay, sounds great," after all, what else could she say. It was obvious that demonstrative affection was not at the top of his 'to do' list. "I went grocery shopping last night, so we shouldn't have any problems finding something to cook."

Leading the way to the kitchen, Sedona opened the refrigerator. But, before she had an opportunity to suggest fixings for a meal, Austin taking her hand, led her over to the azure blue tile counter that encircled the kitchen work area and pulled out one of her winsomely hand painted bar stools. "No, I don't think that you understand, dinner is my treat. I may not be a *stewburner*, but it doesn't mean that I don't know my way around a galley."

Sedona watched with combined amusement and interest as Austin deftly moved about the kitchen. Remembering their autumn visit out in San Diego, she recalled the appealing meal he "threw" together following one of their late night outings. Tonight, she had no doubt that he was going to whip up . . . or as he put it – scare up something as equally wonderful. Noting how he took care in selecting the proper utensil to peel and de-vein a colander of Gulf shrimp, it was obvious that Austin enjoyed cooking as much as she. And, the smile he flashed when he spied the steamer also let her know that he appreciated what some would term her "gourmet kitchen."

When her ex insisted that they outfit the kitchen with only the best in appliances and other appointments, she thought that it was just another extreme example of Gary's penchant for spending money. When they first bought the home, she with newlywed romanticism envisioned the two of them side by side lovingly restoring each room as they planned their future. But it quickly became apparent that Gary had another, less idealistic idea in mind. Pointing out the immeasurable business benefits of using the house as a working model for his architectural design ideas when they entertained potential clients, Gary made it clear that he viewed their diamond in the rough as being more than just their retreat from the rest of the world. So, within hours of closing on the property, work crews were busy wielding their hammers and sanders.

Surveying her surroundings, Sedona, despite her initial feelings had to give Gary credit. She would be hard pressed to find many other architects who were as talented and gifted. Without sacrificing any of the home's Victorian charm, he had managed to innovatively update its space. Skylights were unobtrusively added and walls strategically removed to open up rooms whose beautiful carved woodwork and burnished floors were previously hidden. Only after removing several decades' worth of paint from two century-old fireplaces did they discover that the mantles and hearths were fashioned from intricate inlaid marble.

While Gary dealt with the technical aspects of the renovation, her mind went wild with decorating ideas. With a generous budget and her panache for color and style, she carried the home's updated Victorian styling to the windows by creating beautiful stained glass treatments for the top pane of each casement. Appreciating the Victorian's love of fanciful patterns in rich jewel tones of color, she selected rugs, overstuffed upholstery, pillows, and window seat cushions that carried the theme throughout the house with seemingly effortless elegance.

In the kitchen area, as well as out on the patio and in her studio, she mixed Victoriana with upbeat "whimsy". The combination of her interior design ideas and Gary's architectural work proved to be a resounding success, as evidenced by a spread in *Architectural Digest* and the *Times-Picayune*.

All of the attention did not come without a price though. In order to maintain their promising position in New Orleans' *haut monde*, she had to embrace her husband's definition of a "good wife." A role, which explained to her by one of New Orleans' grande dames; her mother-in-law, included learning how to be the perfect hostess. Being the eager young bride, she wanted more than anything to not only please Gary, but to "earn" his love and respect.

So, she immersed herself in numerous cookbooks, even taking time off from teaching to enroll in The Culinary Institute of New Orleans. To her surprise, not only did she enjoy cooking, but also she discovered that she was quite good at it. Parlaying her talents, personable charm and natural good looks to his business' advantage, Gary insisted that they host a continuous stream of dinner and "after" parties, soirees and informal working brunches. While Gary savored every morsel of their increasingly pretentious and superficial way of life, she grew to loathe the shallow "friends" and the consuming effort it took to simultaneously "keep up" and stay true to her values and convictions.

She did not realize just how much she resented their lifestyle until a symphony after-party that they were hosting. The gathering was made up of their usual guests that included the requisite New Orleans in-crowd, several of the firm's key clients and business associates, a few of Gary's family members and even fewer of her friends. As usual, she spent the evening making her obligatory round about the room while stopping to check on the hired servers and kitchen help. As she paused to make small talk with several of the guests that her husband had made a special point of mentioning at the party's start, she noted how flawlessly she was able to carry on an absolutely meaningless conversation with a group of women who were narcissistic to the point of being comical.

Ordinarily she would not have sought out their company, and she had no doubt in her mind that likewise, they would not have given her the time of day if she had not been Mrs. Gary Chandler, the poor clueless wife featured in many of the rumors that they floated about town regarding Gary and other women.

". . . Sedona?"

Brought back to the present, she offered an embarrassed smile, "I'm sorry . . ."

Leaning across the counter, Austin playfully teased as he swatted her arm with an oven mitt, "The next time you take a trip, let me know so that I can pack you a lunch. You were miles away."

"Years away . . . Austin, have you ever been out to one of the casinos?"

"I haven't visited any over on the river, but I've been down to Rio and out to Vegas a couple of times. Why?"

"No particular reason, I guess my mind is just wandering all over the place . . . the first time I visited a casino, I was mesmerized. You know – caught up in the lights and sounds. It wasn't anything like what I had imagined. Everyone just seemed to be so focused on winning at whatever game they were playing."

Chuckling Austin quipped, "Well . . . yeah! Why else are they there? The whole point of going is to win money, and hopefully a lot of it."

"I know, but I just found it fascinating to watch how each player had his own method of playing. Some would only play a certain "lucky" machine while others would go from aisle to aisle trying them all. Every one of them desperately wishing that the next pull on the lever would be the big win. You know, it's kind of easy to understand how people get caught up in the excitement of it all."

As the quick dicing sound of Austin's knife falling against parsley, onion, celery and garlic filled the quiet that had lapse between them; Austin tried in vain to figure out where Sedona was going with her comments. "You're not trying to tell me that you're a closet gambler, are you?"

This time it was Sedona's turn to chuckle, "No, no silly . . . I was just thinking of how so many people fall for what they think is gold, only to find out that it's just . . . just . . ."

"Pyrite – fool's gold," supplied Austin.

"Yeah, exactly. Take the casino for example, you look around, it seems as if everyone's winning – having a good time. But, if you stop for a minute and take a good long look through all of the hazy cigarette smoke, you see that the smiling hostesses that are eagerly plying you with their "complimentary drinks" and the rolling money changers who make certain that you won't be inconvenienced by having to leave your spot in front of the slots, are all just part of the artificial glitter."

"Selecting an iron skillet to prepare a roux for the vegetables he had just diced, Austin curiously asked, "So what got you thinking about casinos?"

"Well, I was noticing how you seemed to really enjoy tooling your way around the kitchen. Gary just enjoyed putting it on display and being part of the show. Just to show off this place, we constantly use to throw elaborate dinner parties inviting all of . . ." feigning an affected southern accent she continued, "New 'Awlins who's who". Gary would use the excuse that it brought in business, but I think that he was addicted to the contrived energy that sort of party creates."

Continuing to work over the stove, Austin shrugged, "There's nothing wrong with throwing a party every now and then, but having never met the guy I take it that there was something more." Looking up, he teased, "And I bet it has something to do with casinos."

"Ugh!!" she growled in pretend frustration. "I've given you more credit, but at times you are thoroughly the typical male."

"Thank you . . . I think."

"Austin, don't you get the connection? The lure of the casino has the same soulless seductive pull as the high-living, partying lifestyle. And my playing the role of the perfect hostess was no different than being a . . . a . . . casino barmaid."

Shaking his head in amusement, Austin laughed, "Sedona, isn't that stretching things a bit? You should stop beating up on yourself for being human. Believe me, making mistakes and bad choices are things that we all are guilty of at one time or another . . . boy, don't I know that first hand. Besides, I've found most casino barmaids to be pretty darn cute."

Quirking a brow, Sedona's gaze absently fixed on Austin's back as he returned his attention to the stove. Gary was as different from Austin as night was from day. While Austin often proved to be an enigma, with Gary what you saw was basically what you got. That even proved to be true in their relationship. From the very start, it was clear that Gary seldom compromised. Anything that he felt like saying or doing, he did with no apologies or excuses. When they first met, she found what she mistook as being simple forthrightness, very appealing. But over the course of their ten-year marriage, she realized that his unrestraint was just a manifestation of his blatant self-centeredness.

At the time though, Gary was like a refreshing breath of life. She had spent most of her life in a college town in Nebraska, where her parents taught at the state university. Both her mother and father were highly recognized experts in their fields of study and devoted all of their energy and time into writing and research. Always feeling either like an irritant or disappointment, growing up she would despairingly refer to herself as their "subject" gone badly. She could still remember scouring her father's psychology and her mother's anthropology articles to see if her name appeared as a research reference.

Since they were always so submerged in their work, she would often be left to her own devices. In the summers, her mother would be off to some exotic location on one dig or another. So, in order not to burden her father, she would be sent off to a special interest camp, or worse yet . . . forced to tag along behind her mom. The few times she did go along, she always without fail would do something to irritate her mother and get sent home.

Irritating her mother wasn't very difficult. They had two very different personalities. Mother hated conflict or dissension of any sort, so when Sedona disagreed or voiced an opposing thought she would shut her out by ignoring her. Dad was altogether different. She frequently sensed that he appreciated her wit and opinionated comments, even taking some delight in their often times spirited debate. But as she grew older, she realized that he was becoming increasingly frustrated in the fact that she had slowly begun to formulate a different "vision" for herself than his plans for her future.

Ever since she could remember, he had studiously enrolled her in various classes that offered her glimpses of the world that was awaiting her. Early on she realized that her dad did this in part to challenge and broaden her scope, but he also was well aware of the unhealthy tension that always seemed to shadow her relationship with her mother.

Half smiling she humorously thought that Daddy and his classes were his own undoing. For it was through one of those courses that she discovered that she had a natural talent for expressing herself creatively. Art became her passion, the one thing that kept her company through the all too often lonely days. It was how she respectfully screamed out her frustrations at her mother, and how she cried over so miserably disappointing her father.

Dad made no bones about telling her that he thought that majoring in art was a waste of a good college education. To him, art was something that you did on the side. Closing her eyes, she could still hear his words, "Sedona, I've always given you credit for being too bright to do something so foolish. Mark my words; you'll regret the path that this . . . this whim of yours will lead you. And when you do, expect to hear, I told you so."

It wasn't that he didn't think that she had talent. In fact, despite his prediction of doom, he demonstrated that he rather appreciated her talent and enthusiasm – so much so that he agreed to provide for her studies. On the other hand, her mother accused dad of foolishly indulging her. That was mother's stance on everything she tried her hand at, and was further evidenced by the fact that she never inquired or showed any interest in her art exhibits.

The only time her mother feigned moral support was when with uncharacteristic enthusiasm, she applauded her decision to complete her graduate work in France. Sedona, not for one minute believed her interest sincere. In fact, she would even go as far as to conjecture that her mother was elated at the prospects of her being away for several years. Of course, her dad thought that it was a waste a money – at least that what he said, but Sedona hoped that he was just a little proud that she had gotten accepted as an art history fellow in the competitive graduate program at the American University in Paris. She had her doubts though; for it was just recently that he off-handedly commented that he was still waiting for her to make him proud. For years, common sense admonished her that it wasn't healthy to be so eager for approval, but it was far easier said than done.

While in Europe, she met Gary, a handsome outgoing architecture student who was enjoying France on a fellowship, as well. Their friendship sparked when she mentioned that her hometown was located in Nebraska. It seemed that Gary found it quite incredulous that an African-American actually called a burg hidden in the middle of the "Heartland" home.

He was a New Orleans hometown boy. His father was wealthy and prominent in the city's colorful politics. Gary's life was filled with all of the whirlwind that young men fantasize about while growing up. Around him, she felt like the girl who had hit it big on the "Mystery Date" television commercials from the '60's. When Gary rang the doorbell there was no telling what fabulous plans he had up his sleeves. One evening it would be the opera, the next a lazy walk and picnic along the Seine River. Plus his willingness to show affection differed so dramatically from the undemonstrative behavior of her parents. His manner was thoroughly infectious, he laughed and joked, and wasn't shy about expressing his feelings. No wonder she soaked up his attention like a dry sponge. Even though over 15 years distanced that time, she still remembered how wonderful it felt to be loved and thought of . . . in spite of the fact that it was far too brief.

"There you go again . . ." Austin once more cuts in on her

thoughts. "What have you looking so melancholy? Why, a little over a hour ago . . ."

"You couldn't pay me to shut up," supplied Sedona as she good-humouredly smiled.

"Remember, you said it, not me . . . so, what's up?"

"Oh nothing . . ." she forced out a tad too brightly as she silently added, *that is nothing that a few loving words, a hug and kiss wouldn't cure.* "I was just indulging in a trip down memory lane."

"Depending on the memory that can be pretty self-defeating."

"Only if I allow myself to fall into the same old traps . . . which pray to God, I don't intend on doing ever again."

Adding the shrimp to his roux, Austin paused a moment and made a stab at reading Sedona's sober expression. It was obvious that something other than her earlier somewhat rambling anecdotes on party hosting, gourmet kitchens, and off-the-wall casino analogies were on her mind. Deciding to brave the murky waters, he disarmingly feigned nonchalance. "Again I ask, what's up?"

Watching as he measured rice into the steamer, Sedona wanted so desperately to ask the one simple age-old question that she imagined that every woman who had ever found herself head over heels in love begged an answer to – "how do you feel about me?" Even though she would give anything to know his reply, both pride and fear kept her from asking. Instead, she gingerly pried the door open a bit.

"Austin, how do you see your life in let's say five . . . ten years?"

Having some idea as to where his beautiful friend was going with the question, Austin bought time to formulate his response. "You are asking me this question because . . ."

Taking a deep breath Sedona slowly began, "Because, I just want to know whether . . . whether or not you . . ."

Ring, Ring. Grabbing the phone, Sedona sent up a quick prayer of thanks. If she ever needed to be saved by the proverbial bell, this was it. All thoughts of her predicament leaving as she recognized the voice on the other end, Sedona beckoned to Austin. His sister, Stephanie, was on the line letting him know that she had safely arrived. She also wanted to encourage Sedona not to "give up the ship" when it came to her brother. It was obvious that his sister wanted the two of them together, as much as she did. After exchanging pleasantries, she handed the phone over to an eager Austin.

Happy to give him a bit of privacy, Sedona walked over to a cupboard and selected two wine glasses, thought twice about it and put one back. Austin seldom drank anything alcoholic. As she filled her glass with the dry pink hued vin gris, she noticed the tired lines of concern that creased Austin's face and wondered how he was going to handle his sister's impending death. At some point or another, every person seeks refuge from life's grieves and burdens. For some, solace is found in a bottle, for others in their friends and loved ones, or faith.

Quietly replacing the wine bottle, she glanced over at Austin. Knowing him as she did, she was certain that it wouldn't be alcohol, drugs, or any other of the more common vices. Neither would it be family nor friends, for she and Stephanie were the only two that he kept in contact with on a regular basis. Thoughtfully running her eyes across the military crease of his shirt, she suddenly realized that he had found his shelter years ago . . . in the sea.

As she listened to him tell Stephanie that he loved her, she agonizingly wondered if she would ever hear him speak those words to her. After Steph's death, she could very well imagine him simply retreating back to the sea, and out of her life.

Conscious of the fact that she was eavesdropping, Sedona picked up her glass, selected a favorite CD and flipped on the stereo. Walking over to the fireplace, she idly poked at several logs resting on the andirons and ignited the gas pilot. Very seldom was there a need to start a fire in mid May, but she was beginning to feel quite cold.

"So, how is Stephanie doing? She sounds good."

Waiting for a reply, Sedona watched as Austin placed the dish of Shrimp Creole and a basket of warm bread on the dining table. He had spoken little more than a sentence or two after the conversation with his sister. Deciding that it would be cathartic for him to express his emotions, Sedona, moving her place setting from directly across her gloomy guest, to his immediate left – took her seat and made a second stab at conversation. "I think that when I finally see God face to face, I'm going to ask him why He went out of His way to make life so damn unfair."

Caught off guard, Austin let out a chuckle. "When you see HIM, you better leave out the word "damn". It wouldn't be very respectful."

Sensing his mood lightening a bit, Sedona reached for his hand, as she looked him in the face, "You know, you're quite the expert at side stepping your emotions. Ever since this whole cancer thing has come up with Stephanie, not once have you expressed any anger or bitterness. If I bring up your sister, or for that matter, any subject that would force you to betray your feelings, you either close up or change the subject. Squeezing his hand, she continued, "What are you so afraid of?"

Not quite knowing how to begin answering her quiet question, Austin found it difficult to break away from the compelling gaze of her gentle brown eyes. It wasn't that he wished to deny the ache of loneliness and the often times engulfing feeling of sadness. Over the years they had become his constant companions. It was just that he was, as Sedona had so eloquently stated, afraid.

Finally answering, he cleared his throat as he buttered a slice of bread. "I guess, I am afraid of the same things that most people are fearful of . . . fear of facing certain truths about myself. Fear of failing at the very thing that is at the heart of what matters most." Shifting the focus of his intense ebony eyes away from his meal to her face, he softly continued, "Fear of possibly finding out that what I want above anything else in the world, quite possibly may not be mine to have."

Listening to the gentle patter of the rain, Sedona studied his face as she allowed his words to settle and slowly meld into the melancholic strains of music wafting from the stereo." Despite the fact that she assumed that Stephanie was uppermost in his thoughts, she sensed that Austin was referring to a desire quite apart from his sister's well being.

"How do you know if it's not . . . ?"

"Mine to have?" completed Austin, "I don't, but just like you, I'm mindful of falling into the same old traps."

"But that's self . . ."

Once again Austin completed her comment, "Self-defeating. I know. But that is my dilemma."

Slowly rising, Sedona allowed her arm to gently brush across Austin's as she reached for his empty plate. As she leaned across him to retrieve his glass, Austin was afforded the tantalizing scent of her cologne. Noticing, not for the first time during the evening, the roundness of her breast through her loosely constructed sweater, he watched the easy sway of her round hips as she gracefully moved into the kitchen.

Sedona, aware of the seductive web she was weaving, continued the conversation as she entered with a plate of one of Austin's favorite desserts-chocolate almond cookies, and a carafe of coffee. "You know Austin, despite what I said earlier about casinos, there are times when it pays to take a chance, to gamble."

Relieving her of the tray, he placed it on an ottoman near the fireplace, and motioned that they sit on the floor. Teasingly he winked, "Sedona, please spare me. No more gambling analogies."

Leaning over close, Sedona, with the smoldering depths of her eyes and a suggestive smile, coyly invited him into her silken web. As she penetrated the nebulous coals of his gaze, Austin, with only a momentary hesitation, found himself drawing Sedona into his arms. Deciding to temporarily ignore the unflagging sirens of doubt that always seemed to follow him, he inhaled deeply as he savored the comforting warmth and softness of her body. Should he foolishly dare to hope that maybe, just maybe, happy endings were possible? Waving away the somber voices that constantly dogged him, he embraced her with loving tender strength, and offered kisses that spoke of a brewing quiet storm of passion, desire, and want.

His hands went up to her hair, along the curve of her spine and across her breast. Rubbing against the fibers of her sweater, and then under, he played with the nipples until they were pinpoint hard. Drinking in his scent she pulled his shirt from his pants and shrugged it off of his broad shoulders. Slowly falling back onto the floor, he pulled her down on top of him, she felt him hard against her thighs. The crackling fire, his warm scent, the falling rain all melded as she found herself rhythmically moving at his gentle urging. Feeling her stomach quivering, she had never remembered wanting any man as badly as she wanted Austin. No second instinct cautioned her to stop; no inner voice whispered words of guilt or trepidation. Everything felt as it should, her sixth sense assuring her that she could abandon herself in Austin and not fear emotional retribution.

Placing one hand in her hair and the other on her well-shaped rear, he possessively rolled her over until she was positioned under him. Now on top, he allowed his fingers to slowly caress her inner thighs and sweetly kissed her trembling lips. Playfully tugging at the small buttons of her sweater, "Tinney, I know this isn't terribly romantic, but this seems to be the best time to talk about the past six months. I've always assumed that we have had sorta of an understanding between us; but considering how I'm just off deployment, it would only make sense for you to have some concerns about the possibility of me being with someone other than you.

Appreciating his concern, she fingered his collar and looked him in the eyes, "To be honest, I can't picture you not taking care of yourself. As for myself, I haven't 'been' with anyone since the last time that we made love. But just to be safe, we can get ourselves tested tomorrow. As for tonight, her fingers caressed his lips, we can practice a little " safe sex."

Allowing her to first unzip his pants and then slowly finish undressing him, he held her gaze as he slid off her skirt. With smug satisfaction, Sedona watched Austin's face as he realized that she wasn't wearing panties. "Tinney, do you always walk around without your unmentionables?"

"Always? No. Only when I'm not wearing pants."

"Do you mean that all of those times when we've been out together and you've worn either a skirt or a dress, you haven't been wearing . . . ?"

Confirming his question, Sedona smiled, "You don't find that too risqué do you?"

"No, not too." Despite his nonchalant response, it was obvious that just the thought of this newly discovered secret took his excitement to a heightened level. Inhaling deeply as he undid her buttons, she heard his breath catch when he looked down at the lacey bra that she was wearing. Through the intricate lace, the darkened nipples of her soft breast teasingly pressed against the fibers. Undoing the front closure, he breathed in deeply as each breast more than filled his strong hands. Letting out an uncontrollable moan, her body arched forward. Taking delight in her response, he gently took her arms in one hand and held them over her head. "God, you look so good."

Looking up at him, she slyly smiled, "Let me go and I'll make you feel just as good."

Running his free hand across her stomach, he obliged. Doing as she promised, she pushed him down to the floor, and seductively ran her lips down his chest. It was her turn to dominate. Before handing him one of the condoms that he had taken out of his wallet, she stopped her lips at the curly hairs that ran across the lower portion his stomach and slowly inhaled his wonderful musky scent. Smiling, he obliged as she rose before him. Allowing the unrelenting hand of sensuality to guide the way, she slipped over him like a velvet glove. It was now Austin's turn to uncontrollably arch towards her, and as he did so, with her most sensual muscle, she treated him to an incredible hands free massage. Alternatively squeezing and then releasing him, she lifted her arms heavenward as she bore down hard.

Austin, bewitched by Sedona's candlelit form, could not take his eyes off of her full glistening breasts. It was if they each were teasing him, daring him to reach up and pull them into his mouth. No longer able to simply enjoy Sedona's sensuous grasp, he curled his strong thighs about his ladylove's hips and sat forward. "Oh baby, I see that you have been doing your Keigel's".

"How can you tell?" She asked as she wickedly caressed him with a powerful squeeze.

Instead of answering with the obvious, Austin slowly took into his mouth, first one nipple, then the other. As his tongue enjoyed both their taste and feel, he gently sucked them until she could no longer contain her control. "Austin! Austin, please . . ."

If Austin heard her pleading, he didn't let on. Instead he tugged at each nipple with the edge of his teeth. Sedona's groans and gasps of exhilaration rang out. Austin, turned on by how her voice melodically vibrated the room's antique windowpanes, held tight to her hips and watched as she rode each wave of passion.

Wrapped and bound by the pleasure of it all, her soul lifted and she heard herself moan, "Austin, I love you."

CHAPTER FIVE

Awakening, she allowed her mind to come out of it's sleepy fog and slowly focus on the man laying next to her and the scene that had played out downstairs only a few short hours before. Sitting up, she peered over at the clock sitting on the nightstand – four o'clock. Only two, maybe three more hours until sunlight rears its' ugly head and demands a reality check. Sitting in the darkness listening to Austin's sonorous breathing, it would be very easy to disillusion herself into believing that the night's love making had left her feeling happy and satisfied. What they shared was wonderful, no doubt about it. Austin knew how to make a woman feel good. But it was obvious that sex for Austin James was just that . . . sex. Great, but all the same – sex.

Why should she expect anything more than what she had received? After all, Austin in the two years that they dated, or whatever in the hell you called it, never indicated that he was ever interested in any form of commitment. What could she rightfully expect him to say when she, in a fit of utter stupidity, told him that she loved him?

With a despairing glance, she took in Austin's peacefully sleeping form, she wished Cupid and his twisted mean spirited little arrow, that she had the nerve to kick his butt out of the bed, demand that he give an honest account of his feelings, and state his intentions. Intentions, hah! What a word. She was lucky to have been graced with his unemotional friendly little pat on the head. The only thing that stopped him from getting the hell out was the fact that he had been in desperate want of a woman after six months of sea duty. It was clear that he only needed her to fill some type of void, to satisfy his sexual urges.

Sedona, you are some kind of fool. Not caring whether she woke Austin up or not, she threw back the covers, leaving as much off of him as on, and walked over to the closet where she selected a black dress to match her mood. Shoving the door close with a loud thud, she then yanked opened her lingerie drawer, which she also slammed shut. By now, it was obvious that she was not going to get a response from the still sleeping Austin. Just like a man, when you want their attention, you get nothing. So, with a wake the dead slam, she banged the bedroom door closed and headed for the guest bathroom.

The cool shower did little to restore her usually pleasant disposition. If anything, it gave her more time to dwell on Austin's inconsistent and self-serving behavior. Frustrated to the point of tears, she poured herself a cup of strong coffee and threw on her artist's smock. She would deal with the morning's emotions and disappointments the way she had most of her life, by seeking solace in her creative muse.

While the kitchen was one of the rooms that drew the most attention, her personal favorite was her studio. Previous owners had used the enclosed back porch area as a type of combination sunroom and breakfast area. But when she first laid eyes on the narrow room that ran the entire length of the house, she immediately concluded that its wonderful natural lighting and serene view of the container garden would be perfect for her art studio.

Dragging a stool over to the stained glass project that she had planned to temporarily put on hold for the duration of Austin's visit, she soon lost herself in the cutting and soldering of the small jeweled colored pieces of glass. The artwork, commissioned by Gary's architectural firm, was to be used as the focal point of a church atrium. Despite the fact that they were no longer married, Gary wisely acknowledged that his ex was one of the more creative and skilled stained glass artisans in the region. Her pieces were increasingly becoming recognized, and were proving to be a big selling point in his architectural proposals.

This piece, in comparison to most of her previous work, was a daunting undertaking. It measured 12 feet by 7 feet, and depicted several detailed scenes. Despite working on it for over five weeks, she was still only a little more than a quarter of the way finished. But with the vengeance in which she was now working, it stood a good chance to be completed before the week's end.

"I never found a companion that was so companionable as solitude."

Startled at the unexpected sound of Austin's easy voice, Sedona jumped and in the process burnt the inside pad of her finger with the hot iron tip of the soldering iron. "Damn it!"

In a display of concern, Austin crossed the room. "I see that Henry Thoreau has the opposite effect on you than most." Gently placing her injured hand in his, he examined the skin and led her over to the sink that stood at the opposite end of the room. "It'll feel a lot better after we've run some cold water over it." Turning the faucet on, he adjusted the flow of the water and placed her hand under its stream. "Just stay here and let the water cool the burn while I go get my bag."

Sedona, resembling a willful child, withdrew her finger and placed it in her mouth. "Austin, I'm sure that I'll be fine. Soldering iron mishaps are an occupational hazard. Besides . . . I barely singed the top layer of skin."

Slowly smiling at her uncanny knack for the dramatics, he replied, "A singe is still a burn, so humor me. A little ointment won't hurt."

As she did as she was told, Sedona sulkily placed the injured finger back under the cool water and with narrowed eyes, followed Austin out of the room. It was obvious that he was thoroughly clueless regarding how his unemotional reaction to her declaration of love had left her feeling. Not knowing which made her angrier, his insensitive response, or his overall inability and obvious lack of desire to verbally express his emotions, she let out an exasperated sigh. One thing for sure though, by the day's end, she would see to it that dear blasé Dr. James would get a heaping tablespoon of his own nonchalant medicine.

As promised, Austin quickly returned with a travel-sized grip, and retrieved a tube of anesthetic ointment.

His cheerfulness prompted her to quip, "Do you always carry that *bag* around? I thought that only doctors on television carried their medical cases around with them."

"Tinney, you had me fooled. I always thought that you were a "morning person" where's that pretty smile of yours?

Sedona, before flashing a fake smile, snatched the swab that he was using to apply the ointment.

After unexpectedly kissing her injured finger, he walked over to a box of pottery and picked up several items. "When do you find the time to do all of this? You have enough pieces here to open up your own gallery."

Tossing the cotton swab into a garbage can, she glanced around at the potpourri of pottery and art. In one area of the room were a kiln and a wheel where she threw clay. At the opposite end of the studio, was a huge flat table that she used to fashion her stained glass pieces.

And positioned close to a nearby window, were an easel, watercolors and stool.

"Tell me, out of all of this, which do you enjoy the most?"

"Oh . . . I don't know, I guess it just really depends. My mood determines what I tend to work on, along with whether or not I have any commissions to fill. But I guess if I were pressed to choose just one thing, it would be the stained glass. I know that I get the most requests for it. In fact, Gary's firm still uses me quite a bit. I was working on a commissioned piece for them when you walked in."

"Very, very nice," Austin complimented as he admired both Sedona's handiwork and the full size drawing of the window. "I gather that it's a depiction of nature. I see sunlight, trees and birds."

In spite of her mood, Sedona genuinely smiled. Her artwork was near and dear to her heart, and she enjoyed talking about it whenever anyone showed the slightest interest. Joining Austin over by the table she explained, "You're close. The scenes aren't so much about nature, but more about the feeling that one gets while walking at the quiet of dawn. It's my interpretation of Robert Browning's poem "The . . ."

"Year's at Spring," completed Austin as he held Sedona's eyes. "It's the poem that concludes with the two lines from that first Christmas card you sent me. *God's in his heaven – All's right with the world!*"

As they held eyes for several seconds, Sedona heart quicken as she sensed their thoughts connecting. Purposely allowing the perfect moment to kiss his companion to slip away, Austin picked up a paintbrush from out of a nearby cup, "With your teaching, I'm surprised that you have time for all of this."

Once again, she could feel her eyes threatening to mist. "Um . . . during the school year, I'm usually up late. That's one of the things that used to give Gary fits. He wanted me to quit teaching."

"But?"

"Teaching keeps me sane . . . and company. Despite what you hear, kids are really great. They're very honest and they soak up love like a sponge. Besides, I guess it is in my blood."

Realizing that she was referring to her parents, he asked, "Have you spoken to them . . . your parents lately? I remember you mentioning something about them coming down to visit this summer."

"Not this summer, she shrugged as she distractedly handled a pottery implement. They've cancelled their plans. It seems that Dad received an offer to speak before a group of sociologists at some symposium or another in Togo, West Africa; and Mom is going to use the visit as a chance to join an anthropology team who are studying the weavings and pottery of the Kotokolis. At least that's what I think that she said, I loose track after a while."

"Kotokolis? Wow, that sounds impressive." Despite her effort to appear unfazed, it was impossible to miss the disappointment in her face. "Even though their plans sound fascinating, I know how much you were looking forward to their coming down. I remembered you mentioning that they'll finally see your home, and the school where you teach. Why didn't you suggest joining them? I mean, the weaving and pottery thing sounds right up your alley."

"Well, I thought so. But when I brought it up, Mom pointed out that it would be a working trip, there would be, as she put it, 'little time for frivolity. ' So, I just left it alone." Feigning indifference, Sedona brushed off his concern, "It's no big deal really. You would think that during the fourteen years that I've lived in New Orleans, I would learn not to get my hopes up. I mean, it's all so very silly. We talk on the phone every now and then . . . and if I need to see them, they're only an airplane ride away."

Abruptly replacing a paintbrush, he remarked with an unmistakable edge, "When it comes to parents, I don't think that we ever stop hoping."

"My parents I'm used to, it's the other certain some ones in my life that keep setting me up," she mumbled under her breath as she reached for her coffee cup.

Not fully hearing her last comment, he took both of her hands in his and gave her a playful wink.

"Let's say that we ditch this joint and leave all of our ghosts behind. I've already called Loretta and Charles, and the coffee is hot."

Realizing that her comment had sailed clear over his head, and that he had no intentions of even mentioning their "night of passion," she shrugged, "Sure."

The drive over to the DuPree's was pleasant; the rain seemed to have washed the sky a brilliant blue. Driving down Royal towards the heart of the Vieux Carre – the French Quarter to the tourist, Sedona admired, as she had thousands of times, the beautiful iron balconies that adorned many of the old buildings. No matter how often she made her way to the French Quarter, she never tired of the quaint beauty of the ageless elegant old city. Pointing to a parking space, Sedona suggested to Austin that they grab it and walk the block to the restaurant. Heeding her advice, he eased the small car into the space.

As he opened the car door, Austin discreetly admired her well-shaped legs and immediately the secret that he had discovered the night before, came to mind. Sedona was impossible to resist. There was no getting around it; she was by far one of the sexiest women that he had ever dated. With the way she filled out the dress she was wearing, she had better be glad that he didn't drive the car right pass the restaurant, back to her place and carry her up the bedroom. The only thing that stopped him was the one thing that prevented him from kissing her earlier in the studio. He was in no position to fall in love. Not only wouldn't it be fair to Sedona, but also he was certain that his heart just couldn't risk another loss . . . another disappointment. It was for that reason, and that reason alone that he chose to ignore her words of love the night before. There was no point in giving her any false sense of hope.

The walk was pleasant, the couple stopped and admired several window displays and Austin with a bit of pride, did not fail to notice the several admiring smiles his date received. And by the time they had reached the restaurant, Austin found himself not for the first time, totally enchanted by Sedona's ingenuous personality. She was thoroughly uncontrived and open. He found it not only sexy, but it stirred an emotion that urged him to protect her – to keep away the bad, even if it meant himself. Sedona was by no means the helpless damsel. He had a feeling that she fought tooth and nail for those who she cared about, even to the exclusion of her own feelings.

As they entered the private entrance of the restaurant, they walked into a beautiful side courtyard garden that always reminded Sedona of Monet's Giverny. Courtyard gardens, quite common in the Vieux Carre, were a source of pride for many of its denizens. The gardens provided not only a quiet enclave from the hustle and bustle of the streets that lay only a few yards away, but they also provided an intimate spot in which to entertain. The DuPree's garden was especially lovely, for it was filled with a colorful abundance of flowering shrubs and containers. Even the staircase that led up to the second floor residence was adorned with the fragrant climbing vines of the Bougainvillea.

As they entered the courtyard, they were immediately greeted by Charles and Loretta, who were seated and enjoying a pot of coffee under a large umbrella. It seemed that Austin, in typical military fashion, had given them his estimated arrival time, and they knew barring a small disaster that he would be punctual. Accepting the embrace and the kisses of first Loretta, then Charles, she could feel the love that flowed between the pair. As she took in the happy couple locked arm in arm, Sedona felt some of her blue disposition fade.

Just as they were concluding their rounds of hugs and kisses, a stunning statuesque woman, as if on cue, stepped out onto the balcony directly above them. While Sedona had enough well placed curves to tempt even the most controlled man, this woman in contrast was tall, cool and sophisticated, from her smooth cafe au lait skin to her long straight jet-black hair. In the strappy heels that complimented her long lean frame, she was easily as tall as Austin.

Quite used to turning heads when she entered a room, the raven head beauty sensuously leaned over the rail as she drawled, "Austin darling, not only are you back in town, but you've brought along a *little friend.*"

Neither her use of *little friend*, nor her insincere smile passed over Sedona.

With more than a touch of irritation, Austin sarcastically snarled loud enough for everyone to hear, "Hell, just what I need to brighten up my morning."

Seeming to ignore both Sedona's presence and Austin's unfriendly comment, Lorraine who had made her way down the staircase, slipped in-between them and placed a rather possessive hand upon Austin's shoulder. Immediately removing her hand with obvious disdain, he pulled his date to his other side, "Sedona, this is Lorraine, my spurious ex. Lorraine, Sedona Tinney."

As she offered a polite smile, Sedona quickly recalled the few comments that Austin had made regarding his ex-wife. Even though he rarely referred to her, Sedona had always gotten the impression that their parting was not amicable. If Austin's reaction to Lorraine's presence was any indication of his dislike for the woman, then breakfast was going to be a real hoot.

Quickly assessing Sedona from head to toe, Lorraine flashed one of those practiced smiles that Sedona had come to refer to as the "dilettante smile". Then, without even a polite hello, returned her attention to Austin.

Yep, I'm dismissed! thought Sedona humorously as she made a mental note to ask Austin what was on his mind when he married the wicked bitch.

"So Commander, you had us pacing the floor with worry last night. It was very thoughtless of you not to call."

"Now Lorraine," chided her sister, Loretta, "He did call and explain that . . ."

Not caring who heard, Austin coldly remarked, "Lorraine, if you paced the floor, it was probably while you were thinking up ways to add more misery to my life. Just why are you here anyway?"

Already taking an instant dislike to the woman, Sedona decided that enough was enough. So, slyly laying claim to the obvious target of the woman's desire, she offered an apology to the group. "Loretta, I'm afraid that last night was all my fault. I was late picking him up from the airport and then I had car trouble, by the time that we finally made it on over to my place, poor Austin was wiped out. So, I thought that it was best to forgo another trip out into the rain and insisted that he spend the night with me." Possessively patting his arm on the last comment, Sedona smiled up at Austin's dancing eyes.

The logic apparent in her explanation, Charles waved aside

Sedona's apology, "No need for regrets, it was wise not to go back out into the rain. I heard reports of flooding from quite of few of my customers last night. In fact, a couple of 'em even found themselves stranded down here at the restaurant.

"Charles, we can stand out here and gab all morning, or we can go on up and enjoy a bit of breakfast," suggested Loretta as she shooed her guests upstairs. I made a batch of beignets that won't be worth the flour they're made from if they sit around much longer."

Just the thought of Loretta's mouth-watering pastry got the group moving. Austin and Charles, allowing the ladies to head up first, followed close behind. As they climbed the stairs, Sedona couldn't help but notice how Lorraine switched those tight jean clad hips of hers a little too dramatically. It was obvious that she called herself giving Austin a little sampling of what he's been missing since the two of them parted. Despite her growing irritation, she had to give the woman credit, her model's figure showed off the white midriff blouse and jeans perfectly. She looked like an advertisement straight from Vogue.

As usual, Loretta outdid herself, along with fresh beignets, she served a wonderful green onion and red pepper omelet, sausages, and delightfully seasoned potato galletas. Refusing her hostess' offer for seconds, Sedona gingerly sipped the strong coffee that was traditionally spiced Creole style, with chicory.

"Loretta the meal was the best I had since the last time I ate here," complimented Sedona. "But, I'm afraid that I am at my limit."

Feigning empathy, Lorraine, heaping an additional helping of sausages and galletas onto her plate, innocently smiled over at Sedona. "I don't blame you one bit for turning down seconds. I know how easily those curves of yours can turn to fat."

Without a pause, Sedona impulsively retorted, "Oh really, I

would have never guessed that having too many curves were one of your problems, Lorraine."

Loretta, thoroughly oblivious to the tension between the two women, unknowingly added fuel to the fire; "Lorraine has always had what Mama used to call a "coat hanger body". You know, like a lot of those over-priced fashion models. The clothes just hang . . ."

Charles, noticing his sister-in-law's scowl, discreetly interrupted, "Loretta, could you be a dear and fetch me some more of that coffee?"

As Loretta brought over the coffeepot, Austin asked his ex, "So, Lorraine, you never did say as to what we owe the pleasure."

Puzzled by the question, Lorraine shrugged, "I wouldn't think that an explanation was necessary. I'm just here for a friendly little visit, after all Loretta is my sister."

After studying her for several seconds, Austin sarcastically commented. "I suppose, you always did have a penchant for "friendly" little visits."

It was obvious from Lorraine's pursed lips that Austin had struck a nerve. After darting a glance over at Charles who was suddenly busy adding sugar to his coffee, she pushed back her chair and left the table in an angry huff. Although curious at the interchange that she had just witnessed, Sedona kept quiet and politely offered to assist her hostess. Loretta, still unconscious of the friction between her guests, motioned for her to stay put.

When he was certain that Lorraine and his wife had left the room, Charles leaned across the table towards Austin, "I hope that you know that it wasn't my idea inviting her over. As far as I'm concerned, the longer she stays up in Baton Rouge, the better. She telephoned Loretta yesterday afternoon and invited herself down. And you know my wife . . . she's so kind hearted, it didn't even occur to her to say no. She said that Lorraine sounded a bit lonely, so to cheer her up, she insisted that she stay the weekend. I'm sure Loretta's thinking that the hell that Lorraine sent you through is long forgiven and forgotten. You know my wife."

Rising from the table, Austin patted the shoulder of his good friend, "Don't worry about it. Even though I'm not as forgiving as Loretta, as far as I'm concerned, Lorraine is yesterday's news."

As Sedona silently tried to make heads or tails out of the men's conversation, she watched as Austin walked out to the balcony that overlooked the courtyard garden. Not quite sure as whether or not to follow him, she glanced over at Charles for a clue.

"Did I miss something?"

With a sympathetic smile, Charles poured her another cup of coffee, "Give him a little time, he'll tell you all about the exploits of Miss Lorraine. Until then, just try to be a little patient. Austin puts up a good front, but don't let him fool you. The way he'll tell it, he doesn't need anyone. But I've shared quarters with him for close to seven years. I've seen him up and I've seen him when things couldn't get any lower. And despite what that woman in there will tell you, Austin needs love just as much as the next guy, and in some ways, maybe even more.

While dipping a corner of his beignet into his coffee, he continued, "Loretta and I worry about him. We just don't know how he's going to hold up when his sister dies. It's been just the two of them for so long. You're good for him," he pronounced with an affectionate wink. "You have that way about you that gets him out of his shell. Besides, you're pretty damn cute. Listen, I know he has that way about him . . . you know what I'm talking about. But don't let him put you off. He's a decent guy. So, like I've said, just be patient."

"Charlie," Loretta called, "Wasn't Sandifer going to come round with those extra cases this morning? You better think about heading on down."

Looking at his watch, Charles explained to Sedona, "Sandifer is our beer supplier. Usually he's by about twice a week, but this music fest thing that they've got going has been packing them in. I hear that they've got some pretty good talent this year." Calling out to Austin, Charles relayed a bit of news, "Hey Doc, I hear that ol' Jay McShann is scheduled to perform this weekend.

With a look of fond remembrance, Charles referenced his remark, "On one deployment, we pulled into Perth. On liberty, a bunch of us guys would head over to this blues club that would bring in talent from all over the world. Lucky for us, we were there during the height of the tourist season, so we had the opportunity to enjoy some pretty big-time names. One of the acts were Jay McShann and his combo . . . hey Doc, what was that club in Perth called? All I know is that it was some Portuguese name, ran by a guy from Lisbon. Azure Camino or something of the other. "

"Azul A Câmara," Austin fluidly supplied as he rejoined his best friend and date. "It means Blue Chamber."

"Listen to how the Portuguese just rolls off this guy's lips," Charles good-naturedly teased his best friend. "If I didn't know better, I would say that he's trying to show me up, just to impress you."

"Sedona's too smart of a lady to be so easily fooled. She knows that I'm just an ol' salty dog."

Charles, whose eyes had taken on a sudden mischievously glint, slyly gave Sedona a wink. "Say Doc, why don't you take this smart young lady on over to the music fest. Y'all can kick back, enjoy a bit of jazz, while at the same time forget "Little Miss Thang" in there. If it wasn't for this restaurant, that's where Loretta and I would be."

Surveying Sedona's face, Austin offered his date a boyish grin, "Well, what do you say?"

Any other time, she would have accepted the offer, even before the invitation was completely out of his mouth. But, she had just promised herself not to take part in Austin's emotional roller coaster ride. Feeling her resolve melt, she quickly studied his face and remembered Charles' words of advice. Maybe she should reconsider and give the day . . . and perhaps even Austin a second chance. Who knows, with the loving DuPrees setting the mood, she might even be able to convince him that what he sorely needed most in his life was the love of a good woman.

So, taking a deep breath, she smiled, "Just give me a hat, a tank of water, and I'm ready." Having previously attended the music festival, she knew that despite the fact that the sun now looked inviting, in a few hours it would be very unforgiving.

Pleased that his impromptu plan to "help" Sedona and Austin to the altar was in motion, Charles gave Austin's back a fatherly slap. "I'll get Loretta to fix you both right up. 'Retta . . ."

Entering the room from the kitchen, Loretta answered her husband's call as she dried her hands on her apron.

"Sedona and Austin are heading on over to the fair grounds, how about fixing them up with a couple of hats and some water? I'm heading on downstairs." Giving his wife an affectionate kiss on the cheek, he returned his attention to his friends. "I'll expect to see you two back here for dinner. We're open late, so no excuses." With that admonishment, Charles had craftily seen to it that she and Austin spend the remainder of the day in one another's company.

Deciding to use the city's shuttle bus to reach the fair grounds,

Sedona suggested that, along with the water bottles that they each were carrying, that they also take along two collapsible canvas chairs that she kept stowed in her car. Austin, poking through the gear that filled her trunk, asked if she always hauled around such an array of hats, bottles of sun block, camp stools, oversized umbrellas, and other miscellaneous items.

As she slung the strap of one of the folding chairs across her shoulder, she laughed. "I'm not the pack rat that you think I am. Every now and then, I head on down to Jackson Square and paint the scenery. The Cabildo and St. Louis Cathedral, along with the tourists and locals, are perfect fodder for the artistic mind."

The music festival was an annual attraction that each year, drew thousands. It was truly a festival of music and Louisiana culture, with something to offer everyone – jazz to bohemian, R&B to folk, blues to zydeco. Along with the music, there were colorful booths crammed with tempting arrays of goods and foods. The afternoon offered the perfect opportunity to try Louisiana's well renowned culinary fare.

Sedona, who thrived on the free and easy festive atmosphere, fitted in perfectly with the carefree mood of the crowd. Austin watched with amused pleasure as she clapped to the infectious melodies of a gospel choir and swayed with the blues fans. She even shouted her share of accolades to the musicians. As the afternoon wore on, he even found himself loosening up. Sedona made it easy. Without being pushy, she encouraged him to just follow her lead and let the day happen.

As they walked through the bustling souvenir vending area, he watched as she greeted many of the vendors. And with a tiny bit of prompting he even found himself helping her select a beautiful batik skirt. As the sales person handed her their selection, Austin teased, "You are a regular Bohemian aren't you?"

Suddenly, the smiled that had graced her face for most of the day faded as she shrugged her shoulders without comment. It was obvious that he had said something to upset her. "I take it that wasn't a compliment."

"No, no I 'm just being overly sensitive. Behind my back, Gary's family and friend's special nickname for me was "Bohemia." They never thought that I had quite enough class for Gary. Figure that one out. But in all fairness, I guess that I didn't help my cause much when, as Mrs. Chandler so aptly used to put it, "I took to the streets,"

Almost fearful of her explanation, Austin slowly asked, "What exactly does that mean?"

"Don't worry. It's not as wicked as it sounds. It's just that I had this burning need to earn my own money. So, before I got a teaching position, I use to set up shop – you know, draw portraits and caricatures of tourists – down at Jackson Square, the French Market and at special events like this. That's how I know so many of the vendors here."

"I call that being pretty resourceful," he complimented as he plucked a stray blade of grass from her hair. There's nothing wrong with displaying a bit of that good old U. S. of A. entrepreneurial spirit."

With a smile, Sedona, taking his hand, led them over to an informal crowd that was dancing under a huge tent to the rollicking accordion beat of zydeco's prince – C. J. Chenier and the Red Hot Louisiana Band. Austin pleaded for mercy, but Sedona would not relent. Before he knew it, they were a part of an impromptu "couple mixer" dance comprised of free spirits like Sedona. He had never participated in anything so spontaneous. During the course of the dancing, a large circle was formed with couples holding hands. Initially relieved that Sedona had managed to stay to the right on him, he was soon dismayed when she wound up dancing with someone else.

Unlike Austin, Sedona thought the whole situation humorously apropos. The song's title, "Man Smart, Woman Smarter" and the expression on Austin's face said it all. Letting herself go, she totally gave in to the music and temporally forgot all of her troubles.

Suddenly finding himself partnered up with a gal who knew the steps no better than he, Austin gave a quick smile and frantically surveyed the merry crowd for Sedona's face.

"Is dancing with me really all that bad?" teased the young woman.

Looking at her face for the first time, Austin flashed an embarrassed smile, "No, it's nothing like that. It's just that this really isn't my cup of tea."

"Well, that's because neither one of us knows the steps. Why don't we just do a dance that we both know? Here, follow me. "

Before he could respond, his dance partner was leading him through the crowds in a lively trot. Feeling himself relax, he stole a glance at the woman's face. Pretty eyes, soft brown hair, and a cute smile . . . a fella could do far worse. Given a different time and place, there was a good possibility that he would have asked her for her phone number. Almost as if reading his mind, the woman moved them away from the crowd and over to the edge of the tent.

"My name is Carolyn, and yours?"

"Um . . . Austin," answered the doctor as he casually glanced around for Sedona. It was obvious that the young woman intended on making conversation, and with Sedona nowhere in sight, he obliged figuring that it was far safer than being caught up in another round of dance.

As the band changed tunes, Sedona perused the crowd for Austin. Realizing that circle dancing was not exactly his thing, she instinctively scanned the seats along the perimeter of the tent. Almost immediately, she spied a laughing Austin totally engaged in conversation with a rather attractive woman. As she studied the pair, she was totally oblivious of the man who crept up behind her.

"Hello, beautiful," a familiar voice whispered, making the hair at her nape raise. Planting a kiss on her neck, he continued, "If I remember correctly, dancing was one of the two things that we did quite well together. What do you say to a spin?" Not giving her an opportunity to refuse, he spun her around and expertly moved them back onto the dance floor.

Despite the fact that dancing was the last thing that she now wanted to do, especially with this new partner, she gave no hint of protest and purposefully guided her partner in the direction that Austin was seated. She might as well as make use of her 'irritant,' she reasoned. It was time to give 'Mr. Medicine Man' a taste of his own bitter pill.

Noticing that the band was performing a new tune, Austin surveyed the dancing couples once more and found Sedona partnered up with a man that he could only term as, "friendly". As he caught her eye, he was puzzled as to why she made no move to pull away from her partner's close embrace, so he irritatingly watched as the overly familiar stranger brushed a wisp of hair from her face.

"She's your date?" Carolyn stated the question rather than asked. "She's cute . . . with her figure she probably attracts men like flies. It looks like both of you lucked in this time though . . . you both found someone else that might prove to be more your types." Chirping on without pause, the woman misread Austin's darkening expression, "Usually when one finds someone more appealing, the other winds up as the uncomfortable third wheel. Don't get me wrong though, I'm not saying he's more attractive . . . while he's got that pretty boy thing going on, you're more of the rugged type. Every woman looks for something different in a man. In my opinion, you can run circles around that guy. Like I said, it's all about what you're looking for. I have to give her credit though, she has good taste, mighty good taste."

Austin, answering her observation with an annoyed glare, politely excused himself and made his way over to Sedona. Slowly walking up behind her, he heard Sedona let out what he took to be a flirtatious laugh. "In this crowd, how did I have the luck to wind up dancing with you?" she asked.

Listening to her partner's response, he didn't miss how the 'gentleman', with bold familiarity, slowly brushed off a stray blade of grass from her chest. "What makes you think that luck had anything to do with it? You in that dress caught my eye . . . Sedona, you still got it going on."

"Are you trying to pick me up?"

While her partner knew that her remark was not meant as a challenge, Austin couldn't make out who was teasing whom. "I tell you, the spark is still there Sedona. What do you say to taking me back to your studio and showing me some of your sketches?"

Unable to contain herself, Sedona laughed at his corny come on. "Give me a break, my sketches? You don't possibly catch women with that line?"

Feigning hurt, her *suitor* explained, "Please, give me more credit. I know that you're still working on that cathedral glass project. I haven't seen it yet; maybe we can kill two birds with one stone. You know that I am always willing to give things a second try."

"Dr. Austin James!" Turning around in the direction of a woman's familiar, but rather boisterous voice, Sedona caught sight of first, her best friend – Mazey, then Austin who was standing a few feet away. From the expression on his face, it was obvious that he had heard Gary's proposal.

Sedona, catching Austin's eye, greeted her friend, "Mazey, Gary hadn't said a word about you being out here." As she gave her dear friend a sisterly hug, Sedona stole another glance over at Austin. She could tell from his brooding expression, that up to that moment, he had not a clue that her dancing partner was her ex-husband.

Unaware of Sedona's efforts to get under Austin's skin by milking the role of innocent ingénue for all that it was worth, Mazey commented, "It took me only a second to recognize your face. Gary was so interested in your backside that he had no idea that it was you that he was gawking at."

"I figured as much. Mazey," Sedona teased, "I have a feeling that you were doing your fair share of scoping out the crowd as well. You seemed to have had no trouble finding Austin."

"Girl, you know me too well. Don't tell my husband, but a tall, good looking man always did have a way of turning my head." Playfully patting Austin on the arm, she teased, "I had you picked out in the crowd way before I even recognized Sedona."

Not missing Austin's markedly quiet mood, Sedona couldn't help but take some pleasure in sensing a bit of jealousy. Affectionately looping her arm through his, she introduced the men to one another, "Austin, this is the infamous Gary Chandler, Mazey's cousin and my ex."

In response, neither man extended a hand but simply nodded a cordial hello as Austin coolly added a polite "nice to meet you."

"I don't know if I can say the same," chuckled Gary, "I'm trying to figure out why I am "infamous" and you're "tall and good looking? I'm starting to feel like yesterday's leftovers."

"Well . . . honey, could it be that it's because you are," teased Mazey.

Quite used to the pair's familial bantering, Sedona shook her head with a bit of amusement, and admonished the cousins, "Ok you two, there's no reason to get ugly. I have a hunch as to why Gary's out here without a date, but Mazey, where's Miles and Carly."

Glancing around for her husband and daughter, Mazey explained, "The two of them spied the turkey leg concession, so I got stuck with old leftovers here."

"Again, I ask, why must the two of you only refer to me in the most negative of terms. Now I'm old. Man, you've got to feel sorry for me, I tell you, I get no respect. I don't know why I put up with such abuse."

"Austin, don't you dare feel sorry for him, gibed Sedona as she gave Gary a reproving slap on the arm. As soon as the first "hootchie" walks past that will give him the time of day, he's outta of here." At Sedona's comment both women laughed, and Austin quickly gathered that Sedona and her ex had amicably resolved any rifts between them. It was obvious that they still were good friends and on friendly terms . . . perhaps a little too friendly, but it seemed innocent.

Breaking into his thoughts was the heartbreaking sound of piteous wailing. As the group turned towards the sound, Mazey was dismayed to learn that the cry was that of her six-year-old being carried by her husband. "Miles, what happened?"

Handing over to Gary the food that he had some how managed to carry along with his sobbing daughter, Miles quickly explained. "Don't ask me how, but she got a splinter of some sort caught under her nail."

Fishing for all the sympathy she could get, Carly interrupted, "I was walking my fingers along the fence next to the food stands, and then . . . and then . . . oh, Daddy it hurts so bad." Holding out her hand she let out another cry.

Mazey, in an attempt to get a closer look at the injury, inadvertently brushed the injured hand causing the child to let out another wail.

Austin, who had been quietly observing the goings on, spoke up. "Hey, Carly remember me?"

Nodding the child, looked at him intently, "You're Aunt Sedona's friend, Dr . . ."

"James", supplied Sedona.

"May I?" Austin asked Miles as he took the little girl from her dad's arms, and sat her down on the ground. Sitting next to her, he asked, "May I take a look at the finger?"

Nodding the little girl slowly handed over her hand, "See it hurts right here."

"I see . . . it's stuck way up in there isn't it? But, you know what? I have had a lot of practice at this sort of thing. On the ship where I work, men much bigger than you manage to get splinters stuck in their fingers all of the time. And guess what?"

"What . . ."

"They come to me . . . on some days it seems that all I do is take care of splinters."

Carly's eyes were fixed on him, "Do you think that you can take care of mine?"

"I can try . . ."

"Will it hurt?"

"Well, I'm not going to lie to you, it may hurt just a tiny bit for just a tiny while, but it'll hurt even more, especially if you leave it in there."

Nodding, Carly gave her permission for Austin to continue. Watching intently as he reached in his back pocket and took out a small leather case that contained a pair of tweezers. "What's that?"

"A pair of tweezers. What I'm going to do is use them to pull out that nasty piece of wood. Now, you're going to have to try to hold your hand absolutely still, ok?"

"Ok."

With deftness, he grabbed hold of the piece of wood and slowly eased it out from under the girl's nail. Then he opened the case back up and took out a small bandage and wrapped it around the tiny finger. "Carly, you are as brave as you are beautiful."

"Thank you Dr. James . . . look Mommy . . ."

Stooping down to pick her up, Miles kissed the hand and patted Austin shoulder as he said thanks.

Gary, who had smirked the whole time, ate a French fry out of one of the bags that he was stuck holding, "The man's a regular Boy Scout."

Mazey taking the food from Gary waved a reprimanding finger at her cousin. "Oh you're just jealous!" Turning her attention to Sedona and Austin she apologized, "If you ignore him, he'll go away. Why don't you two stay and join us. Miles brought back enough food to feed an army . . . or in your case Austin, a navy. It'll give us a chance to catch up . . ."

With a smile, Sedona begged off, "Thanks Mazey, but we promised Austin's friends, the DuPree's, that we'd join them for dinner. Besides . . ." Nodding her head towards Gary who was now in an enlivened conversation with Carly, "With you-know-who over there in prime form, none of us would get a moment's rest."

"You've got a point. You two go and have fun, but promise me that you'll stop by the shop next week. Austin, I've set aside a couple of first editions that I think you'll be interested in adding to your collection."

Flattered that she had remembered that he collected American poetry, he gave his word. Taking the time to say a special goodbye to

Carly, who waylaid him with a kiss, they said their farewells. Gary, Austin noticed, brandished Sedona with a rather affectionate kiss.

"Listen, at this point, all of the music is starting to sound like noise. Let's go put in our appearance over at the DuPree's, and head on home." Without giving her a chance to voice her opinion, Austin started for the park's exit.

Sedona, who had had about enough of trying to take his moodiness in stride, stopped dead in her tracks, "Excuse me *sir*, but don't I get a say in any of this. You know, I'm not one of your "privates" aboard ship."

Patience tested, Austin, despite his irritation, smiled. "I think the term you're looking for is "seamen," there are no privates in the navy. Sedona, if you're not ready to leave, it's not a problem. I'll simply return you to your friends."

"Privates, seamen, it doesn't make a difference, the point is *not* that I'm not ready to leave, it's, it's . . . You know, it wouldn't hurt you to ask *whether* I'm ready to leave."

Austin, blankly staring at her as if she was speaking a foreign language tiredly rubbed his brow, "Sedona, it is late. Maybe it would be best if we just . . ."

"Just what? Go home? Fine Austin, whatever you want," Angrily walking ahead of her date, she led the way towards the car. Listening to the crunching of gravel beneath his shoes, she became increasingly infuriated at his smug silence. Typical male passive aggressive behavior, well, he wasn't going to get her angry and then walk away. Taking several more steps, she stopped in her tracks and exploded, "What's with you? Up until a little while ago, I thought that we were having a good time?"

"We were . . . that is until we met up with 'Our Gang. '!"

"Our Gang? Austin, that's pretty mean. Since when do I refer to that "F Troop" mix of your friends so despairingly?"

No longer able to keep down tight the lid on his emotions, Austin stuffed his hands in his pockets, "None of my friends have ever tried to make a play for my girlfriend."

"A play?" Thrown by his response, she vainly searched, "What the . . . who tried to make a play? Suddenly, with a burst of incredulous laughter, it donned on her that he was alluding to her ex. "Austin, you're not referring to Gary are you? Surely you figured out by now that he flirts with every woman he meets."

Furrowing his brow, Austin grabbed her forearm, "Sedona, if it's one thing that I hate, it's being purposely made to feel jealous. After Lorraine, I vowed never to allow anyone to manipulate me like that again."

"Well bully for you. But, I'm sorry, if I've made you jealous, I'm glad!"

Tightening his grip, Austin through clenched jaws, narrowed his eyes and spate, "Glad?"

Undaunted by his obvious irritation, she persisted, "Yes, glad because it worked. If I hadn't made you jealous then I doubt if you would have ever gotten around to calling me your *girlfriend*. If you don't like being manipulated, than you are just going to have to open up and say what you feel."

Although reluctant, he could see her point. In Sedona's mind, the jealousy bit all made sense, and he had to admit, that in some convoluted nonsensical way, he could see her point. Drawing her to his chest, he chuckled, "Tinney, what am I going to do with you and that exasperatingly feminine mind of yours?"

Responding with a husky whisper, Sedona softly suggested, "Kiss me."

Sitting across the table studying Austin, Sedona once again found herself wondering what was going through his mind. At first glance, he appeared to be caught up in the rather good-natured rambunctious conversation of Charles and a group of their old navy buddies. A planned reunion could not have come off any better than this chance spur-of-the-moment meeting of shipmates. It seemed that over the years, The Blue Fish had become the natural weekend hangout for many of Charles and Loretta's friends; and with the music fest going on, tonight it had become the impromptu after party.

Initially, Sedona was somewhat grateful for the party's reprieve. Despite the fact that they seemed to settle their differences on the ride over, Austin's mood still hadn't completely lifted out of its earlier funk. She had hoped that the group's good-humored frivolous conversation, and Loretta's down-home cooking would do the trick. But the longer that he sat and talked, the more it became obvious that his smile was just a bit too well practiced.

As their eyes momentarily met, she softly smiled as she remembered the kiss they shared earlier in the parking lot. But, if Austin shared her feelings, he offered no signals – not even a smile, he simply returned his attention back to the buddy sitting next to him. It had been that way ever since they arrived at the restaurant. Other than to politely introduce her when to do otherwise would have been pointedly rude, he had made no attempt to draw her into the group's conversation. In affect, he was basically making it a point to ignore her. Well, she wasn't going to have it. Her first inclination was to stir things up a bit and have a little party of her own with the guys seated around her. Or better yet, she could leave and let him find his own damn way home. Sedona swallowed back her vengeful streak, reached for her purse and made her excuses to no one in particular.

Studying her dejected reflection in the ladies' room mirror, she freshen her lipstick. Damn the roller coaster ride! Realistically though, what should she expect? If a man – a lover, couldn't say I love you, in the midst of "lovemaking," what made her think that he would offer an inkling of that emotion in the midst of a crowded room. Face the hard cold fact, the smartest thing to do, would be to bow out grace-fully while there was still pride and dignity left.

"The course of true love never did run smooth . . . at least that's what Shakespeare seemed to have thought. Personally, I think that there's got to be a better way," purred a woman's voice.

Sedona, startled by the unexpected sound of the husky southern drawl, dropped her lipstick case.

Picking it up, Lorraine with a humorous raise of an eyebrow momentarily fingered the delicate small swivel mirror attached to the antique filigree case. "Figures . . . you wouldn't carry just a simple tube of lipstick like most women."

Good Lord, what now. Taking the case from Lorraine's out-stretched hand, Sedona quietly murmured thanks. She was hardly up to a conversation of wits with Austin's ex. "Listen Lorraine, I'm not in the mood for . . ."

Lorraine, non-fazed, brushed aside the other woman's words with a chuckle. "Believe me honey, I do understand. I have actually lived with the man, remember."

Not quite sure of what to make of the woman's concern, Sedona stared back in the mirror at Lorraine's flawless reflection. For a brief instant, she caught a flicker of empathy in the woman's eyes, but emotionally tired and spent, she left the restroom without further comment. Walking over to Loretta, who lovingly had her arms draped around her husband' neck, Sedona forcing a note of brightness into her voice, and thanked her hosts, "Loretta . . . Charles, as usual the food and company were wonderful. But, it has been a long day and I'm beat . . ."

Austin, noticing Sedona standing near the bar with her purse, hastily stood and threw down their share of the tab, "Well guys, it looks like it is time to hit the road. I'll try to get back over here before I leave town." After exchanging a couple of pats on the back, Austin made his way over to his date.

Loretta, noticing Austin reaching for Sedona's hand teased, "Sedona was just telling us that you two are about to cut out on us. It's a bit early isn't it?"

Both surprised and annoyed at Austin's newfound attentiveness, Sedona flashed a tight smile, and out of the corner of her eye, spied Lorraine watching at the end of the bar. "Austin, you don't have to leave on my account. I wouldn't want to keep you from your friends."

"Old age must be catching up, because I'm – how did you describe last night, *dog tired*." As he said the last phrase, Austin gave Sedona an affectionate wink.

Last night, humph . . . Last night was last night; don't expect more of the same. With a misleading smile, Sedona gave Austin no clue as to the thoughts going through her mind. *Talk about assumptions! What made him think that she even wanted him back at the house? Surely this man wasn't obtuse.* As she half-listened to his conversation, and took in the meaningful squeeze to her hand, in spite of her earlier anger, she found herself more than just a little curious as to why he now was being so attentive after having ignored her while with his pals? Was he purposely sending out mixed messages, perhaps attempting to pay her back for their misunderstanding at the music fest? Or was she just being overly sensitive? After all, in fairness, he couldn't be expected to direct all of his attention towards her, some of the guys over at the table he hadn't seen for years.

Making up her mind as she adjusted the strap of her purse, she self-consciously glanced over at Lorraine, said a quick prayer and decided to give him the benefit of the doubt. Besides, they were going to have a little talk about 'feelings'.

On the drive back to her home, mellow soulful strains from the radio settled in the air. Austin occasionally glanced her way and smile, but made no attempt to initiate conversation. Several times she started to bring up what had transpired at the restaurant, but stopped herself. At times she could be all too blunt, and she didn't want to kindle another argument. As ballads of love both found and lost filled the quiet between them, she thought of Lorraine . . . *The course of true love never did run smooth.*

Were she and Austin on the course of true love, or was it all just lopsided wishful thinking? She would give anything to have the strength to ask Austin that question – straightforward and direct. Looking out at the dark, perturbed she stared at her reflection. Maybe last night was the answer to her question. Sighing she closed her eyes, maybe . . . maybe . . . maybe . . . so what if he never expressed the depth of his feelings for her. His inability to express his love, if that was indeed his feelings, did not diminish or negate the realness of her love for him. Besides, if he never said, "I love you", would she stop loving him?

As they pulled into the garage, she wondered of the outcome of others that made it their habit of loving without the guarantee of ever being loved in return.

Resting against Austin's chest, Sedona took in his scent. Every morning she tried to make it point to wake a few minutes before he stirred. In some ways, this early morning interlude was even more sensual than their lovemaking. She felt as if she truly had him to herself – no internal unspoken demons or distracting memories to fend. Somehow the quiet seemed to assuage, at least temporarily, all of the reminders of the tenacity of their relationship. Silently reminding herself not to get too used to things, she closed her eyes and willed him to sleep just a bit longer.

CHAPTER SIX

The days that followed could not have been better for Sedona. Despite the fact that Austin still had not declared those three little words that she longed to hear, their time together was romantically wonderful. Mindful of not placing pressure on him, she made a genuine effort to be laid back and allow nature to take its course. In return, Austin was relaxed and affectionate, and he made no effort to hide his genuine fondness for her.

Even though their feelings were never verbalized, Sedona and Austin explored New Orleans like a couple in love. Mid mornings found them enjoying beignets and Creole coffee at any one of the French Quarter's cozy courtyard restaurants. Their brunch was often followed by an afternoon of treasure-troving at the various antique shops along Magazine Street, or scanning the produce stalls a little further downtown at the French Market for provisions for their quiet evening meals. This particular evening, after a pleasant walk along the riverfront, they hopped a trolley over to Mazey's bookstore, The Book Café. She had telephoned earlier with news of a book that had just arrived on James VanDerZee, a highly respected black photographer made popular by his portraits taken during the Harlem Renaissance. Austin was quite eager to take a look at the books, along with several other collected works that Mazey had thoughtfully set aside over the previous months.

As they entered the shop, Sedona inhaled, "Mazey, it always

smells so good in here."

"It's either the pastries or the coffee," Mazey greeted both of them with an affectionate kiss. "Today's theme is orange and cinnamon. I have the flavors featured in the scones, coffee, as well as the tea. I'm partial to the coffee myself, but a lot of customers will drink nothing but the herbal stuff.

With an eager glance over at the photo art books, Austin teased, "I see why you have the busiest shop on the block. Not only do you cater to the eclectic taste of your customers, but you ply them with warm baked goods and cups of herbal tea."

"Laugh all you want, but the idea has done wonders for business. A quiet repose gives people an excellent excuse to come in to browse and hopefully buy."

Glancing around the softly lit store, Sedona noticed a healthy sprinkling of customers settled in comfortable upholstered club chairs with refreshment in hand. From the looks of things, quite a few loved the idea of whiling the time away with a good book.

"Everyone's reading, but how many buy?" queried Austin

"Let me put it this way. What would you do if you found yourself engrossed in a book that was too good to put down? Would you put it back on the shelf after you've had your tea, or would you purchase it?" replied Mazey.

"Why, it depends on how many were on the shelf?" chuckled Sedona.

Mischievously smiling, Mazey quipped, "That's why I only display maybe two, but no more than three copies of a book. Besides, much of what I stock are one-of-a kinds that are no longer published, therefore hard to find; or are put out by small presses. At least once a week I find myself mediating a squabble over a book that someone has claimed to have set down just for a moment." Interrupting their conversation, Mazey excused herself to turn her attention to a rather attractive male customer waiting at the cash stand.

Erotic Poetry for Lovers, is this for your wife or girlfriend?"

"My girlfriend . . . hopefully soon to be fiancée."

Reading aloud several verses from the book, Mazey winked, "If you plan on reading her any of this, you won't be for long, you better go with ring in pocket. There's nothing sexier than erotic poetry being read by a good looking man."

". . . Or being flattered by a beautiful woman," flirtatiously returned the gentleman.

Handing him his purchase, Mazey walked him to the door and accepted his compliment with a soft smile and an admonishment not to be a stranger.

"Mazey!" admonished Sedona. "You better be glad that Miles has a healthy ego. I don't know many husbands who could handle your unabashed flirting?"

"Aw, flirting keeps a man in line, ain't that right, Austin?"

With a polite smile that didn't quite reach his eyes, Austin brusquely quipped, "I see that you and my ex must've gone to the same school."

"All women have, Austin you know that. It is affectionately called, *Why Should Men Have All of the Fun?*"

Any humor in the remark was completely lost on Austin. Sedona, noticing the tightening of his jaw, changed the subject, "So, Mazey, where are those books that you were telling us about?"

As they waited for their friend to return from the storeroom, Sedona quietly eyed Austin as he perused the well-stocked stacks. Slowly the frustratingly complicated pieces to the puzzle that comprised Dr. James were beginning to fit. She had long suspected that his apparent aversion to commitment had something to do with "love lost", or in the case of Lorraine, love sullied, stained and besmirched, now she was certain. If she had any chance of ever connecting with Austin's heart, she was going to have to talk to the two women who probably knew him better than anyone, Stephanie and Lorraine.

True to her word, Mazey had stumbled across five books to add to Austin's collection. Without hesitation, he decided to purchase all of the books, and watching the two of them agree on a fair price was comical. Austin insisted that one of the books, the 1960's era, table-top compilation on the works of VanDerZee could easily garner tripled the price that Mazey was asking for the entire collection. It was obvious that her friend wished to offer the set as a gift.

Stepping in, Sedona suggested, "Listen you two, you're never going to settle on a mutually pleasing price. So, Austin, why don't you just donate the difference to a charity of Mazey's choice?"

Both seeing the logic in the compromise, agreed. "Well, since he's being inordinately headstrong about this, the young writer's group that meets here at the store could use the money."

"Sounds like a winner to me," Austin smiled and planted a kiss on Sedona's forehead as he took out his checkbook. "Wise, as well as beautiful. Now you see why I love her so much."

Dumbfounded, first by his unaccustomed display of affection, and then by his comment, Sedona could only offer a broad smile in return. Unaware of the havoc that he just wrought on her emotions, Austin sought a quiet corner to further study his books.

Playfully thrusting a compact mirror at her friend, Mazey chuckled, "Take a look at your face. I ask you, can that grin get any wider. I'm waiting for you to break out in a chorus of 'I'm In Love, I'm In Love with a Wonderful Guy. '

Embarrassed, Sedona quickly snapped shut the compact, "Austin must think that I'm no better than some silly school girl." Smoothing her dress, she muttered, "Look at me, I'm worse."

"Don't worry, he was so tickled over those dusty old books, I don't even think that he noticed." Overjoyed for her best friend, she impulsively gave Sedona a hug, "So, he finally used the "L" word."

"Please, you're making way too much out of this," whispered Sedona. "His using the word *love* in passing is hardly the same as his saying, *Sedona, I love you*, you know that."

Amused, Mazey placed her hands on her hips. "Sedona Tinney, I don't get you. One minute you're 'Oh my God, my ears can't believe' and the next second you're little Ms. Cynical. Why don't I just go out and find you a large bottle of Prozac."

"What you need to find me is the bitter pill of reality." Glancing at Austin who was now completely enthralled in his book, Sedona lowered her voice. "Austin never said that he "loved me.""

"Yeah he did. I was standing right here."

"So was I. Believe me, what he was really saying is that he loves me like a friend, no different from the way that he loves you."

"Okay, yeah, right. Sedona, I don't get you. Anyone would have to be blind not to notice the way he watches you when the two of you are together. If you don't believe me, go ask him," suggested Mazey as she pointed in Austin's direction. "After all, the direct approach is the best approach."

"Will you lower your voice and stop being so dense. You know that he needs to say it unprompted."

"But he did," loudly whispered Mazey making no bones to hide her exasperation.

"Don't you get it, whether I like or not, if this relationship is to progress past this visit, it's up to him. I've extended my feelings as far as I dare. I'm not going to set myself up for hurt, not this time, never again."

Shaking her head, Mazey refused to back down. "It sounds like you're giving up to me. With your attitude, he is going to go back out to sea, while you die here of writer's cramp pen paling – waiting for those three magic words in correct form."

As tears welled up in her dear friend's eyes, Mazey softened her tone but not her message. "Hey, I don't mean to mean to make you cry, I just want to see you finally get your bit of happiness. After all that crap that Gary put you through, don't you think that you deserve it?"

She understood where her friend was coming from. She too wanted that bit of happiness for herself. But over the years, reality proved that wanting and getting were often two very different things.

While her friend went to repair her face, Mazey brainstormed possible solutions to Sedona's predicament. She had half a mind to go over and talk to Austin herself, but Sedona would never forgive her. In her opinion, Austin was like a lot of people – afraid. Not so much afraid of a commitment, no . . . once you had him, she had a feeling that you had him for life; but he was afraid of being hurt, putting it all on the line and leaving it up to God and His divine will. In a lot of ways, it was easy to understand. Life is tough and unpredictable, and seldom fair – people even more so.

Sedona was a case in point, in the name of love; she had been through hell and back. Looking at the closed restroom door, she immediately thought of Gary and his extramarital exploits. How over the years, in his attempt to mask his own fallacies, he set out to purposely make her feel inadequate. Sedona's parents, albeit, without the maliciousness, employed the same abuse. She had long lost count of the number of times Sedona had extended herself, only to be rebuffed. Unacknowledged gifts, returned airline tickets, and cancelled visits were the Tinney's guise. The last such "visit" was especially heartbreaking. The previous Christmas, they had agreed to fly down, even made reservations and Sedona was on top of the world. She'd bought presents, planned a fabulous meal, decorated the house, and bought a beautiful tree. On Christmas Eve morning, an hour before they were to arrive at the airport, Mrs. Tinney called from the Caribbean to say that they had opted to spend the holidays with some "dear and special" friends. If it had not been for Carly, who on Christmas Eve, had insisted on dropping off a last minute present, they would not have found out about her thwarted plans; and Sedona more than likely would have spent the holiday alone, painting in her studio – her usual way of dealing with disappointment. Glancing over at Austin, still deep in his book, she recognized the same emotional weathering that prevented Sedona from recognizing and accepting proffered love.

Going into the restroom to further force the issue, Mazey thoughtfully watched as Sedona re-applied her smudged makeup. "Okay, now that you've had your little cry and have felt sorry for yourself, you can find your backbone and take control of this situation. Listen to my plan, follow it through, and you *will* get your man . . . or at the very least have the satisfaction of knowing that you tried."

Mazey, I pray that this works, thought Sedona as she studied the network of veins that bridged the bronze hand guiding the steering wheel. Wondering where Austin's thoughts were resting, she mulled over his face as she took in the attractive crinkles gathered at the corners of each eye, the strength of his jaw, and the sensuous curves of his lips. Concentrating on his eyes once more, she silently prayed that God would one day allow her to help rid them of their sadness.

Austin, as if sensing her petition, suddenly turned and smiled, "Hey beautiful, what are you up to?"

"Oh, nothing. I'm just appreciating the scenery." *If only he knew.*

"I know what you mean, springtime in the bayou. Mother Nature outdoes herself every year. I would be lying if I didn't say that the moment Mazey suggested that we come out here and use her family's cabin, the idea appealed to me."

Sedona agreed, "I have to admit, this is one of her better ideas. But, I have to warn you; if you're expecting to stay in a jury-rigged fishing shack you'll be sorely disappointed. The Chandler's idea of a cabin is quite a bit grander than yours or mine."

"Just as long as I can enjoy the clatter of the herons and warblers, I won't complain."

"We're going so far in the deep, you'll enjoy all that along with the alligators, cottonmouth snakes and black bears. I hope that you brought your trusty side arm."

Laughing aloud at her penchant for colorful expressions, Austin took hold of her hand. "Don't worry, as long as I'm around, you'll always be safe."

"Oh yeah?" Without thinking, she jibed. "How long will that be?"

"Well, Tinney . . ."

Holding his gaze, she felt her breath catch; maybe this was just the opening for the heart to heart that she so desperately wanted. *Please Lord; let him say what I need to hear.*

Honk, honk!

Interrupting what Sedona had hoped to be the long awaited expression of love was a bright red convertible recklessly hurtling up the middle of the highway driven by an obviously drunk woman.

"What the hell," muttered Austin as he dodged the hurtling automobile. Deftly pulling the convertible over to the side of the road,

Austin quickly picked up his cell phone. "Let's hope that the police catch up with her before she literally runs the next driver off the road."

Hoping to get the offending driver's license plate number, Sedona walked to the rear of the car to study the other auto's quickly disappearing weaving tail. There was something oddly familiar about the car and its vanity plate.

"The state police promises to send a car after her. I hope that they do, she's going mighty fast. Drunks, I don't have time for any of them. While you, on the other hand," his voice softening as he pulled her into his arms, "I'll make all of the time in the world." As he kissed her with a languid patience that left her heart racing, he drew her closer. "You're not too badly shaken, are you?"

"No . . . other than my racing heart, I enjoy any excuse to have you hold me in your arms . . . um, Austin, what were you going to tell me a few minutes ago in the car?"

As soon as she asked the question, the pace of Austin's heart matched that of his date. "Sedona," he murmured as he kissed her once more, "as much as I want to continue to hold you and talk, I can't. It's getting late and these bayou back roads are tricky enough in the daylight, but at night they are downright treacherous." Kissing her lips lightly before releasing her, he successfully stalled any further conversation. Behind the wheel and once again in full control, Austin surveyed the small lakes of water that bordered each side of the roadway. "With all of the rain that we have been getting, I hope that the side roads to the cabin are clear."

Only half-paying attention to his concerns, Sedona made one more attempt at trying to bring the conversation back around to her topic of choice – their relationship. "Austin . . ."

"Excuse me Sedona, where's that map that Mazey drew for us?"

Fishing it out from in between the seats, Sedona impatiently remarked, "If I remembered correctly, our turn should be coming up shortly. See . . ." pointing to the map, "we make a left turn right after the old barn."

As Austin made his way down the dusty clamshell road he took in the murky swamp only a few yards away, "I hope that Mazey got the map right? How far do we go?"

"Oh, for about 20 minutes – that is, if it's dry, an hour or more if we have to ditch the car, find the boat and row." In the name of fair play, she purposely added the last bit of information. Why should Austin call all of the shots in setting the emotional mood of their conversation?

"What?"

"Yeah, the Chandlers keep a boat hidden in the underbrush in case it floods. It's usually under the big old oak that should be coming up ahead."

Turning on the headlights, Austin slowed as a possum darted across the narrow road. "I tell you, if we have to go find a boat, and row for a hour, we need to make this little jaunt another time."

"Hey, where's your sense of adventure and courage? I thought that you navy men joined up to see the world, to blissfully drift about in boats?"

If he caught the full gist of her sarcasm, Austin did his best not to let on. "The operable word is "world", not the bayou. Do you know that we haven't seen another car since we turned off the highway?"

Sedona, thoroughly amused, spotted another small animal scampering across a massive cypress knee that jutted from out under the misty waters. "I doubt very seriously if we'll see another car the whole time that we are out here. This is a private road. I tell you, ain't nothing out here, but us and nature . . . the occasional hunter or loon."

Easing his way down the dark winding road, under the headlights,

Austin caught sight of what appeared to be recent tire tracks. "Well, it looks like Cudzo's waiting for us. Look at the tracks, someone or something has been up here recently."

Unconcerned, Sedona suggested that perhaps someone had taken the road by mistake, "Probably a fishermen looking for a good spot."

Unconvinced, Austin pulled up outside the cabin. "All I can say is that I am glad that I brought along my gun. With people as crazy as they are these days, you can't be too careful."

"You are totally correct Austin, you can't be too careful." Pointing a finger to the stand of moody moss laden cypresses that stood alongside the cabin, she continued as she unlocked the front door. "But you know, I'm learning that you need to be just as wary of those smiling at you dead in the face, as anything that may be out there lurking behind one of those trees." As she pushed open the door, she flipped the light switch and noticed a still figure sitting in the shadows by the fireplace. Letting out a shriek, she reached for Austin, who already had taken out his revolver. Immediately recognizing the figure as it turned, Sedona yelled, "Gary! What in the world . . ."

Unperturbed and laughing, Gary held out a wine bottle. "Boy, I wish that I had my camera. If I could've just gotten a picture of your faces."

Putting aside his gun, Austin retorted, "You better be glad that I didn't shoot that fool head of yours."

"Why are sitting in the dark, better still, why are you here?" demanded Sedona, still angry.

"The answer to your first question my sweet is what else is there to do; and to your second, I had planned a night of wining and seduction, but my plans were foiled."

As she crossed the large room towards him, she stopped when she noticed a dark red stain seeping across his shirt's sleeve. "Gary, you're bleeding! What happened?"

Seeing the blood, Austin quickly headed towards the door, "You better get out of that shirt while I go get my bag."

As Austin was leaving out, Gary chided just loud enough for him to hear, "Ben Casey takes his woman on a tryst in the woods and packs his medical bag? Brother, what kind of freaky sex are you into? A little doctor and nurse, or doctor and patient?"

"Oh, shut up. You'd better be glad that he brought his bag."

Quickly returning with his case, Austin set about examining the wound: Reaching for antiseptic and a bandage, he dispassionately studied Gary's face. "It looks like you'll have some explaining to do. You have been grazed by a bullet."

"I could've told you that . . ."

"Wait a minute, a bullet? Who did you piss off this time?" Sedona demanded. "Knowing your track record, it had to be either a woman or her husband."

"Well, let me put it to you this way. Wrath knows no fury like a woman scorned."

"I knew it." Knowing the history and exploits of her ex-husband, Sedona was quickly able to put two and two together. "I bet she was the reckless witch that ran Austin and I off the road a little while ago. It was Katrina Bonham wasn't it? I knew that the car looked familiar."

Still nonchalant as ever, Gary explained, "I had a game plan and she didn't want to play. It's as simple as that."

Snatching the wine bottle from his lips, Sedona found no sympathy in his plight. "I don't even know what you did, but more than likely, you deserved everything that you got." Any empathy that she had initially felt had vanished.

Not deterred, Gary good-naturedly appealed, "Austin – brother, man help me out here. I tell you – women . . . when things don't go their way, there's always a tantrum and hell to pay." Raising an eyebrow, Gary caught the other man's eye, "Tell me, why can't they be more like us? You know how we are, when things get uncomfortable, we simply check out, just like that, without a word. Ain't that right?"

Austin, ignoring the question, finished dressing the wound and gave his prognosis. "Well, it looks worse than it really is, like I said, she just grazed your arm. It'll be as sore as heck for a few days, but you'll survive."

"I figured as much. She's an expert shot, if she wanted to kill me, I'd be dead by now."

"Both of you are nuts," Austin pronounced. "An average five-year-old knows better than to play around with a gun, let alone a grown man. It's not any of my business, but I'm sure that the police will want to make out a report."

"Police? Who said anything about calling the police? I'm not pressing charges."

"Well, when we get you over to the hospital, under the law, they're supposed to contact the authorities. Actually, since I've treated you, I'm supposed to."

"Man, you're crazy. There is no way in hell I'm going to the hospital."

Sedona tersely interrupted, she had more than enough of her ex, "Let me guess, your woman friend is a wife of a client." His sheepish smile only further aggravated her. "I wish that she was a better shot. You're still the same sorry old bastard."

"Yeah, but this time, I'm not married."

Finding no humor in his comment, Sedona held his gaze and as she remarked, "We should've let him bleed to death." It was wrong she knew, but she couldn't help but glean a bit of perverse delight as he struggled to shrug on his shirt. "How long were you going to sit here

— why didn't you call for help?"

"Katrina took my cell phone. And it would've been pointless to try walking. There's no one out here for miles. Besides, I figured she'd be back. . Half way to New Orleans she'd realize that she doesn't want me going to the hospital and risking her husband finding out."

That was it. Sedona had heard all that she cared to hear. "Well, you can sit your sorry ass out on the porch until she gets here." Grabbing up her purse, with no compassion whatsoever she ordered, "But first, clean up the blood. It's beginning to stain the chair."

Austin, silently bemused at her uncharacteristic coldness, quietly watched as she climbed the staircase.

"I see that you still have that same loving touch," Gary yelled as her figure retreated up the stairs.

At the sound of the bedroom door slamming shut, he let out a laugh. Gary, drunk and talkative, turned to Austin. "Fun, isn't she? She just makes you want to walk the straight and narrow. Has some distorted crazy disillusioned fairy tale notion about love. . She always treated me square though . . . I truly loved . . . love her. During our marriage, I put her through H-E-L-L – HELL! No doubt about it. Ask me why, I couldn't tell you, except maybe she had all of these expectations . . . assumed that I was ready to settle down-become responsible, become some sort of family man. Nope, I wasn't up for that . . . determined that I wouldn't have any of it. Got my wish too. Did she ever tell you that we had a baby together – a little girl – Lilie?"

Austin, expression darkening, crossed his arms. "Sure did . . . we lost her less than a month before she was due. Sedona had just found out that I had been having an affair. I always blamed myself, figured that the stress must have been too much. Once again, I fucked up, and there wasn't a damn thing for me to say or do, except to leave. Sometimes that's the best favor that you can do for someone." As he turned to Austin's hooded gaze, Gary's statement silently turned from comment to implied suggestion.

Aware that the last sentence was directed towards him, Austin tossed him his cell phone. "Why don't you call yourself a ride?" Sitting down in a chair across from the drunken man, Austin impatiently listened as Gary smoothly cajoled his "lover" to drive back and claim him. As it turned out, she was already on her way back to the house – had just turned down the swamp road.

"Before the night's over, she'll be back in my arms – apologizing, *Gary baby, what can mama do to make you feel better?*" As he gathered up his overnight case, headlights shone through the window. "There's old "Frankie" now. "Frankie and Johnnie were lovers . . . oh how they played . . ." he sang aloud when he opened the door and grabbed the woman about the waist.

Making a half-hearted attempt at freeing herself, the attractive woman surveyed Gary's bandaged wound. "You know, I could have killed you if I wanted to."

"But you didn't, and that's the point."

Gary with a nod said his good bye. "Thanks man for patching up the arm. Take good care of Sedona, or I just might sic ol' Frankie on you." Despite the humor, it was clear from his suddenly lucid gaze that he fully expected Austin to break her heart. "Don't hurt her."

"Tinney . . . ?" Not hearing an answer, Austin stepped into the now dark room. Stooping down towards her still form, he slowly smiled when he realized that she had fallen asleep. Gently placing a throw over her, he quietly sat in a rocker near the bed.

She looked so vulnerable. Taking in her tear stained face, he pursed his lips and mulled over the drunken ramblings of Gary. Listening to Gary was like listening to his dad when he was in one of his drunken moments of reflective soul-searching. After he would dispense with the usual diatribe on the unfairness of life, he would rework the problems of life by using self-hate and recrimination as his variables. The only solution to his woes was shame filled might-have-beens. All the while, not once thinking of the personal hells that those around were experiencing. Different baggage, same sorry equation.

Sedona, just how much had she cried over the years? Sometimes you get so wrapped up in your own pain, you never realize that those around you may be going through their own personal bit of hell. He loved her, that was for sure; and he wasn't stupid. Ever since that first evening when they made love, she had wanted to hear him say those three magical words, I LOVE YOU. It wasn't that he didn't want to tell her, Lord, if anyone was entitled to hear them it was Sedona; it was that he just couldn't. He was no better with her feelings than Gary, maybe nicer – but no better. Worried about falling prey to love – running in fear that a commitment would leave him open and vulnerable. In the bed so still, her expression was like her heart, trusting and open. He wondered of the heart that could sustain such breaks of unhappiness, but still able to give love another try.

In the past, his own heart had only been a tenth as strong. He never offered it fully – always fearful . . . expecting disappointment and usually getting just what he deserved – in spades. In the darkness, he could hear his old conversations with Lorraine – her pleadings for him to stay stateside, her expressions of loneliness and depression, her desire to have children. At the time, he didn't hear a word, chose to ignore her unhappiness. In the process, he had made her life miserable and unfulfilled. No wonder she found herself turning to other men –

he hadn't been there – not even in spirit.

Chest tightening with emotion, Austin realized that he was no better than the disappointing piece of a man that he unconsciously strove to be *unlike* – his father. Dear old dad . . . selfish, unloving, and undemonstrative – caring only about himself – and not doing that very well. As he forced the pent up memories back to the recesses of his mind, he vainly tried to stem the tears that fell from his eyes. Oddly, focusing on Sedona's sleeping form, he could feel her loving spirit about his shoulders. With her near, his emotional trepidations slowly ebbed away.

Reaching for his handkerchief, he felt surprisingly renewed at the uncharacteristic let of emotions. Crying was something that he did very seldom, and never in the presence of anyone – conscious or otherwise. "Oh Sedona, how I do love you," he whispered as he kissed his sleeping beauty's forehead, leaving as soon as she stirred.

What in the hell is wrong with you? Never had he done anything so stupid. Here he was, a grown man taking off down the staircase because he was too afraid to tell the woman that he loved that he loves her. The opportunity was perfect to profess his love, to explain his distance. To put everything right. But, his head simply refused to listen to his heart. His heart knew without a doubt that she could be trusted with his feelings . . . with his love. There was a part of him that wanted to tell her just as badly as she wanted to hear it. Back in the car, it was obvious that she wanted to know if they had a future together. He was going to say yes, the words *I love you* were finding their way out. But, he knew that her look of reciprocated love would trap his heart into asking her to marry him.

Trap, oh but what a prison – waking up to her soft body each morning, and caressing her at night. What a wonderful release it would be to share life . . . dreams and fears with someone who actually cared about you.

Staring up the stairs, wondering at the irony of it all, he acquiesced to the fear that kept him rooted.

If the plaintive pleadings of a Delta blues man streaming from the kitchen radio were any indication, Sedona knew that Austin was in the kitchen, busy cooking.

"I see that *he's* gone – thank God. I am in no mood to put up with "An Evening with Gary", no matter how entertaining. What are you cooking?" Sedona peered over his shoulder as she grabbed up a broccoli floret from a colander of just steamed vegetables. Before Austin had a chance to answer, she asked, "You didn't wind up depositing him on the highway did you?"

"Nope, didn't have to," chuckled Austin," His lady love collected him, bullet and all."

"I'm not surprised. No matter what he does, how awful and juvenile he behaves, Gary always finds a way to worm his way back into everyone's good graces. It is truly his greatest talent."

Wanting to delve a bit into her and Gary's past, and perhaps ask about the baby that she lost, Austin carefully chose his words. "I see that you have kept a pretty healthy attitude in dealing with him. I imagine that he must have put you through a lot of pain."

Sedona shrugged, "Yeah . . . a lot of pain . . . but you know, things happen for a reason. Reasons that aren't always so readily apparent."

"Hmmp, sometimes the hands of fate are pretty twisted and humorless," agreed Austin as he tossed the dinner salad.

"I guess that is one way of looking at it, but for my own sanity, I have to believe that it is the omnipotent will of God. Things happen in life as a way of preparing you for a greater task or blessing."

"Do you view everything in life like that."

"I try, sometimes it's hard though, real hard."

While handing her the holders for the paper plates, he quietly commented, "Gary mentioned that the two of you lost a baby."

"Too much wine always did get Gary talking," setting the table, she swallowed hard. "What made him bring that up? I mean, we haven't really talked about it since we put away her nursery things."

As he took a seat across from her, Austin shrugged, "I call it alcoholic remorse, excuse me . . . Lord, please bless this meal, amen.

"Amen."

"He seems to blame himself," Austin continued.

With a surprised raise of a brow, Sedona sat down her fork. "Still, after all of these years? I never said anything that would make him feel that he was the blame. The doctor explained to both of us that . . . that . . . Lilie's death was simply an act of God. There wasn't anything obviously wrong with her, her organs were developed; I took good care of myself . . . tried to eat right. I didn't smoke or drink . . . it was just one of those things. Even the doctor was surprised. On the sonogram, everything looked fine. During that last checkup, her little heart was beating so strong, even after I was rushed to the hospital . . . and then it stopped . . . just like that."

Moved as much by the detached tone of her voice, as the story itself, Austin cleared his throat. Lilie, I haven't heard that name is long while. It's very pretty."

"Yeah, we thought so. We hadn't really agreed on a name, we thought that we had a bit more time. To be honest, we hadn't agreed on too much, you know the story. Lilie was Gary's idea; he said that it reminded him of the classes that we took together in Giverny on the

River Seine. We used to walk the gardens, and soak up the peaceful beauty of the water lilies, and afterwards sit and talk about all sorts of things." With a short mirthful laugh, Sedona shook her head, "I know, it doesn't sound like the same Gary that we all have come to know and love."

After taking several bites, she closed her eyes as her voice softened. "That whole period of time feels like someone else's life. I used to think about Lilie quite a bit. I have tried to remember her face, but as time passes, it gets harder and harder. One thing that I will always be able to remember is how she felt in my arms. They let us hold her . . . she was so perfect . . . so still." Refusing to dwell on the memory, she took a sip of her iced tea, "Like I said, another lifetime."

Suddenly wishing that he hadn't asked about the baby, Austin reached for her hands. "Sedona, I'm sorry that I made you dredge up all of those memories. I know that they must hurt. It's just that when Gary brought Lilie up out of the blue, I was a bit surprised. Sometimes, I look at you and feel as if I have known you forever. I have to remind myself that you had a life prior to meeting me."

Before considering her words, Sedona exploded, "It has always interested me how two people can share the same experience and walk away with two totally different perspectives." Not knowing whether or not her sudden gray mood was being fueled by Gary's earlier intrusion or Austin's thorough cluelessness, she hurtled forward. "Here you are "alluding" to our closeness and emotions that you have yet to express, while most of the time, I don't know which way is up with you. Talk about the humorless and twisted hands of Fate."

This time her arrow had found its target, bulls-eyed and centered. Finding her remark totally unexpected and stinging, Austin fiddled with his silverware. "What are you talking about? I would think that it has been rather obvious how I feel about you."

"Really? Obvious to *whom*? It has almost become sort of like a game. You take me to the edge, and then you leave me – hanging. So, Austin, I really don't know how you feel about me." *There, she had finally said it.*

Concentrating on his food, he silently wondered how in the hell he had managed to open the door that he had been so desperately holding shut. Mentally racing through options of what he could tell her, he resigned himself to the fact that there was no way to go, but straight to the heart of the issue. With feigned nonchalance, he responded, "What do you mean you don't know how I feel about you?"

"Well, I know that you enjoy my company. I know that you find me attractive, and if the past week has been any indication, I even know that I satisfy you in bed. But I don't know if you . . . if you . . ."

"If, I love you?"

"Yea, if you love me."

"Sedona, what do you think?" Silence, nothing but the tick, tick, ticking of the wall clock. He wasn't going to be left off of the hook that easy. "Okay, okay, I love you . . . how about that?" *There he had said it.*

"I'm sorry, that is not going to do it!" Sedona, offended by his attitude, felt her temper snap. "*Okay, okay,* what am I suppose to do with that?" Never had she heard such a tired declaration of love. Where were the fireworks, the music, and the tambourines?

Silently wondering how far she planned on taking the topic, he shrugged; even to his own ears, his words sounded lame. Knowing that she had expected more, he stumbled about, "Sedona, I don't know what you want me to say." *Liar, his heart shouted.*

"I want you to say . . . oh forget it," she sobbed as she pushed

105

away from the table. "Why do I keep on trying?" She hadn't wanted to cry, in fact, she had promised herself not to get emotional. She was a big girl, all grown up. From the very first moment that they had made love, she knew what she getting into. "I'm sorry. I should know by now that you feel what you feel. I can't turn it into anything else. With all of the talk about Gary and the baby, I just allowed myself to get a little too emotional. Let's just forget that I even brought the damn subject up."

Austin, wishing that he had the courage to say the words to make it all right, drew her into his arms and kissed her with all of the passion that his unemotional sentiments failed to explain. "Tinney, don't ever apologize for expressing what's in your heart. Just be patient with me, just a little while longer. Please."

Returning his kiss, she accepted his hand.

CHAPTER SEVEN

Wrapped in one another's arm, they were able to enjoy the first truly restful sleep in more than a week. All of the unexpressed emotions that had cloaked them like a pervasive veil, were now gone. More than anyone, Sedona understood the importance of allowing a relationship time to develop – to mature. But, by the same token, in order for her to make sound personal decisions regarding their friendship, she had to know where she stood. And, now she knew. Yes, using his own lips, in his own way, he told her that he loved her, perhaps as much as she loved him. Just knowing this validated her decision to give him time and a bit of room.

By the same token, Austin now felt as if he could breathe, at least partially. It was a lot of pressure to be with someone who had such intense feelings of love, especially when you weren't yet comfortable with verbalizing those same feelings in return. No longer did he feel as if he was using her, nor was he in fear of misleading her always mindful of having to choose every word carefully. Sedona knows that he loves her, but she also knows that he is not ready for a permanent relationship. Maybe now, things could grow naturally, without force. As things stood, time was no longer an enemy – that is until the cell phone broke the early morning silence.

Ring! Ring! Ring!

Certain that it had to be an emergency, Austin reached for his cell phone. Outside of a possible wrong number, no one that he knew would have the audacity to call at 3:00 in the morning. Upon hearing the stricken voice of his brother-in-law, Mitchell, on the other end, he wished that it had been a wrong number. It seemed that Stephanie was missing, presumed dead.

When she first woke to the ringing, she assumed that it was Gary stirring his usual pot of mischief. So she was stunned when she realized the true nature of the call. At a loss for words, she listened as Austin called directory assistance and asked to be connected to a regional airline. Gathering her wits, she gently took the receiver from him, and indicated that she would make the necessary travel arrangements.

"We will be arriving at Houston Hobby in ten minutes, if you have not already done so, please stow all personal items and fasten your seatbelts . . ."

It had been an hour since they boarded, and Austin had barely spoken than a few monotone words. Wishing that she knew how to ease his fear, she turned towards the window and looked out into the clouds, "What a difference a day makes," she murmured to herself.

"I was just thinking the same thing myself," quietly responded Austin. "Life sure can be a bitch."

Taking his large hand into hers, she gave it a loving kiss. There weren't any words of consolation that she could offer, why even bother. From what they could piece together from Mitchell the night before, and again before they boarded the plane, it seemed that Stephanie had taken her boat sailing and simply didn't return.

According to Mitch, they had just gotten in from the Caribbean the day before, and Stephanie was feeling a bit tired and under the weather. So, she agreed to take a nap while he made a run to the grocery store for dinner. When he returned, he immediately noticed that their sailboat, Tranquility, was gone. In the house, on the refrigerator, was posted a note explaining that she thought that getting back out on the water would rid her mind of her aches and pains.

He wasn't too worried; Stephanie was an avid sailor and often took the boat out – always returning before dinner. But, when dinnertime came and went, he began to worry and contacted the Coast Guard before going out in a neighbor's boat to search for her himself. Before Mitch had hung up, he made the heartbreaking comment that Stephanie had died on her terms, and for that he was glad. Looking over at Austin, she was tempted to ask if he thought that his sister's disappearance was merely an accident or a planned suicide. After Mitch's comment, surely the thought must have crossed his mind as well. Not knowing how to bring it up, she took in her companion's fatigued sigh, and instead volunteered to pick up the rental car while he waited for their baggage.

Making their way towards Galveston Island across the Gulf of Mexico on the 1. 7 mile Galveston Causeway, both Sedona and Austin couldn't help but look out onto the gulf and think that somewhere out there, in all of that water was Stephanie. Feeling tears well up in her eyes, she focused on the palm trees and brightly colored buildings that were coming into view. Taking in the throngs of carefree vacationers, it was hard to believe that Galveston Island was once Texas' financial and seaport hub. Under more pleasant circumstances, she would have asked Austin to take her around to his old neighborhood. Maybe encouraged him to share some stories from his childhood. He seldom spoke of that time of his life, and she was a bit curious of how things were for him growing up. As if reading her mind, Austin turned up a narrow street of colorful Victorians. Despite the fact that most of the yards were lovingly cared for with oleanders and angel trumpets it was obvious that it was one of Galveston's less prosperous areas.

"I thought that I would take a short cut through the old 'hood' over to Stephanie's. The tourists seldom make their way back through here."

"So, this is the neighborhood where you grew up in?"

"Yup, the one and only."

Stopping in front of a tree filled lot, Austin rolled down the windows and turned off the car. "Do you see that huge live oak, towards the front of the lot?"

Turning to where he was pointing, Sedona nodded.

"That was our hangout. Stephanie and I used to climb up in that tree and sit for hours. It was the perfect spot to check out what was going on with the neighbors. Even though we could see what everyone was up to, eavesdrop on a few conversations, or spy on whom was cheating on whom, no one could see us. We knew more about what was going on with the block than the neighborhood gossip, Mrs. Jenkins, down the street."

"So, which house did you live in?" Sedona smiled as she imagined the pair spying on their neighbors.

"That one, right next door. We lived on the second floor, the owners, Mr. and Mrs. Goodly, lived on the first – they still do. I think Stephanie told me that they she had stopped by there a little while ago."

His former home was elevated above the sidewalk on stilts like most of the other residences and businesses on the island. She could tell from the worn shutters, designed to be battened at a moment's notice, that the house had probably withstood a good number of hurricanes. Continuing to take it in, her eyes lit as she openly smiled at the owner's choice of color scheme. The wooden clapboards were painted a bright yellow, and even though the vivid blue and red trim was not done up in more traditional colors, the overall effect was oddly pleasing.

"Wow," chuckled Sedona, searching for the right words to describe the imaginative color combination, "It's . . . it's . . . dazzling."

"Dazzling, is not the word that I would have chosen, but apropos. If you think that this combination is something, when we were growing up, the shutters and trim had this sort of lime green and bright yellow thing going on . . . now that was dazzling."

As their conversation lapsed into a comfortable silence, Austin leaned his head back against the seat rest and continued to study the house and its neighboring lot. "It seems just like yesterday . . . the Goodly's were what I guess you would call our surrogate parents. After our mother died, they pretty much looked after us; Dad was of little help. He paid the rent and that was about it." Again, silence.

Intuitively sensing that he was using their stopover as time to get his head together, Sedona sat quiet. Right now, Austin could still view his sister as simply being missing, a bit late returning home. But once they met up with Mitchell, he would have to face the reality that his sister may be dead.

"I will never forget the last time we were both up in that tree. It was the summer that I finished my internship over at UTMB . . ."

"UTMB?"

"I'm sorry, the University of Texas Medical Branch, it's here on the island on the other side of the Strand. I forget; you're not a native. If we ever make it here again, I'll have to show you around. "

Sedona, picking up on Austin's condition of 'if', nodded. It was obvious that he had already accepted the likely fate of his sister. "I did-n't mean to interrupt, you were in the middle of telling me about the last time that you and Stephanie were up in the tree."

"Oh, I was just thinking that back then, at that moment, we both realized that in a few weeks our lives were going to be totally changed forever. The Navy assigned me to a ship out in San Diego, and Stephanie was going to be graduating from college the following spring. Up in that tree we talked for hours. I told her that even though when at sea, I would be thousands of miles away; I would always be there for her. We were all that we had." With a chuckle that almost sounded like a stifled sob, he resignedly shrugged, "What's the line from that old Gilbert O'Sullivan song, "Here I am, alone again . . . naturally."

Wanting so desperately to correct him, to remind him that he wasn't alone, that she loved him, that they had one another, as they sat, Sedona forced back her own words.

It was impossible to ignore the parked state police car, when they turned off the narrow coastal road onto the driveway that ran along-side Mitchell and Stephanie's stilted terra cotta stucco. The presence of the car, along with the dark colored military vehicle parked along-side it, gave the couple pause. Tapping the steering wheel, Austin took a deep breath, "Well, here goes."

Instead of entering the home through the front door, they followed the voices around to the side of the house that faced the dock. There they found Mitchell, two Coast Guardsmen, and a Texas State Trooper. Upon seeing the couple, Mitch – obviously relieved, walked over and gave his brother-in-law a warm hug.

"Austin, Sedona, this is Sgt. Marks – Texas DPS, and Chief Petty Officer Sanchez and Petty Officer Blackman, they are with the Coast Guard's Search and Rescue Team. Returning their salute, Austin not expecting to be recognized queried, "I gather that Mitchell has spoken of me?"

"Yes, sir. He gave us the expected time of your arrival. We thought you would want to be immediately brought up to speed regarding the progress of our search."

From the expression on Blackman's face, as well as his choice of the term "search", instead of the more positive word "rescue", Austin surmised that the news would not be good. Always in control in spite of any situation, he turned towards Sedona and quickly introduced her to the group.

After the courteous nodding of heads, he got straight to the heart of their visit, "Well, let's hear it?"

Solemnly glancing first at Mitchell, then at the state trooper, the senior ranked Coast Guardsman responded, "Lt. Commander James, when Mr. Frazier mentioned that you would be flying down, we hoped that we would have better news. Thus far, things aren't looking very promising."

"They found the sailboat . . . ," interrupted Mitch.

"And she wasn't on it," flatly surmised Austin.

"That's correct, sir," answered the second Guardsman. "The boat was recovered, anchored in fact, about 35 miles offshore. At this point, with the amount of time that has elapsed, we have no other choice but to treat the case as a drowning."

Accepting the news unemotionally, Austin simply nodded, "I assume that you have done the standard search?"

"Yes sir. With recovering the boat that far out, as you know, it is now a matter of waiting until the body washes up on shore."

"We explained to Mr. Frazier that we will continue to search the beach daily," empathetically offered the state trooper. "I am sure that you know better than anyone that it is impossible to know exactly where to search. She appears to not have been far out enough to go out to sea. As you probably already know, we are dealing with two sets of currents here, one runs southwesterly off Louisiana, and the other runs northeasterly from the Mexican coast. So pretty much everything stays here in the Gulf. Keeping this in mind, along with the tide and weather of course, I have been able to come up with a broad, general area. I've brought copies of a map showing the coordinates where the boat was recovered, along with the areas we will be paying special attention to. But, again, like I said, we could find her almost anywhere."

Handing copies to Mitch and Austin, the trooper continued, "If you have any questions, please give me a call at the number on the attached card."

"Um . . ." Austin paused to clear his throat – the only visible indicator of his shaken emotional state, "I assume that you have notified the media and the other local law enforcement agencies, just in case she's spotted?"

"Yes sir," hesitantly answered Sanchez. It was apparent that Austin's question was of concern. Feeling the need to reiterate that Stephanie more than likely drowned, the Guardsman continued after an uncomfortable pause. "But sir, if I may, despite the fact that she was a strong swimmer, at this point it's not very likely that she is still alive. Any boater that may have picked her up, would have radioed with news by now."

Visibly irritated that the man had misunderstood his question, Austin dug his hands deep into his pockets and snapped, "Chief Petty Officer Sanchez, I fully understand that it is more than probable that she did not survive. I was asking the question in reference to the possibility of her *body* being found by a vessel, a swimmer or someone along the beach. I just want to ensure that those in the area are aware that we are searching for her – to have a description of what she was wearing, so that when she is found, there is no confusion."

Quickly apologizing, Sanchez explained, "I'm sorry, sir. I misunderstood. It's just that when a loved one is missing, we find that for many, it is hard to give up hope."

With a nod, Austin thanked them as he shook the hands of the three guests and quietly excused himself.

When Austin was out of hearing distance, Sedona spoke for the first time. "You really must forgive him. He's taking the loss of his sister quite hard. I'm sure that he appreciates all that you have done."

"No need to apologize ma'am, Sanchez responded. We do understand. Please assure him that we are giving this our upper most attention."

Thanking them again as they left, Sedona turned her attention to Mitchell. She had never formally met the man, only spoken to him over the telephone; but because of the loving way that Stephanie often spoke of her husband, she felt as if she knew him quite well. Steph had described him to the "T" – a little shorter than Austin, husky build – almost like a teddy bear, and always ready with a warm friendly smile.

"Mitchell, I'm so sorry about Stephanie, Sedona comforted as she hugged him. You must be just overwhelmed by all of this."

Mitch, looking over the rail, out at the sea, simply nodded. "It is a bit much, but to be honest, I half expected for her to do something like this. Right when Steph was diagnosed with cancer, she said that she didn't want to drag her illness out. She died the way she wanted to, quick and peaceful . . . with dignity."

"So you're thinking that she killed herself?" Sedona quietly verbalized the implication of his statement.

Resignedly shrugging, he continued to stare out into the Gulf, "Sedona, it's the only thing that makes sense. That evening, the water was peaceful, she had been out literally thousands of times before – when they found the boat, there was absolutely nothing wrong with it . . ."

"Maybe she fell overboard, or dove over for a swim," Sedona vainly offered.

"I doubt it. The boat was right there, she could have climbed back on board; she has lived on this water all her life. She knew better than to go swimming alone."

"And you don't think that someone could have abducted her?"

With a no, Mitchell offered a plausible explanation, "Again, the possibility would defy her common sense. Think about it, she had a radio, flares and cell phone on board. She could have easily heard or seen someone approaching. Believe me, I know my wife, if anyone had bothered her she would have called for help in a New York minute."

Before continuing, he glanced behind his shoulder and lowered his voice, "Besides, I didn't mention it to Austin, but she took her "Float Plan" down from off the refrigerator before she left."

"Float Plan?"

"Yeah, it's a form that she picked up at the Coast Guard Station a while back. Before you take your boat out onto the water, they ask that you fill it out with details regarding your vessel, your destination, that type of thing. You're supposed to leave it with a friend just in case something goes wrong. She *always* filled it out. With her going out alone so much, she would leave it posted on the refrigerator. It was a little system that we had worked out, so I wouldn't worry."

"So, what you are saying is that her removing the form was her way of telling you that she wasn't coming back. But, I thought that the cancer was in remission? Only last week she told Austin that she was beginning to feel like her old self."

"I think that she forced herself to ignore the symptoms, she wanted to get better so badly. But, a couple of nights ago, Steph felt some of the old pains return. She was insistent that it was overworked muscles from all of the diving that we did out in the Caribbean. She had me convinced, but now I suspect that the pain had come back sooner, she just didn't want to admit it."

"Or relish the thought of going back through chemotherapy. I know that it was an ordeal. Oh, poor Steph." Sedona accepted Mitch consoling arms as they both quietly sobbed. After there weren't any more tears to spend, she soberly asked, "So what do we do now?"

"Wait."

Looking out onto the vast Gulf, she humorlessly thought of how much she had come to hate that word – how it had ominously preceded every change in her life. With an earnest prayer to God, she asked that this time, He would show special mercy and see to it that the wait wouldn't be very long.

CHAPTER EIGHT

"Well, where is he?'" Sedona asked with more than a hint of concern.

Mitchell had suggested that she go into the house and get settled. He wanted very much for them to stay with him instead of booking a hotel room. Otherwise, he argued, he would spend all of his time dwelling on "what ifs." More than happy to oblige, Sedona helped him retrieve the baggage from the car. She was certain that Austin would have no problem staying at the house.

"Sedona, I wouldn't worry, Austin just needs time to take in all that has happened. I tell you, I've been out searching for almost two days, met with the police and Coast Guard, walked the beach, and I still can't get use to the idea that she is . . . is . . . gone. Austin, well – he has just walked in on all of this."

Sedona knew that Mitchell was right and did her best not to worry. After settling into their room, she took in her surroundings. It was obvious that Stephanie truly enjoyed life on the waterfront. The portion of the house that faced the Gulf was a seamless line of windows. The coolness of the modern furniture betrayed the steamy heat sizzling outside. All of the rooms were painted in fresh pastels, and accessorized with finds from the beach – sea-shell filled glass containers, abstract art integrated with driftwood, along with shelves and table tops adorned with miniature sail boats and lighthouses.

While Mitch answered a phone that seemed to ring endlessly,

Sedona enjoyed the view from the window and appreciatively smiled as she took in the faint, soothing sounds of several rhythmic wind chimes. When Mitch hung up the phone; she joined him over at the wet bar and watched as he took out a pitcher of iced tea from the refrigerator.

"Has Austin ever shown you a picture of their mom?" asked Mitchell as he handed her a glass.

"No, Austin speaks very little of his parents. What I have been able to gather is that he's not on speaking terms with his dad."

"That's an understatement. Here's a picture of their parents right after their marriage." Accepting the beautifully framed photograph of the couple, Sedona took in the woman's face. "Wow, she's quite striking."

"Her and Stephanie both had that same kinda crooked smile, sorta mischievous. Stephanie got her looks honestly."

"I see," Sedona found herself drawn to the face of the father. Even though he embraced his wife with loving assuredness, it was hard for her to overlook the sadness in his eyes. Somehow the gentle smile on his lips didn't quite make it to his eyes – they were very melancholy.

As she set the frame down, Sedona placed a compassionate hand on Mitchell's shoulder, "I bet that you haven't had a thing to eat today? I could whip us up a light lunch . . ."

"Thank you but no, I couldn't eat a thing. I'm thinking of taking that map and heading on out to . . . hey, here comes Austin. Hopefully the walk did him some good."

Hurrying over to the window, Sedona spotted Austin coming up the drive, and quickly opened the door. Before he even entered, she took hold of his hand and gave it a tight squeeze, "Oh, I'm glad you're back, I was starting to worry. Are you feeling a bit better?"

Oddly annoyed by the question, he shrugged, "How do I answer a question like that Sedona?"

"Excuse me, poor chose of words." Not knowing quite what to say, she walked over to the bar and poured him a glass of tea as she tried to explain. "It's just that when you left without a word, I couldn't help but get a little concerned."

Desperate to rid him of his brusque mood, she changed the subject. "Are you hungry? I noticed that you didn't eat a thing on the plane. I could whip us up a salad to go along with one of the casseroles that Stephanie's and Mitch's friends have been nice enough to bring by. If that doesn't sound good, there's spaghetti, enchiladas, and even a chocolate cake. Or, if you're restless, we could head back towards town and try Landry's. The last time I was here, the seafood was wonderful. In fact, they give you so much food; you wind up taking half of it home. What sounds good to you Mitch? I know that you just said that you weren't hungry, but maybe we can share a platter. Like I said, they serve you more than enough . . ."

Austin, so utterly lost in his sorrow, heard himself snap, "Damn it Sedona! I'm sorry, but enough with the prattling on about food. I'm not hungry. I don't know about Mitch, but eating is the last thing on my mind right now. The *only* reason I came back to the house was to see if Mitch wanted to take the boat out to search a bit along the coast. High tide should be over in about fifteen minutes, maybe with a little luck, we'll be able to find her."

"Oh . . . ok, that's fine. I only mentioned eating because I knew that the two of you hadn't eaten. Just let me change my shoes, and we can get going."

Mitch, reading between the lines of his brother-in-laws remarks, had a good suspicion that Austin really wasn't yet up to Sedona's well-intended company. "Um, Sedona, I know that you're just as anxious as both of us to get out and search, but would you mind staying here at the house? I wouldn't want to miss the authorities if they try to call."

Tempted to suggest that they forward the telephone to one of their cell phones, Sedona, glanced over at Austin who had turned all of his attention to a map, and realized that Mitch was thoughtfully trying to spare her feelings from her companion's dour mood. "Sure, I can do that," Sedona shrugged as she studied Austin's profile. "Um . . . I've noticed that the phone has been ringing all morning. I assumed that they have been from your family and friends. Is there anything specific that you want me to tell them?"

"No, just that . . . that nothing has changed . . . we're still searching."

As she walked them out, Sedona self consciously touched Austin's arm. When he turned, their eyes held briefly. Thoroughly at a loss for words, she wished that she knew what to say – anything to ease a bit of his grief. So, for want of anything else, she wordlessly mouthed, "I love you."

The look in his eyes told her that finally she had struck a chord. It was obvious that he was barely holding on by little more than a thread. She knew for him that it was essential that he maintained a strong front, so she didn't press for a verbal comment, but made do with his brief kiss on the cheek.

At the window, she watched until they were long out of sight.

As the afternoon drug on, it became increasingly obvious that Stephanie had enjoyed a much more social life than her brother had. The calls inquiring about her search had been so numerous, that answering the phone was almost therapeutic. The more she brought the caller up-to-date on the situation, Sedona found the more she adjusted to the idea that Stephanie had taken her life. It was no longer some type of surreal event, but a sad fact.

Just as she was about to settle down to watch the early evening news broadcast, the phone rang once again.

"Hello, the Frazier residence."

"Yes, may I speak to Mitchell, please?"

Trying to filter out the voice from a sudden blast of static, Sedona shouted into the receiver, "Sir, I can barely hear you. Your call is breaking up; we must have a bad connection. May I take a message?"

"Yes, ask Mitchell to call Michael James. He has my number."

As she wrote down the message, Sedona immediately picked up on the last name. "Sir . . . sir"

Dead silence.

Grabbing up the message pad, she looked at the name once again, Michael James. *I wonder . . .*

Not giving herself the opportunity to talk herself out of calling the gentleman back, she glanced over at the caller id box positioned next to the phone and dialed the number.

"Hello, Platform C."

"Um . . . may I please speak to Mr. James . . . Michael James?"

"Hold on." In the background, over the sound of heavy machinery, Sedona could hear Mr. James name being announced over an intercom. As she waited, she wondered if her intuition was correct – that Mr. James was Austin's father.

"James here."

Determined not to be put off by his curt tone, Sedona cleared her throat.

"Mr. James, this is Sedona Tinney. I was the one who just took your message. Mitchell is out with Austin, and I'm answering the phone while they're gone."

"So, Austin made it in. Good, then Mitchell's not alone."

"That's correct, he asked that we stay here at the house."

Always direct, Michael commented, "We . . . you must be that girlfriend that Stephanie told me about. How is Austin?"

Pleased that Stephanie had referred to her as Austin's "girlfriend," Sedona's trepidation melted. "He's doing as well as can be expected. He was thrown by the suddenness of all of this, but he's coping."

"Good. I gather that there's still not any word on Steph?" Despite the sharpness of his tone, his concern was evident.

"No, they're still searching. In fact, that's what Mitchell and Austin are out doing right now."

"Good . . . good. Well, tell Mitchell that I'll be coming on in shortly. Since Austin is there, I won't drop by the house without calling. Mitchell will know what I'm talking about – you just tell him that. He can call me on my cell phone when there's further news. You take care now, Ms. Tinney."

Not yet ready to end their conversation, Sedona quickly inquired, "Um . . . sir, you wouldn't by any chance be Stephanie's and Austin's father? I mean if you are, I thought that you might want a little more information about the search."

After a rather lengthy pause, Mr. James slowly answered. "Ms. Tinney . . . ."

"Sedona, please."

"Ok, Sedona, yes I am their father."

With her heart pounding, Sedona barreled forward, "I had a feeling that you were, from the last name and . . . and your voice."

"My voice?"

"Yes, sir. It reminds me of Austin's."

"Don't let Austin hear you say that," he commented with a dry chuckle. "I'm sure that he would want any similarities between the two of us kept strictly to last names. You have more news about Stephanie . . ." his tone a bit hopeful.

"I don't know how much Mitch has told you, but they still haven't been able to locate her body. The authorities were here this morning and have resigned themselves to the fact that she's . . . that she's . . ."

"Dead," bluntly supplied the man.

"Yes, sir."

After a long length of silence, the older man allowed little to be betrayed in his voice. "Maybe the storm will bring her on home."

"The storm?"

"Well, yea, there's a pretty bad one brewing. We've been dealing with it out on the rigs for most of the afternoon. It's been pretty rough, I suspect that's why our call broke up earlier."

Wanting to reach out in some type of the way to the voice on the other end, Sedona picked up the photograph and continued the conversation as if they were old friends.

"So, you're out in the Gulf?"

"Yea, about 136 miles off of Corpus."

"Austin never mentioned that you were in the area, I had always gotten the impression that you were half way across the country somewhere. Have you been in the oil business for long?"

Like most, Michael found himself warming up to Sedona's easy manner, so he settled into what was evolving into a friendly conversation. "Oh, I've been working out on the rigs for about six or seven years now. Before that, I worked out of the Houston Shipping Channel, at one refinery or another. As I'm sure that you know, Austin and I haven't spoken in years. So, I'm not surprised that he hasn't said too much about me. The only way he would've known that I was working out on the rigs is if Steph had told him."

"So, I gather that you and Stephanie were pretty close. I mean, you mentioned earlier that she told you that I was Austin's girlfriend."

"We were getting there. Over the years, she and I have been able to put the past in perspective. She's forgiven me for not being the proper father for her and Austin while they were growing up. It's kinda funny, but when they announced your call over the system, for a sec there, I thought that it was her calling – telling me some funny story or the other. She's one of the few that call me regular. She's always clipping some interesting story out of the newspaper . . . listen to me, still talking as if I'll hear from her tomorrow. I tell you, it's going to be hard."

Her heart hurting at the despondency of his voice, Sedona sympathetically offered, "I know that your heart must be just about breaking right now. But, thank God that you two were able to put things right. Now, you have fond loving memories – that will keep you going, not regret."

"You're right about that. Don't get me wrong though, there will always be that wish to be able to go back in time and change things, but least ways she knows that I love her . . . well, Sedona it was mighty good talking to you. Mighty good."

"Mr. James, if you wish, I will be more than happy to keep you posted on the search. I know that you and Austin aren't on the best of terms, but maybe I could convince him to . . ."

Not allowing her to finish her thought, Michael cut in with a sad chuckle, "You're sounding a bit like my Steph, ever hopeful – up till the very end. You can't change or fix people Sedona, don't break your heart trying. You take care."

Staring at the receiver after she replaced it on its hook, Sedona couldn't help but feel very, very sad. Sad for Mitchell, Stephanie, Austin, his dad, and for herself. Resisting an urge to give her parents

125

a call, Sedona sat on the couch and turned on the television.

"Clunk."

Jumping at the sound of the front door closing, Sedona quickly sat up, "Austin?"

"No, it's me, I didn't mean to wake you," came the apologetic voice from out of the shadows. "Coming up the drive, when I saw that the lights were off and the TV on, I should've guessed that you had fallen asleep."

As her eyes narrowed to make out the moving shadow, they slowly adjusted to the dark room. "What time is it?"

Switching off the television, he turned on a lamp. "Oh, it's about midnight. Did . . ."

"Midnight! Is it that late already? I never seem to be able to watch a movie all the way through. The last thing I remember is Steve McQueen asking Natalie Wood to marry him." Propping a pillow behind her head, she chuckled, "Its not like I don't know how it ends, I can almost recite the movie verbatim. "

"Really . . . what were you watching?" Mitch asked with half interest as he checked the telephone caller id box.

"*Love with the Proper Stranger,*" massaging the kinks out of her neck, she glanced out the window, "It's starting to rain pretty hard, where's Austin?"

"I don't know, and to be honest – at this point, I really don't care. A couple of hours ago, we had – how do they say – a parting of the ways." Irritably throwing his keys on a side table, he pulled up an ottoman across from Sedona. "If he wasn't Stephanie's brother, Sedona

I tell you-I swear to God, I would have killed him. It took all that I had not to . . ."

Thoroughly alarmed at the dramatic change in his usually easygoing demeanor, Sedona sat forward, "What? What happened? What did he do?"

"It's not what he did, but what he said. He insinuated that, no I take that back, he blatantly accused me of turning a blind eye regarding Stephanie's cancer. Of either not paying attention to her conversations regarding her remission or worse yet, ignoring any hints that she was going to take her own life. Do you believe the audacity? He actually said *to my face*, and I quote, *judging from your casual acceptance of my sister's death, I'm beginning to think that you are somewhat relieved that she killed herself.*" With his head in his hands, the weary man sighed deeply. "I keep telling myself that they are brother and sister, close brother and sister. But, Jesus help me, I am her husband. Austin hasn't cornered the market on loving Steph. Besides, what right did I, or anyone for that matter, have to ask Steph to continue struggling with the pain?"

It was impossible not to feel his anguish as she instinctively knelt beside him and offered words of solace. "I know that you love Stephanie, and Austin knows it. He has never said anything to suggest otherwise. So you don't have to convince anyone that you love her; no one is questioning that fact. Austin is just looking for someone or something to blame. Even though he's a doctor, he truly wanted to believe that Steph's remission was permanent." Patting his arm, she softly asked, "I gather that you told him of your suspicions?"

Mitchell took out a handkerchief and wiped away quiet tears, and nodded. "I had to. It just tore me up listening to him go over and over the possibilities of what could've happened on her boat to cause her to go overboard. He had to know."

Only imagining how Austin's heart must have broken, Sedona quickly said a prayer before continuing. "Listen, despite what he said, I'm sure that Austin had already suspected that Stephanie had taken her own life. I know that it was the first thing that had gone across my mind, and he knew her much, much better. She was in pain, and it was her choice not to suffer. No one can fault her for that. Right now I think that Austin is angry with God, Stephanie for getting tired and giving up, himself for hurting so much, and with you for being the last one to see her, to touch her, to say I love you. Outside of his mother, Stephanie is probably the only person that he has ever freely said those words."

Damn! Unseasonably dry for over a month, and now it decides to rain. Glancing back over his shoulder, northwards up the beach towards the house, he momentarily considered heading back, but quickly decided against it. Mitch was probably already back sobbing on Sedona's shoulder. The last thing he was in the mood for was a continuation of their argument with the added bonus of Sedona acting as some kind of self-appointed mediator. After the way Mitch had unceremoniously deposited him at the pier – hell, kicked him off the boat – he doubted if he would be welcomed anyway.

Perversely laughing at the memory of the usually affable bear of a man shoving him off the motorboat, Austin wondered what would have happened, if he had pushed him back. He hadn't had a good "fist-a-cuffs" since high school, his graduation night to be exact. Angrily kicking away a piece of driftwood as the memory came wandering by, he remembered the empty feeling that stayed with him long after those bruises had healed.

His eyes following the flashlight as he traipsed its light across the water, then back onto the brown sand, Austin noticed the glint of abalone shell mixed in with the crushed rock that littered the beach. As he reached down to unearth what the sea had brought in and abandoned, the light caught the muted rainbow of colors. It seemed like only yesterday that he and Steph were playing along the beach, picking up shells, poking around the broken pieces of sand dollars and weathered driftwood for anything that looked interesting. They used to be amazed at what they would stumble across – auto parts, relics from the many oilrigs that dotted the gulf, sometimes even old appliances. Over the years, they had accumulated quite a collection. The months immediately following their mother's death, when they had had their fill of treasure hunting, they would hold hands and walk hip deep into water and imagine that they could join the untroubled sea gulls and fly away far to some idyllic island.

Turning his head in the direction of laughter wafting from a young couple's playful conversation, Austin inquisitively searched out the guilty party from a row of elegant beach homes. When he spied the devilish pair lounging in a chaise behind a screened in loggia, he enviously wished that he could wave and in turn, be extended an invitation up to share a bottle of wine and the rainy night. As their mirthful play heartlessly filled the air, Austin unconsciously furrowed his brow and walked deeper into his past.

Idiotic laughter – he hissed with disparagement. *Nothing ever changes, you move away, come back – and there it is, still hitting you upside the head – those same lousy feelings.* If he didn't know better, he could've still been thirteen, staring out from behind the hazy windows of school bus #114 creaking up Seawall Blvd. Living in a beach town was fun if you were the seasonal tourist, spirit bruising if you were an impoverished resident, too poor to frequent the flamingo pink and neon clad souvenir shops; and unwelcome at the endless island celebrations and festivals. Looking bleakly out into the water, his heart remembered how as a child riding that smoky old bus, he along with the other kids would point and laugh at the tacky tourists wearing their flashy clothes and too small swim suits. The ten mile long seawall, boasted as the longest continuous sidewalk in the world, was always enlivened with music and fun activities. Despite the reproachful remarks and rounds of laughter, if the truth had been told, any one of them would have gladly traded places, if just for the afternoon.

Strands of music drifted from yet another house, and he vainly tried to shut out the bizarre surrealism of death. Even though, as a physician, he had tussled with death, smelled death, and even forestalled it's inevitability; the acceptance of the painful contradiction that in spite of death, life continued to pirouette with unwavering resoluteness still gave him periods of consternation. None of it made sense. His sister, the only real family he had left was out there, adrift on the sea, while giggling couples clueless to the ache of loneliness drank wine in the rain. Chilled by the callousness of it all, he thought of Sedona and the remark that she made the first night that they had made love. She said that she was going to ask God why He went out of the way to make life so damn unfair. Well, he was going to be right behind her, waiting for an answer.

As he reached down to toss a hermit crab back into the sea, Austin bid a reprieve, *there you go buddy, a second chance*. Where was Stephanie's second chance, her reprieve? If she had just kept on with the chemo – had just a little more faith, just maybe she would have stayed in remission. The world is full of cancer survivors, who says that she couldn't have been one of them . . . at least for a little longer . . . at least until *he* was able to say goodbye. Fixated on a series of waves that seemed to approach the shore like huge dark moving stair steps, Austin allowed tears of grief to slide down his face as he remembered the goodbyes in his life. None he had understood, from the father who never loved him to the ex-wife who stopped. In between was his mother, now his sister. Kicking a shell, he sadly wondered why for some, life was family gatherings, Sunday dinners at mother's, with father and uncles sitting around sagely dispensing advice. He never expected a "Norman Rockwell" life, but he deserved better than being alone, always being the one *told* goodbye. "It's always much harder for the one being left," Mom smiled. Mom smiled, said I love you and died. Was there a smile on Stephanie's face? Hell, why wouldn't she have smiled? No more pain, no more surgery or therapy . . . no more uncertainty.

Unmindful of the strengthening rain, he walked closer to the water's edge, scanning the fluorescent foam of the rough surf for any signs of his sister. Stopping, he stared out at all of the blackness and willed himself to become one with the sea – silently begging its clutches to give her up. Feet cold from the chilly water that seeped into his shoes, he mournfully wondered if Stephanie too was cold. As his consciousness melded into the seamless black horizon, Austin remembered expressing that fear to his father when his mother passed. Is she cold? Despite believing that her soul had gone on to heaven, he was so unable to live with the idea that his mother was to be buried in the cold dark ground – alone, he petitioned his father to have her cremated. Surprisingly his dad agreed. Closing his eyes, he remembered it like yesterday. Together, all three of them, cast her ashes on the wind and watched as she was carried over the water. "*The lark's on the wing,*" his sister whispered as the ashes flew away.

Quickly turning in the direction of her soundless voice, Austin felt their warm presence. So tangible were they – his mother and sister, he could smell the freesia from his sister's cologne. All at once, glad that they had joined him on the beach, sad that he couldn't see and touch them, he closed his eyes and allowed them to encircle him. As soon as his mother and sister released him, Austin instinctively knew that there was no need to worry. Stephanie was doing just fine.

Aware of the cold for the first time that night, Austin stuffed his hands in his pockets and braced his back against the wind. Walking rearwards, he continued on his journey away from the house. Although his heart wanted more than anything to return home to Sedona – his last respite, his head refused. Love was just too precarious; there were no guarantees, not even from those who were supposed to love you for life. They too leave. Leaving you behind, alone. *Sedona, I love you. I truly do, but I have to be smart.* Hardening his heart against the pressing desire to rest in her warm embrace, he desperately tried to shut away the desire to touch her soft body, to smell her hair, to test her smile. Oh, how he miserably envied Stephanie and his mother. He wished that he too no longer had to deal with the cruel realities of life's uncertainties.

Away from the increasing tide of water, he stopped and scanned the lightening filled sky. From the looks of the brooding clouds and rumbling thunder, it would only be a matter of moments before the deluge. He should have turned back hours ago. Now, cognizant of how foolhardy his trek along the deserted beach had become, Austin looked around for cover. It didn't take years of living at sea to know that a beach was the last place to be during an electrical storm. He had walked too far from the island's entertainment strip to be near any kind of night spot, short of knocking on someone's door and asking for shelter, his only hope was to find an open bait shop.

In a futile attempt to protect himself from the rain that had progressed into a steady drizzle, Austin pulled up his collar and looked around to get his bearings. It had been years since he had been this far down the beach; most of the homes that he was familiar with were long gone. Not sure whether he should turn around and go back the way he came or continue, he chose the latter; for all that he had passed for several miles were homes – most of them empty and battened. Ahead, he soon found out, were only more of the same. It seemed that his only recourse was to find an empty house with a covered porch and wait out the downpour. Several yards along a bend in the shore, he caught the distant twinkling of white lights, Harland's Fishing Pier! It had been over twenty-five years, but it was still there.

Cold, wet, and miserable, Austin ran the half-mile, praying that it was still open. Even if the pier was closed, he reasoned, he could take cover under the structure. Several feet short of the steep stairway, Austin prematurely sighed. Just when he thought he had made it, his ankle betrayed him and he found himself slipping down on the wet sand, into the incoming surf.

"Hey buddy, you need help?" boomed a vaguely familiar gruff voice.

In the darkness it was impossible to make out the face obscured by sheets of rain. Gratefully reaching up towards the helping hand, Austin nodded thanks. Following the rain-slicked figure up the steps into the bait shop, Austin noticed that the helpful stranger was almost his height. The raincoat made it impossible to make out much else.

As they neared the landing, the man commented, "Thank God for Harland, he's been keeping this joint open twenty-four/seven ever since I can remember." Opening the shop's door, he stepped aside to allow Austin to pass.

Without looking at the man's face, Austin gratefully nodded thanks and ducked into the toasty shop.

The helpful stranger took in Austin's profile and caught his breath. Quickly recovering, he pointed towards the rear of the store, "There's a rack of clothes – souvenir stuff, on the other side there, back near the bar. Why don't you buy yourself a dry T-shirt and a pair of shorts? You've got money don't ya?"

"Yeah, I got money." Focused on finding dry clothes, Austin, without looking in the Samaritan's direction, brusquely nodded thanks and headed for the rear of the store.

Dry clothes never felt so good. Rolling his wet jeans and shirt neatly into one another, Austin directed the nozzle of the electric hand dryer upward and allowed the hot air to dry his still wet back and hair. Looking down at his newly purchased "beach ensemble" – a flamingo pink T-shirt and a pair of shorts decorated with turquoise palm trees, he chuckled for the first time all day. *Good thing Sedona isn't here to see me in this get-up. I would never hear the end of it, especially after that crack I made about her appearance at the airport.* Feeling a bit like his old self, he decided to buy his "Good Samaritan" a beer.

In search of the stranger, Austin followed the sound of the bar's television set and ducked into the dark lounge. Save for the short spindly bartender who had his head buried in what looked like a Bible, the room was empty. As he settled onto a stool, he peered out of a dirty window into the night. The rain showed no sign of letting up, from the creaking and shuddering of the pier, it seemed to have intensified since his coming in.

"This must've been like what those boys out on the Sea of Galilee a-felt like," commented the Bible reader. "Can ya imagine bein' out at sea on a night like this . . . all vulnerable like . . . waves crashing . . . thunder a clappin' . . . ya rockin' to and fro?"

Not wanting to encourage the talkative stranger, Austin intently stared into the television set and simply nodded. *God, this is worse than listening to Sedona when she's lost in one of her painful meanderings.*

Just my luck, a Bible-thumping bartender – just who is he talking to, the bottles or me? Austin slyly avoided eye contact by looking every place else but at the old fella.

Either not picking up on his non-verbal disinterest or simply not caring, the Bible reader slid both himself and his Good Book towards Austin. "But, *Peace be still,*" saith the Lord – sure did, that's what he said. You know, it's all about trust. Trustin' God, trustin' God, trustin' God . . . puttin' aside that old demon named Fear." Pointing a skeletal mahogany hand heavenwards, the evangelist passionately continued, "If you trust *Him,* what harm can come to ya? Tell me, what real harm? Oh my son, my son, it's a simple fact – ya got nothin' to fear when ya got God and ya just allow yourself to trust."

The bar keep, catching Austin's eye only in the way that those who you try to avoid can, lovingly closed his well-worn book and placed it under the counter. "Don't mean to preach and carry on, but the good Lord told me to tell ya that."

Not knowing whether to say thanks or to ignore the well-meaning man, Austin gave another non-committal nod.

"Now that I fed your soul, what can I get for your thirst?" asked the bartender, placing a coaster and basket of tortilla chips and salsa before Austin.

"Well . . . Austin replied, taking a chip, "How about a pot of hot coffee – black?"

"Good answer," came the familiar gruff voice from earlier. "That was a trick question. If you would've answered any differently, old Harland here would have pleasured you with another sermon."

At the touch of a heavy hand upon his shoulder, Austin turned to face the man who had just come out of nowhere, and his easy smile froze.

"I see that you remember me. How long has it been?"

Unable to speak, Austin felt his heart pounding in his ears. It was his father, Michael James.

Not surprised at the response, he took in his son's narrowed eyes, and answered his own question. "Twenty-four years if I recall. You were eighteen," Staring into the face that could've been his almost twenty years earlier, Michael casually placed his hands in his pockets. "Listen, about your sister . . ."

No longer hearing, Austin yelled for the old bartender to give him a shot of bourbon – straight. Ignoring the preacher's disapproving frown, he swallowed the liquor back, quick and hard.

"I guess your girl – Sedona, right? – I guess she knew what she was talking about when she said that we shared some similarities. Bourbon, if you remember, was always my drink of preference. That is until old Harland here, and Jesus got ahold of me."

Wanting with all of his heart to go back out into the storm without a backwards glance, Austin found himself inexplicably rooted, he chased the liquor with a gulp of scalding black coffee. Not caring to hear the tale of his father's road to repentance, he ignored the reference regarding his *glorious salvation.* "What do you know about Sedona?"

Slowly positioning himself on the stool next to Austin, Michael shrugged, "Oh, nothing much, she sounds like a lovely girl, that's all. I phoned Mitch and she answered. Very friendly – nice voice. She said that you were out looking for Stephanie." Not put off in the least by Austin's demeanor, he watched as his son clenched and unclenched his jaw. "You and your sister were always close. Through the years it helped to know that you were looking out after her when I couldn't."

"Or wouldn't," Austin supplied sharply.

Helping himself to a cup from the pot of coffee, Michael again shrugged. "It doesn't matter much now, I can't go back and change things. Stephanie was able to understand that. Like Carissa, she understood a lot of things." After a sip or two of coffee, he reached inside his shirt pocket for a cigarette and took his time lighting up. "You know, I had just about quit these things, but forgive me Lord, the way I'm feeling – it's either this cancer stick or the liquor." Studying Austin's tense profile, he drew out a few drags and continued with characteristic deliberateness, "I know you're hurting son."

"*Don't* call me that," Austin quietly hissed. "Besides, what do you know about me?"

"Sorry . . . I had that coming." Gazing up into the smoke spirals, he turned and searched his son's heart through the dark hurting eyes that matched his own. "No matter how you feel about it, you are *my son* . . ." Allowing the words to purposefully fall between them, Michael continued undeterred. "Look, I know that you don't need me now – I'm over twenty years too late for that. There is nothing in hell I can say to put things right, so I'm not going to waste your time or mine by even trying. I just want to tell you what I had a chance to tell Stephanie . . . that I love you and I am sorry. I don't think that she ever fully understood why I failed so miserably at being a father, but she forgave me. She . . ."

Outraged at the audacity of the man whom he should have only felt loving regards towards, Austin incredulously demanded, "Is that why you're here . . . asking for forgiveness? You want me to ease your sorry conscience? To help you make peace?" Picking up a match book cover, he angrily tapped it on the counter top, "Listen, I'm glad that you and Stephanie had your . . . your "reconciliation", your "moment of 'epiphany', but you're *not* going to get it from me. As far as I'm concerned, you're as dead as you were the last time I saw you." Flicking the matchbook to one side, Austin, calling on all of his reserves for control, tightened his forearms and leaned forward. "Do you remember that last time *Father*? My high school graduation night?"

Quietly reaching for his pack of cigarettes, Michael's eyes sadly took in his son's reflection through the mirrored Lone Star Beer sign that hung behind the bar.

For some reason, it felt good to see his father discomfited. So with a bit of perverse pleasure, Austin beckoned the old preacher to come closer so that he could hear all of about the sins of his father. "Now Harland, you're the preacher here, tell me, how do you forgive a *father* who gave more attention to the bottle than to his own children, to his own dying wife?" Turning his attention back towards his dad, Austin looked Michael straight in the eyes. "Yeah, mom understood. She understood that she was married to a drunk, a sorry ass drunkard. Do you even remember that night?"

Other than to flick his cigarette ashes into his empty coffee cup, Michael showed no emotion and continued to study his son's reflection, and said nothing.

Meeting the object of his disdain eye to eye in the mirror, the younger man unmercifully continued, "You came to the ceremony drunk." Nudging Harland's arm, Austin humorlessly laughed as he elaborated. "Here I was, class valedictorian right, ready to make my big speech, and my *father* strolls up the aisle, not to take a picture like the other proud parents, but he comes to share his woes and short comings with the world." He didn't have to dig far to remember details, for his memory gladly turned them over. Eyes fixed on Michael's profile, Austin narrowed his eyes. "As I looked out in the crowd, all I can remember is seeing poor Stephanie sitting there, crying. She was mortified; embarrassed for me and wishing that she could disappear. You know, that was the only time I remember being glad that mom was dead."

Michael, looking down into the ashes in his cup, massaged his temples as if the effort would sooth away the memory, "I'm sorry, what can I . . ."

"I'm sorry, what can I say . . . you know, the last time you said that to me I tried to kill you."

Not missing Harland's surprise look, Austin angrily explained without apology. "Yeah, I did, I tried to kill my own father. You see, after the ceremony, he comes back to the house. The Goodly's trying to make up – always put in the position of trying to make up for dad's mess, gave an impromptu graduation party in that little side yard of theirs. The whole gang from the block was over, the Henderson's, Mr. and Mrs. Williams and all of their kids, old Miss Canady, Rev. Easterly, even some of my teachers . . . and here comes my old man, stumbling from around back. *Son, I'ma, I'ma sorry* . . . man, what did he say that for?" Transported back in time by his own words, the memories that refused to fade, Austin half stood and refocused his attention onto his father, "I walked over, grabbed that $35 suit of yours, and whupped your . . ."

Harland, convinced that Austin was going to do a repeat of that long ago night, quickly grabbed his sleeve as he soothed the younger man's arm. "Sit down son, c'mon . . . that's it." It was easy to empathize with the anger, to understand the bitterness. Words to quiet his soul escaped him, so he slid Austin his mug, "Here, take another swallow of that coffee."

All of his control long gone, Austin felt tears fall as he stared blindly into Harland's cat like eyes. "I could look in his eyes and tell that he was sorry, he was always sorry. But this time, this time, I just couldn't take it anymore, just didn't want to hear it anymore." With a glower that chilled Michael's bones, Austin turned and faced his father. "Haven't you ever heard of the expression, sorry just doesn't cut it?"

Still patting his arm, Harland fervently cut in, "II Corinthians 5:17. *'Therefore if any man be in Christ, he is a new creature: old things are passed away; behold, all things are become new.'* That's what I told your father when he came in here one night 'bout fifteen years ago. He had hit rock bottom pretty hard, really on the skids he was, but when he heard, I mean really listened to how he had a second chance coming, he turned his life around – never been the same since."

If Harland meant for this little insight to exact some understanding, he was sorely disappointed, for Austin's response was callous. "Well hallelujah, wonderful for you!" he applauded. "So you had a little talk with Jesus, my, my, my." Sarcasm dripped from every word as he waved his hands in the air. "Praise the Lord and thank you Jesus. It is testimony time." Laughing he nudged his father, "Is that what you say now, Pops? Praise the Lord?" Caught up in the anger that kept his past connected to the present, he stood over his father and mocked, "I can see you now at one of ol' Harland's barstool revival meetings, 'I traded my bottle in for the Bible. Now I can say I'm sorry without the guilt, without the sh-a-me!'"

Austin certainly felt no guilt, no shame in mocking his father's salvation. Why should he? He was the one that had been wronged, had been robbed of a good portion of his childhood. Undaunted by the consequences of his words, he now sermonized, "I John 1:9. *'If we confess our sins, He is faithful and just to forgive us our sins, and to cleanse us from all unrighteousness.'* Well Pops, I believe that God did forgive you. That's what I've been taught, that's what I believe. But, you see, I'm not God, therefore I choose not to forgive you of the sins that you've committed against *me*. I guess that makes me neither just nor faithful, but in my book, the book you co-wrote and edited, you get as good as you give. Therefore you are as dead – as non-existent – as the night I laid you out cold."

As he turned to leave, Austin wearily took in his father's gray hair, weathered brow and sad eyes. As far back as he could remember, his dad always had those sad eyes – heavy-laden and disappointed. Well, they couldn't be anymore disappointed than he was that moment.

Turning away, he walked down the dim aisle, out the door and back into the rain.

The night could not have gone any worse. This wasn't the meeting that he had planned. He knew better than to think that his son would greet him with open arms, in fact he had expected some bitterness, but not this. "Lord Jesus," Michael called on his strength as he took a draw from his cigarette. Up through the smoky wisps, he looked heavenwards, "Lord, this is the closet I've come to going back to the bottle since that night You led me in here fifteen years ago. Help me, Father!"

With a hand on his friend's arm, Harland reached over for his Bible. "Proverbs 26:11. *As a dog returneth to his vomit, so a fool returneth to his folly.*'" Pointing a stern finger at his brother in Christ, he pronounced, "For *you*, that's what that whiskey, that bourbon, that rum is – vomit. Ya know that don't cha Mike, I ain't telling you nothin' new." Stating the question, rather than asking, Harland rewarded his friend's agreeing nod with a pat of praise.

Determined to fortify his friend, he impassionedly continued, "II Timothy 2:22 – come say it with me Mike, ya know it by heart." Together they recited, "*Flee also youthful lusts: but follow righteousness, faith, charity, peace, with them that call on the Lord out of a pure heart.*'"

There was no doubt in his mind; Harland knew that his special

141

brand of alcohol rehab had once again stuck. Satisfied, he replaced his Good Book back under the counter and took out two clean mugs and filled them with coffee. Each, enjoying the renewing Spirit that seemed to have settled over them both, said not a word for several minutes. Finally with a serene smile, the old man remarked, "Peace sure is wonderful – ain't it Mike."

"You're right, peace is wonderful," Michael agreed as he stubbed out his cigarette and reached for the coffee. "It is something that I use to think that I would never find. But I have it, in spite of."

"In spite of," Harland concurred. "That is what you need to get that boy of yours to understand for himself, otherwise he'll be walking in rain until the day he dies."

Michael turned and frowned thoughtfully at the door from which Austin had recently exited. "You're right, I owe it to him. Maybe in turn, he can teach me a thing or two about strength."

Not completely understanding, Harland leaned forward, "How do ya mean, Mike?"

Michael, settling in to tell his story, stretched his long legs along the length of several stools adjacent to where he was sitting. "Oh, you've heard my story before – at least most of it. When I first met his mother, Carissa, I truly thought that the world was my oyster. Man, I had plans – dreams. At one time, I even wanted to be a pharmacist. Here me tell it; I was going places, first off of this two-bit island, then out of 'Texas Ain't Got Nothing for a Black Man', USA. This place held no luster; back then, it only had a way of beating a man down. Carissa was game; she had her bags packed – she wanted outta here as much as I did. There was one problem though; the only way her mother would give us her blessing was if we got married before leaving. I loved her, so sure I said; no problem. But I made it clear; there would be no babies until we had all of our ducks lined up. Nothing was to be allowed to hold us back."

"But it didn't work out that way," Harland supplied as he sat a burlap sack of roasted peanuts on the counter."

"You got that right, it didn't quite work out that way. Before the ink was dry good on the marriage certificate, she was pregnant. I don't fault her none, it was just as much of my doing as hers, but at the time, I sure didn't see it that way. All of our plans were out the window, and the little that we managed to sat aside went to doctors. As fate would have it, not only was she pregnant, she had some pretty serious female troubles that required special attention – that was more money, not to mention things for the baby, a place to live, food, you name it, we needed it."

"Why didn't you just leave her with her mama, go off on your own and send for her?" inquired the older man with practical male logic.

"Don't think that I didn't contemplate it. The thought was appealing – too appealing. My father had done it when I was a boy, and never did come back – not even to be buried. I tell you, at the time, I knew that if I had left, I would've done the same. It's too easy to forget your responsibilities when they're not right there staring you in the face. Besides, I barely found work to keep food on the table, let alone for a ticket and some pocket change. There are mighty poor pickings on a sand bar for a black man, especially if all you got are a high school diploma and no real skills."

"Who you telling? And that's with or without our slavery benefits," pronounced Harland with an indignant huff.

"Slavery benefits!" snickered Michael as threw a peanut shell in Harland's direction. "Man, what are you talking about – slavery benefits? Never heard anything so crazy."

"Ya know what I mean – affirmative action, school busing, the right to vote, equal opportunity – all of that jazz."

"Those are rights man, God given basic rights. A benefit is something extra – on top of what you've got coming."

"I know all of that," Harland interrupted. "I was just being, how do you say, facetious." His feelings hurt because he was misunderstood; Harland brushed invisible dust off of the counter top. "Everybody comes in here making jokes, and as soon as I *attempt* to do the same, all of a sudden no one knows what I'm talking about."

Well used to Harland, Michael teased as only a good friend can, "Man, what are you talking about – facetious. I didn't even know that that word was in your vocabulary."

"I read things other than the Bible, you know."

"Yeah, I know." After a chuckle and a pause, Michael continued on with his pitiable tale. "Well, as the years went on, I got tired, frustrated, and tried less and less. By that time, the cancer had gotten a hold of Carissa and I had given up completely. If I had known then, what I know now, I know that if I had just been stronger, tried just a bit harder and not given up, I could've gotten us off of this sand pile. Maybe not have become a pharmacist, but at the very least, moved on to Houston." No one had to beat him up; for it was obvious that Michael had been down this road of recrimination more than once. "Every once in a while, I would find work at one of the refineries, but nothing ever steady or well paying enough to move us away. And by the time that I had – well, the liquor had gotten a hold of me – I was a bona fide alcoholic – a drunkard."

Harland leaned forward, fully understanding the path that Michael had chosen. "Satan will try every way that he knows how to bring you down. He had found your Achilles Heel."

"That he did. That's why Austin was well within his rights on his graduation night. I knew it then as sure as I know it now, I was jealous of my own son. At eighteen, he had managed to elevate himself off of this sand bar – he was on his way. Instead of being happy for him, I was jealous. Jealous that he had been stronger than me. Strong enough to overcome, to succeed. Not only that, he was leaving and I was stuck. Instead of being happy for him, all I could see was the irony – the unfairness. The very reason for my being stuck and left to die, had found himself a way out."

"You've gotta stop beating yourself up over this man." In a way that only someone who had trod the same bitter road can, Harland pointed out valid reasons for his friend's plight. "Michael, you gotta remember, it was a different time when me and you were coming along. We didn't have the opportunities. You know the toll a man's soul takes being called 'boy' by a *white boy* who knows no more than you do. And at the end of the day, after busting your backside, you look up to find that you still only got what he wanted you to have. Every man at least got to have the hope that they can do better. If not, it beats you down, I tell ya, it beats you down."

Both men, momentarily loss in their own painful memories, sat silent. Harland cracked open another shell and munched, "Do you know, the only reason *they let me have* this place was because it kept the brothers down from the other end of the beach away from the tourists? And even with that, it took God to see fit to send me a blessing when my oldest brother, Cooper – you know the one who made it up to Chicago and found that job at the steel mill, passed on. When he died, he left me a small policy. It's a good thing too, cause I tell you, the money couldn't have come at a better time. I suppose getting ahead, sometimes has to do with strength, but a whole lot of times, it has everything to do with the breaks. And man, when the breaks don't come your way, when they wouldn't know you if you ran up to it, touched it and called it by name, it beats a man down. Nobody can tell me different, I see it everyday." Harland couldn't help but shake his head as he thought of all of the broken men that had come in and out of his bar. Men that unlike Michael had never been able to get their lives together.

"Harland, I don't doubt a word that you just said, but I still had no right – no right to be jealous of my own son. No right to have despised his presence, to feel ill towards his mother because I thought that they had taken away my opportunity. It made me no better than my own father. Other than finding salvation as an answer to my burden – the 'onlyest' other thing I have to be grateful for out of all this, is that Austin is bent on being a better man – a stronger man than me – his father.

CHAPTER NINE

A Channel 11-KHOU News Update – *Drifter seeking shelter under carport, discovers a woman's body, apparently washed ashore* . . .

Ring . . . Ring . . . Ring!

Not the phone again. Every since the word had gotten out regarding Stephanie's disappearance, it had rung off of the hook nonstop. What Mitchell wanted more than anything was to get some sleep. Sedona, restless because Austin was still out, kept him up far longer than he intended. If he hadn't started drifting off to sleep, they probably still would be in the living room talking about Austin's foibles and strengths.

Ring . . . Ring!

The caller id, now flashing with the incoming call information, caught his eye; it was Michael.

"Mike?

"Listen . . ."

Mitch rousing himself sat up, "Sedona told me that you called, I was going to call you back, but it was way too late . . ."

"That's not why I'm calling. I've got some news . . ." the words that followed had the effect of a cold bucket of water. "I don't want to raise your hopes, but there's been word of a body washed up." It was just on television – maybe it's Stephanie's, maybe not, I don't know."

Mitch, now fully awake, frantically grabbed his pants. "Did they say who has the body?"

"No, but I'm assuming the morgue over at UTMB. That's where I'm headed for now."

"Um, I tell you what . . ." Finding the business card that the state trooper had given him earlier, Mitchell threw on a shirt. "I'm going to call the State Trooper's to see if they know anything about the body. But, you go ahead on over to the hospital, and keep your cell phone on. I'll call if I'm told anything different.

"Mitchell?"

"Yeah," hurried the distressed husband, already with a shoe in hand.

"I ran into Austin tonight, over at Harland's. The meeting wasn't too good. Has he made it back?"

At that moment, the emotional state and whereabouts of his brother-in-law were the least of Mitchell's concerns; and it came across loud and clear in his tone. "Mike, I . . . he wasn't here when I went to bed. I don't know what to tell you. Say, let me get dressed and I'll see you in a few."

Austin, Austin, Austin . . . if another person expressed concern about Austin or mentioned his name, Mitch was going to lose it. After all of his mouthing off and all of his accusations, he could give a rat's ass about the man. Quickly lacing up his shoes, he swallowed, took a deep breath and dialed the state police. Not sure as to whether or not he should be hopeful that the found body was that of his wife or praying that it wasn't, he sat on the edge of the bed." Um . . . Mitchell Frazier here, Trooper Marks please." Waiting to be connected to the officer, Mitch mentally prepared himself to hear the worse. "Marks,

Mitchell Frazier . . . um . . . about the body . . . the morgue . . . yes, I know the building. I'll be over in a few minutes . . . No, I mean yes, someone will be accompanying me, Stephanie's dad, Michael James – he's meeting me there. Lt. Commander James? . . . no, he won't be with me . . . thank you."

Not wanting to wake Austin in case he had returned, Mitch hesitated at their bedroom door. If Austin had made it back, he would be sure to want to go. *God, if you have any mercy, please let Sedona be alone.* "Sedona . . . Sedona . . ." he whispered as he knocked gently.

"Austin?"

Thank you, he mouthed upward. "No, it's me, Mitch. I just got . . ."

"I heard the phone ring," Sedona interrupted as she opened the door. "It wasn't Austin was it?"

"No. It was Mike, he thinks that they've found Stephanie."

"Oh, Mitch," she touched his arm not quite sure how to ask her next question. "Is she . . . is she alive?"

"No, he was calling from the morgue." Before he could finish the sentence, Sedona began pulling out clothes, it was clear that she intended on accompanying him. "Say, Sedona, it's sweet of you to want to drive over there with me, but I would much rather that you stay here. Austin might show up and I would hate for him to hear about something like this via a note. Besides, Michael is already down there by now. It seems that he heard a news story about the authorities finding a body on television. There's really no point for a crowd . . ."

"Maybe we can try calling him again, he's carrying his cell phone?" In her concern for Austin, she had missed Mitch's subtle but quite pointed hint that he rather Austin not join them. Before Mitch could respond, she had already grabbed up the bedside phone, and quickly punched in the number. To his relief, there was no answer.

"That's strange, I wonder why he doesn't pick up? It's almost 3:00. Surely he's not out there still looking in all of this rain? I hope that he has had sense to find decent cover somewhere."

"Yeah, maybe, I don't know. Michael said something about running into him earlier tonight. From the sounds of things, it didn't go too well." Heading towards the door, he continued, "In any case, you've got my cell number. We'll be at the morgue, over at UTMB."

"Okay, you drive carefully." What else was there to say? Somehow offering a sympathetic hug and a 'take care' seemed hardly enough to say to a man about to face the grim task of identifying his wife. As he pulled away from the carport, she watched the tail lights slowly disappear. Alone in the early morning quiet, there was little else to do but to settle back down on her now familiar perch and wait.

After several minutes, the sound of the surf hitting the black beach carried her off to a restless and foggy sleep. It was a slumber filled with faces and voices so familiar that she found it impossible to discern where the reality of life ended and the parallel life of dreams began.

In the midst of waves crashing overhead, there's the sound of a wailing buoy, broken loose from its mooring. Its cries are both pitiable and heart breaking. Struggling to silence it, she bests the current and reaches out to bring the lonely object home. Not satisfied until she has silenced the sobbing, she first soothes and then caresses as together, she and the buoy, float across varying levels of sea – both mild and turbulent. Onward they swim towards a beckoning steady beam of light. The buoy, no longer forlorn has now become her weightless companion and lifesaver. Her newfound friend now is keeping her anchored and on a path – free from drifting.

Inexplicably aroused from the wakes of the sea, Sedona heeded a silent voice and rose from the sofa to check the front door. Curled up on the porch is Austin – disoriented, cold and wet.

More concerned about the man on the porch than the spirit that moved her to open the door, Sedona urged Austin to get up. "Austin . . . Austin what are you doing out here? You're soaking wet. Why didn't you ring the bell, or better yet, use your key? Mitch and . . ."

When he didn't respond, she stopped mid sentence and took a closer look at his face. It was an Austin that she didn't recognize; only a shadow of the usually self-assured man stared back mutely into her eyes. Immediately pushing all questions aside, she reached down to help him to his feet. "Oh, baby, let's get you in and warmed up, you must be exhausted."

Once in the bathroom, she turned on the shower tap. As warm steam filled the small room, she, as if assisting a three year old, undid his clothes. "Listen, you get in and warm up . . . just take your time. I'll bring in some dry things for you to slip into."

Satisfied when he obeyed, Sedona walked into the light of the kitchen and took a closer look at his wet clothes. The brightly colored shorts and T-shirt that she had helped him out of were not what he had worn when he left out on his search. In fact, it was unlike anything that she had ever seen him wear. Reaching into a sand filled pocket, she retrieved his wallet and a soggy matchbook cover – "Harland's Bait and Souvenir." From the looks of things, he must've had some night. Tossing the clothing into a nearby laundry basket, she filled a teakettle and waited for the water to boil. The soggy clothes, his disoriented state, none of it made sense. Surely a chance run-in with his father could not have caused such an emotional upheaval, it just didn't fit the Austin that she knew. No, there had to be something more, as she picked up the matchbook cover, her thoughts were interrupted by the phone.

"Sedona . . . Mitch. The search is over. We have Steph. Michael identified the body before I got here. He said . . . he said, that the water had her beat up pretty bad."

"Oh, Mitch. I 'm so sorry." Even as she spoke, she knew the words fell flat and offered little consolation.

"Well, we all knew that it would only be a matter of time. I'm just thankful to the drifter who pulled her in. It looks like he found her out on the beach; at least that's what the police seem to think. Whoever he was, he didn't hang around to offer any details. Odd thing though, they found the cell phone that they assumed that he made the call from."

"What?"

"Yeah, it was laying right there next to . . . the body. Has Austin made it back?"

As she answered, her eyes settled on the clothes hamper and the sand encrusted shorts. "Um . . . yeah, just a little while ago. He's taking a shower. Are you on your way back?"

"Not yet, I'll be here for a little while longer. Seems as if there's quite a bit of paperwork they need for us to fill out, plus I still need to get a hold of a funeral director . . . all of this is pretty surreal."

Truly sympathizing with his task, she asked if Michael was going to stay and help him take care of the details.

"Oh, yeah. Mike is here. In fact, he's helping to speed things up down in the morgue. He's been a big help. He does quite a bit of volunteer work upstairs in the hospital, so everybody knows him. Say, be sure to tell Austin that there's really no need for him to come down."

Not wanting to add to the burden that Mitch had to deal with or upsetting Michael, Sedona saw no real point in sharing Austin's current state. "Okay, I'll make sure that he knows that everything is being taken care of, you hang in there and give Michael my regards . . . bye."

Good Lord, what next. This evening was definitely like none other that she had ever experienced.

"Austin? Honey?" No answer. Ready to knock, she instead pressed her ear against the door. Over the sound of the shower, she heard what sounded like sobbing, a soul wrenching letting that flowed from the seat of the emotions. "Au . . ." she began again, but stop short. Not knowing quite what to make of what she was overhearing, her mind turned to the clothing that he came in wearing, the sand filled pockets, and the unanswered calls to his cell phone, suddenly everything made sense. Austin was the fathom drifter – he was the one who found Stephanie's body.

It took all that she had not to tear into the bathroom and pull him into her arms. God, how she wished that she had the words that could make everything okay; words magic enough to erase the memory of what he discovered. A simple kiss and a promise to love him forever wouldn't do it; life seldom presented problems that could be solved so easily. At any rate, who was she to think that her love would be enough to ease anyone's pain. No longer able to listen to the tears that echoed the ones that she cried in her own heart, she left the door and tended to the kettle calling her on the stove.

A cup of chamomile tea, it was all that she had to offer with any kind of surety. If she could get him to drink it, maybe talk about the past few hours, perhaps he would relax enough to sleep; sitting down the tray; Sedona rearranged the blanket and pillows and mentally prepared herself. When she heard the bathroom door open, she swallowed hard and listened for his quiet footsteps to make their way up the hall.

"Sedona . . ."

"You found her, you found Stephanie, didn't you?"

In response to his silent nod, she crossed the room and pulled him into her arms, "Oh, you poor baby. You poor thing. God only knows what you've been through these last couple of hours." Austin, too wrung out to return any kind of emotion, simply accepted the affection and prayed that nothing more would be demanded of him. All that he wanted to do was to go to sleep and forget.

For once, not questioning his detachment, Sedona took his hand and led him over to the bed talking nonstop, "I've made you some chamomile tea, it'll help you get to sleep. I sat out some honey and lemon if you want to sweeten it up a bit. I prefer mine without anything, but some people insist on adding sugar. If you want sugar instead of the honey, just tell me. You've tried chamomile before, right?" Without waiting for a response, she answered her own question as if she was the only one in the room. "Yea, when I was out in San Diego. I was so keyed up after that long plane ride. Do you know what else that works? Valerian. Usually I have to go over to the health food store to find it, for some reason the grocery store only carries chamomile. I didn't ask you, are you hungry? You know, there's . . ."

"Sedona, shut up! For Christ's sake, could you just stop talking, please?" He didn't mean to sound so cruel, Lord knows he didn't want to hurt her feelings. But he just couldn't handle the prattling, not now. Not after what he's been through, not after seeing his sister so beat up.

"I'm . . . I'm sorry," her voice trailed, stunned by the outburst. What else was there for her to say? She knew, even as the words were coming out of her mouth, that she was running on about nothing, saying all of the wrong things, expressing her concern in the most wrong of ways, after all, it was her forte. It was what she did best. "I . . . um . . . listen, you get some sleep; you're tired. If you need me, um . . . I'll . . ." Already he had closed his eyes to tune her out, so she slipped out the room wishing that she could truly disappear.

When he opened them, she was gone. "Sedona . . ." He didn't

mean to chase her away, in fact, if she could have read his mind, she would've known that was the last thing that he wanted. If he ever needed her presence, it was now. He needed her to help chase away the smell . . . the picture of . . . Jesus, when was it going to stop! Every time he closed his eyes, he kept seeing Stephanie. Not the loving sister that he played with and teased, but Stephanie, dead and unrecognizable as any a number of 'floaters' he had helped to grapple out of the water while on deployment. The only difference was that this body was his sister – swollen, skin beginning to slough from the friction of the sand and the water. When he first spotted her coming in on a wave, he had to look twice. His eyes didn't want to believe what they were seeing, but he had seen enough bodies to know. That is why he hesitated before reaching out for her; he knew how her skin was going to melt into his fingers even before he touched her. At first, he was going to let her be, just pray that her body floated back out, maybe all of the way out to the sea. But she was his sister, coming back to him.

The funeral was oddly comforting. Mitchell, Austin and Michael shared their love for Stephanie with those who attended the service. They each spoke of her many endearing traits. Mitchell spoke as an adoring husband who thoroughly loved and appreciated the essence of his wife. Austin's fond sentiments were equally as loving, but his remarks were sprinkled with anecdotal stories that painted Mitch's observations with color and perspective. It was obvious that Austin had always taken his role as loving and protective brother seriously. Michael, on the other hand, pointed more to her future. He saw her departure from earth as her home going to heaven. His words were filled with God's assurance that this belief was real. Michael's expressive eyes, filled with their wisdom and silent tales of hard living, offered credence to his comforting words. He pointed out the irony of her faith – the faith that so helped her mind and body battle a similar type of cancer that fell her mother, was the same faith that made dying something that she never feared. What peace she must've had in God's promise of eternal life. By the end of the service, it was poignantly clear that while she had loved and enjoyed both life and those around her, she recognized no sorrow in dying.

"I'm sure glad to see that Austin is holding up under all of this," commented Charles DuPree as he helped Sedona and Loretta serve coffee to the gathering of friends that met back at the house. "It looks like he is going to weather this pretty much as he has done everything else in his life."

"Strong as a brick, he is," added his wife, "at least that's the front he puts up."

A front all right, even bricks have been known to crumble, thought Sedona with a grimace. If Loretta and Charles knew only half of the changes that she had seen Austin go through over the last few days, neither one of them would be referring to him as a brick. Not knowing how to or even if she should dispel the myth regarding his unflagging strength, Sedona bit her tongue and instead, took in the number of people that dropped by to pay their respects. It was obvious that what Stephanie lacked in family, she more than made up for in friendships. Not surprisingly, several of Austin's close friends, including the DuPrees, Mazey, and even Lorraine, made the trip in a show of support and sympathy.

"I'm sure that Austin takes some comfort in you all making the trip out here. Having friends close by helps to remind him that he is not alone."

"No, he's not alone," Loretta reiterated as she poured coffee for a guest. "After everyone leaves, and he gets off to himself and start feeling low, you remind him of that. Even though Stephanie is gone, he still has people who love him."

"Has he said if he'll be staying on here for a while?" asked Charles. "I'm sure his brother-in-law is going to need some help going through Stephanie's things."

"He hasn't said, but I wouldn't think so," Sedona hesitated, debating on whether or not to bring up the contention between Austin and Mitchell. "Mitch pretty much has things under control . . . I think that what he wants more than anything is some time alone to make sense out of all of this."

Loretta, always thinking of Austin, expressed concern, "Hmmp . . . even though they're putting on a good show of it, I've noticed that he and Austin don't seem to be talking too much. Austin has always given me the impression that they were close, it doesn't seem like it though."

"They're just both tired," shrugged Sedona. "With Austin finding his sister and his dad the way that he did, and considering that in less than a week Mitch has gone from being a carefree vacationer to being a widower, I think that they are just both stressed out."

"It just goes to show you how changeable life is. Charles and I try never going to bed angry; you'll never know what's on the other side of the sunrise. Or if there'll even be one for that matter."

Sedona wished that things could be so simple. Most of her relationships were far too complicated to even think as far as the next day's sunrise; she did well if she could just make it to the day's sunset. Be it Austin, Gary, or her parents, everyone involved in the travails of her life had a rationalization, a sorry chapter of their own that entwined with hers in a way that often left her with feelings that were wrung out and a soul crying for love and comfort. Unlike a good book, with chapters that lent understanding, insight, and a clear plot, her chapters refused to be closed and settled; not even upon the setting of the sun.

She wondered, not for the first time as she watched Austin's father pick up a framed photograph of his wife, if Carissa ever discovered the story that lain behind the unhappiness in her husband's eyes. Even though it had only been a few days since she had gotten to know Michael, it was obvious that he was a far different man than when his wife was dying of cancer. When he first came round to the house to assist with the funeral plans, she was struck by the uncanny resemblance between he and Austin. Not only did they share the same sensuous smile and heart stopping baritone timbre; there was the same sense of unaffected self-assuredness that they both wore like a pair of easy fitting gloves.

Oh what she wouldn't give to get him into a conversation, to ask the myriad questions that she had formed in her mind since first discovering his existence. But, this was neither the time nor the place; it had to be done in private and more importantly, away from Austin. Despite the fact that both he and Austin respected the difficulty of the occasion by calling a truce, Austin had said very little to his father. And on more than one instance, she found herself acting as a type of buffer between the two. She was certain that it had not gone unnoticed by Mitch and Michael that Austin had made a point of keeping her close by his side. Whether he found her presence comforting or simply convenient, she could only guess — for in terms of conversation, he still expressed very little.

Stepping out onto the porch, she leaned against the railing and took in the blue green waters of the gulf. Little more than an hour before, they had been on the Tranquility, casting Stephanie's ashes out to sea. As requested by Michael, they moored the boat at the bend of a cove, in the area of the Point Bolivar Lighthouse. According to the Goodlys, this was the exact position that Michael had set anchor when they buried Carissa, close to twenty-nine years before. As Michael sang "Amazing Grace," Mitchell and Austin released her ashes to the wind. "Like a lark on the wing," whispered Austin. In affirmation, a nearby buoy chorused its approval.

Lost in the hypnotic sound and gentle stirring of the water, Sedona looked out at the peaceful vastness that surrounded her. With the lap of each wave, all of life's problems and disappointments seemed so removed, somehow much less critical, and a bit more surmountable. No wonder Stephanie, as well as Austin and his father, sought the sea's refuge. It soothed like nothing else on earth.

"All of that pretty blue water, just look at it. Don't tell me that it has you fooled as much as the others?" Clued in by the sharp clicking of high heels, she recognized the scathing voice before she had even turned around.

"Excuse me?" Sedona frowned as she turned towards the elegantly dressed intrusion.

"Given the chance, it eventually claims everything and everyone as its own. I can attest to that sad and sorry little fact first hand."

Unclear as to how she was expected to respond to that little snippet, Sedona waited for Austin's ex to continue and silently wondered if the woman had ever taken acting lessons. If not, she was definitely a natural – slim figure casually posed against the rail, lighting a slender cigarette with unhurried style. Somewhere along the way, she had polished the technique of 'pause and effect'.

"You are so unlike your sister, it ain't even funny."

"I can only take that as a compliment," smirked Lorraine, totally unfazed. "Sedona, what exactly about me don't you like? Was it some

159

passing comment of Charles or Stephanie, or are you just calling your-self being loyal to Austin? For some reason, you don't strike me as the type to judge a person based solely on the word of someone else. I've given you more credit. So what's the deal, Sedona? Do you see me as competition, someone here to lure your lover away?"

Laughing would have just been plain rude. Any other time, she would have taken the woman on, round for round. There were some people that you scrunch down on the first blow so that you don't have to deal with them later, but at the moment, she was just too tired. Over the last few days, there had been enough dramatics thrown her way, there was no need to borrow any. So instead, she employed a tac-tic that she perfected during her marriage. "Listen Lorraine, I'm not in the mood to play games. I have gone through enough drama these past couple of days to last a lifetime. So if you've got something to say, a point you're just dying to make, then for God's sake, just go ahead and do it."

Lorraine, understanding that Sedona's offensive front was as much about self-protection of her emotions as it was about keeping her at arms length, empathetically smiled at the woman's sharp tone. Years ago, she too had been where Sedona was now standing. So, the well-chosen words, the strategy to somehow put her on notice, to ruf-fle her feathers, were needless. A point emphasized by the thin wisps of smoke that she casually blew into the evening sky before turning to face the Gulf. "I don't know what I can say to convince you, but believe it or not Sedona, I am on your side, I don't want to make your life more difficult, quite the contrary."

"My side?" God, what she wouldn't give to have the woman swirl away up into one of her thin wisps of smoke. "Just cut to the chase Lorraine and answer the question of the hour. Why are you here? It just doesn't make any sense. You weren't especially close to Stephanie, and with the way things are between you and Austin, you could've saved the expense of the plane fare and sent a sympathy card."

"You're right, I could've; it certainly would have been easier. But I know Austin better than anyone, at least as best as anyone can, so I know how important it is for him to know that he has people who love and care for him." Responding to Sedona's raised brow, she paused and smiled, "Contrary to popular belief, I still do love Austin. I have never stopped, and quite possibly, never will. I've just learned how to love myself more."

"Lorraine . . ." Sedona broke in, truly tired of the conversation.

"You know, this was the last gift that Austin gave me," Lorraine talking over Sedona continued as she fingered the heavy silver bracelet that adorned her wrist. "We picked it out at one of those little shops along Mission Bay back in San Diego. That was a whole other lifetime ago. I guessed looking out at all of this water just brought the memories all rushing back."

Not a clue as to where the woman was going with the conversation, Sedona kept silent. It was obvious that Lorraine was not egging for a cat fight – verbal or other. Besides, there were other, more appropriate opportunities for such a confrontation. And even if this were an attempt to endear her to Austin, picking a fight with the girlfriend at his just buried sister's repose would hardly do the trick.

"From the very beginning, I've always thought Austin intelligent, handsome, funny, charming, sexy, gentle, responsible, God-fearing – everything that a woman could want. But all of those glorious traits weren't enough; they just didn't do the trick. In fact, sometimes I would just stop and look at him and wonder how a man so perfect could be so incomplete."

Sedona, studying Lorraine's classic profile, felt a bit of her hostility melt, the woman did not have to go on any further; they were now on common ground.

"It is almost as if he is an . . . an . . ."

". . . Anomaly," quietly finished Sedona.

Amused at her pedantic description, Lorraine quirked a brow and recalled the unusual antique lipstick case that Sedona had dropped in The Blue Fish's ladies' room several weeks before. If anyone had the ability to get to Austin, she would be the one. "I guess if you were going to be polite, that would be the term. Personally, I've always thought of him as being more 'engineered'. Almost like the million dollar man without emotions."

With the sound of the surf filling the silence between them, Sedona searched for the words to defend Austin. Her Austin wasn't quite the cold machine that Lorraine depicted, she had heard him cry, seen the care and love that he possessed for his sister. But, by the same token, she knew his remote behavior, all too well.

"My sister mentioned that you and Mr. Spock vacationed out in San Diego a couple of months back. That's one thing about southern California, it's beautiful no matter what time of the year." When Sedona didn't comment one way of the other, Lorraine made a casual assessment of the other woman's dress – the linen fabric, the simple but expensive sandals, handcrafted jewelry. Everything confirmed her initial impression, so with a tap of her cigarette, she offered a disarming smile. "I bet I can guess how your vacation in paradise progressed. Each morning you woke in his arms, spent from the love making but never feeling loved. Never quite able to put your tumbled emotions into words, not because you couldn't, but because you didn't want to risk losing what you've found, you instead opted to paint some seascape or the other while Austin read one of his stuffy old books. In the afternoons, let me guess . . . you hit the beach and went shell collecting. Or if Austin was in a lighthearted mood, you were able to entice him into a sexy romp out in the water. And maybe, after supper, if the night was clear and the stars were out, you enjoyed a moonlit walk along the shore, all the while hoping that his feelings for you were as intense as yours for him." Flashing a Cheshire grin, she asked, "Did I get it right?"

Sedona, suddenly angry, felt tears well up behind her eyes. Knowing that the woman had found her button and pushed it, she indifferently shrugged. "I don't see how anything that you've just said has to do with . . ."

After a parlous chuckle, Lorraine ground out the cigarette with the sharp heel of her delicate black pump. "Oh, but it does, Sedona. It does. Don't you see; it has everything to do with everything. In the after glow, when you can't quite believe your good fortune of being blessed with the perfect man in the perfect setting, you can't escape that nagging certainty that always looms in the back of your mind. The certainty that Austin could, and most likely will, leave both you and your beautiful little beach without a backwards glance."

Angry at both the undeniable truth and the harshness of her words and at the woman herself, Sedona crossed her arms and moved to a corner of the porch – a deep alcove hidden by the shadow of the setting sun. Telling herself not to let the woman get the best of her, she felt her throat tightening.

"One day Sedona, you'll look out and see that pretty blue ocean for what it really is – nothing but cold suffocating water. And when Austin leaves, runs to it – and he will, you'll curse both it and him."

Just as she was about to tell Lorraine how wrong she was – insist how things were different with she and Austin, the DuPree's stepped out onto the porch.

"What are you doing out here by yourself?" asked Loretta.

Sedona, catching her breath, shrunk further into the shadows of the alcove. Realizing that the couple hadn't yet spotted her, she stood perfectly still. She dearly enjoyed their company, but not right now. Silently pleading for Lorraine to get rid of them, she composed herself just in case she was drawn into a conversation.

"Oh, just taking a smoke," shrugged Lorraine. "Why, what's up?"

"Well, it's getting late, that's all," answered Charles. "Everybody's leaving so we were thinking of doing the same. I tried looking for Austin and Sedona to say our goodbyes, but nobody's seen them in a while. Best I can figure is that they took a walk somewhere. Can't say that I much blame them. These types of gatherings are always difficult. You're glad for the support, but you sure as hell don't feel too much like being bothered."

"You're right," agreed Loretta. "You gotta feel sorry for him – for all of them. Stephanie's death was a shock – just a shock."

"I'm sure that Austin will handle it like he does everything else," dryly commented Lorraine.

Per usual, the sarcasm was lost on her sister. Nodding, Loretta's brow furrowed with concern. "Well, at least this time around, he has Sedona and his father. Michael seems like a nice man, and my word – what a beautiful voice."

At the mention of Sedona's name, Lorraine glanced over at the corner and let loose a sly smile. "I guess, hopefully he'll hang around. The way I hear it, he's one of those rolling stones – has a real hard time with staying put. I suppose that the apple really doesn't fall too far from the tree."

If Loretta didn't catch the cutting comment regarding Austin, Charles did. To him, it was more of the same old same old, so he took hold of his wife's hand and cut the conversation short. "C'mon, let's tell Mitch and Michael good night. We can give Austin and Sedona's our goodbyes in the morning. Lorraine are you coming, or are you taking that broom of yours?"

When she was certain that they had stepped back into the house, Sedona quietly eased out from the shadows and slid into a chair. As much as she wanted to, it was impossible to dismiss Lorraine's stinging comments, they had found their mark. She was all too familiar with the bitterness of unrequited love not to know that there was some semblance of truth in her words. Suddenly finding the sound of the surf irritating, she wondered if things weren't already too late. Had she indeed lost Austin?

"Hey girl, what are you doing out here? We thought that you had left with that man of yours."

Rising as her best friend sat beside her, Sedona walked over to the railing. "No, I'm still here. Um . . . Charles said that everyone had left?"

Even though Mazey could not clearly see her friend's face under the darkening sky, the tearful timbre in her voice was hard to ignore. "Well, yea. Just about everybody's gone. Mr. and Mrs. Goodly have just left, Loretta and Charles – I helped them put away the food, and they're saying their goodbyes now. I was just about to head on back to the hotel myself. I told Miles I was going to get back before Carly gets out of school tomorrow. Say, why don't you drive back to the hotel with me? We can hang out in the bar and visit a while."

. "Sure." Not wanting to seem overly concerned, Sedona turned to look down at the beach. "You said something about Austin having left. Did he go out for a walk?"

"I assumed that's where he was going. He walked out with the Goodly's and another couple, but didn't come back in. I guess it's been about twenty minutes or so," she shrugged as she glanced down at her watch. "Poor dear, you can tell that the strain is starting to get to him. He probably just needed some fresh air. I can't say that I don't much blame him with that ex of his switching around. What was she trying to prove with that dress anyway? It was cut so low that every time she leaned forward, you could see all that God didn't give her. She ain't got nothing up there."

Sedona, although well aware that Mazey's critical appraisal of what she thought was a very elegant outfit was an effort to show loyalty, found herself defending the woman. "There was nothing wrong with Lorraine's dress. I thought it was nice."

"Yea, nice and expensive. What does she do for a living anyway? Surely she's not just living off of what Austin sends her."

"I have no idea. Austin makes it a point to talk about her as little as possible. In fact, we both were a little more than a bit surprised to see her here."

"I wasn't. I know her type. She loses interest in a man, but wants no one else to have him. In fact, she gets off on trying to make him miss her."

No longer sure that Lorraine's presence was entirely motivated by reasons so selfish, Sedona shrugged, "I don't know about all of that."

"Girl," Mazey crossed her legs, confident that she had the woman figured out, "give me a break, I know that you are not that naive. Why else would she have shown up dressed so provocatively?"

"Provocatively? She just wore a simple v-neck dress. Perhaps it emphasized her shape a bit more than necessary, but it wasn't in bad taste. Besides, what makes you so sure that she was the one who lost interest, why couldn't it have been Austin? I mean, to hear her tell it, Austin was the one who ran cold."

"And you believe her?"

Turning to face the gulf, Sedona rubbed her arms and stared out into the water. "Well, what she said rang just a little too true to ignore. She seems to know Austin down to the letter. She knows him so well that she even knows how things are between us – every scene, every verse, every line. I figure that she knows because she lived it. I wouldn't be surprised if he loves me no more than he loved her."

Mazey, trying her best not to walk over and shake a bit of sense into her troubled friend's head, joined her over at the rail. "Sedona, just listen to yourself. I can't believe that you've bought that woman's line of garbage hook and sinker. I don't know what she told you, but I know Austin. He is hardly the sort that would lead you on – take advantage of you. All you need to do is to pay attention to how he looks at you. There's nothing but love in those eyes. Besides, you are not Lorraine. Sure, she can tell you how Austin treated her, but did she ever mention her own shortcomings?"

Despite the common sense behind Mazey's question, Sedona refused to stray from her course. "Austin doesn't even trust me enough – trust our love enough to express his feelings. The one and only time Austin has ever told me that he loved me was a week ago. And then I had to drag it out of him. You would have thought that he was going to choke. It was so pathetic that I told him not to bother. I truly believe that there is nothing on this earth that I can do or say that will ever convince him that I am worthy enough for his trust. Do you know how much that hurts?"

"Sedona, snap out of it," Mazey admonished as she grabbed the woman by the shoulders, "you are not making sense. I am not going to allow you to do this to yourself. Do you love Austin?"

"Yes."

"Can you honestly say that you know beyond a shadow of a doubt that he doesn't love you?"

Taking in her question, Sedona shook her head. "No."

"Then just stop this silliness. You are not Lorraine. What went wrong between them was between them; it has nothing to do with you

and Austin. If you feel that Austin is afraid to love, is just plain scared
– then deal with that. For crying out loud, don't allow Lorraine, or
anyone else to color it any other shade."

Wiping at her tears like a chastised child, Sedona, moved by her
friends concern, allowed herself to feel the certainty that Mazey
demanded – at least a little of it. "Yes ma'am."

"Now let's go see if Mitch and Michael want to go out for a
drink."

"I don't think that Michael can, he's an alcoholic."

"Well . . . he can watch."

CHAPTER TEN

Going through Stephanie's closet opened a floodgate of memories. When volunteering to help Mitch, Austin and Michael sort through Steph's belongings, she had no idea how emotionally draining it would be. Unexpectedly, it took her back to the morning when she and Gary packed away all of Lilie's baby things. Gary and Mazey had suggested that they place the clothing and furniture in storage before her return from the hospital. But she had insisted that the nursery be left intact. Putting away the layette and never used toys would be the only activity that she would ever have the opportunity to do for her daughter.

The task made the passing so final. At the service, with friends and family about, she made a conscious effort at being strong and holding back the tears. But with each fold of clothing and wrapping of tissue around keepsakes, the realization hit that there would never be new memories shared.

Oddly, she found the more mundane the object – a pair of socks, a comb or a hairbrush, the more her heart tore. It was for that reason that she usually begged off when invited to attend estate sales. Going through someone else's belongings, judging their value and worth, made life seem just a little too temporal. It even made her wonder of the importance of her own existence.

Each lost in their own thoughts as they muddled through the task of sorting and folding, neither Michael, Austin nor Sedona noticed

Mitch's increasingly darkening mood until he suddenly picked up a large box of books and hurled it against a wall. "Damn it, damn it! Damn you Stephanie! Oh, God what am I saying? Forgive me! . . . Just tell me why?"

Standing stock still, everyone was taken by surprise by Mitch – calm, sweet, laid back Mitch. Michael, the first to react, walked over to the sobbing man and drew him into his arms. "Go on son, He understands. Just let it on out," his embrace silently giving him permission to cry.

Both Sedona and Austin, familiar with his anguish first hand, quietly slipped out the room and closed the door behind them. "Poor guy," said Sedona, as she wiped away her own tears. "He no more understands than any of us."

Austin, looking down at the hatbox that he still carried, frowned. "You wonder why God would . . . what good does it do to ask questions? We can ask all the questions in the world, but it won't change a damn thing. She is not coming back." Abruptly changing the subject, he lifted the lid of the box. "This used to be my mother's, I still remember the hat that she used to keep in it, a little blue thing with pink flowers."

"Is the hat still in there?"

"No, just some old letters and pictures." Pulling out a bundle of envelopes, he frowned when he noticed one that was stamped with his name and address neatly scrawled on the outside. "She must've forgotten to mail it." Opening the envelope, he pulled out a stack of pictures and a letter.

"What does it say?" When he didn't immediately answer, she resisted the desire to peek around his shoulder and instead shifted through the remaining envelopes. "She had ones made out to Michael and Mitch as well. I wonder when she wrote them, better yet, why didn't she mail them? I mean, they're all stamped and everything."

Whatever was in the letter, held his attention for again, he made no response. So when he took a seat on the sofa, she sat down next to him and soothingly rubbed his leg as he silently continued to read.

"Based on what she wrote, it seems as if she had everything planned for quite some time. She explains that she had been out of remission for weeks – even before I left San Diego. She didn't tell anyone, not even Mitch because she didn't want anyone to try to change her mind about . . . about her *decision*. She wanted to be remembered as being happy and well."

"Wow," Sedona whispered as he grabbed a hold of her hand.

With an air of dejection, Austin sat back and soaked in the implication of what he had just read. "So, on the phone, the last time we spoke, she *knew* that she wouldn't see me again. She *knew* that she would be leaving, but she was still able to say goodbye, just like that, as if she would be simply taking a trip. I meant nothing more to her."

"Oh, Austin, I'm sure it wasn't that easy for her. You two were so close. I bet you that was why she didn't mail the letter. She probably realized that knowing would only make things worse for the three of you. Come on, put yourself in her shoes. You've got to be fair . . ."

"Fair?" He quietly asked with such vehemence that he might as well as shouted. "Fair? What's fair in all of this? Is it fair that someone that you need, the only person that you truly love, just decides to up and leave?"

Taken aback not only at his anger, but even more so at his words, Sedona shrank back into the couch as if he had struck her. *The only person that he truly loved.*

The words had slipped out before he thought about what he was saying, it was too late to retrieve them, and there was no way to dress them up in order to make them more palatable. "Sedona, honey, listen, I didn't mean that the way it came out. You know how I feel about you. It's just that things are all just so mixed up in my head right now."

Silently nodding, she quickly stood. "Maybe . . . maybe I should go and make us some tea." Over the running tap, she heard the front door slam.

"Austin?"

When there was no response, she hurried over to the window. She knew before she saw the empty sofa that he had left. Making out his figure – hunched shouldered and hands in pockets, walking up the beach; she asked God for a lifeline, some chance to bring him back.

After their goodbyes to Mitch, Michael and Sedona turned to walk back towards the house. "I hate to see him go like this, but I can sure understand him wanting to get away so fast," remarked Michael. "I've done it many a time myself, believe me. When you feel as if all control is snatched away – that no matter what you do, what you want, say or feel, not a single thing will make a difference, the only option left is to fly away. But, unless you fly away like Stephanie, you have to come back and face the music sometime. Mitch will find that out soon enough. The memories that he made with Steph might fade, but they won't completely disappear."

"Sometimes a little time away is good though," commented Sedona, making little effort to hide her melancholic mood. "Who knows, his aunt and uncle may be able to lift his spirits and help him think about getting on with things. Seattle is a long way from Texas. Besides, there's a lot that can be said for having a safe and warm place to run to. Otherwise, even when there are friends around, you find yourself feeling lonely and stuck with trying to sort through every-thing yourself."

"You talk like you know a thing or two about being lonely," gen-tly eyed Michael.

"Yeah . . . I guess I do." Sighing, she wished not for the first time that she had someone to run to; a warm home with someone waiting to hold her and to tell her that everything will be all right. Someone to assure her that even if it wasn't in the cards for Austin to love her, life will still be okay.

Conscious of Michael staring down at her, she shrugged with nonchalance, "Well, I've just been there myself, that's all. After losing a baby and then going through a divorce, lets just say that I have a pretty good idea how Mitch is feeling. Sometimes it is good to have someone else to help put everything into perspective for you. Someone who you know loves you no matter what and won't steer you wrong. I imagine that it would make life a little more bearable."

"You imagine? You don't have anyone like that, no parent?"

With a hard laugh, she shook her head. "I wish. No, my parents are more of the 'you-go-and-sort-it-out-for-yourself' type. They don't mean any harm, so I don't take it personally, that's just the way that they are."

Picking up one of the boxes that they had set by the door, she fol-lowed the older man into the storage area that Mitch had cleared for Stephanie's belongings. "I suppose that you're right, nine times out of ten, you usually wind right back up with what you tried your best to leave."

Michael, guessing that she was alluding to Austin, sat the box in a corner and studied her for a moment. "I'm assuming that you're referring to Austin and me?"

Conscious that she had spoken her thoughts aloud, Sedona shook her head. "Maybe I should have worded that a bit better. Sometimes I'm guilty of speaking without thinking."

Michael, not offended, thoroughly enjoyed her openness. "There's no need to apologize. Austin and me, the two of us are quite the pair, aren't we? Most of what troubles Austin can be pointed back to me. So, don't be too hard on him. He didn't get too good a lesson on loving and trusting, least not from me."

At the mention of his name, Sedona glanced down at her watch and wondered where he had walked off.

Without her having to say a word, Michael knew where her thoughts had wandered. "He'll be back. He just needs time. That letter really blew him away. It's probably why his sister decided against mailing it. He just needs to let everything sink in. Death hits people differently. When you get old like me and seen more than what you think is your fair share of trouble in this life, you realize that death is part of the package. You can't escape it. Sometimes it hits hard and fast, and for some, well it just takes its time. There's no accounting for it. It's simply how we pass on to that next life that God has in store for us." Turning his long body to face her, he reflectively smiled with his dark sad eyes. "I've always said that mourning is for the living, not the dead, a least not for the Believer."

After they moved the last of Stephanie's belongings into the storage room, Michael started for his car. "Well girlie, it looks like it's about that time for me to head on home. If I don't see Austin and you before you leave, just . . ."

"Don't, please don't go yet." Not wanting to see the man leave, Sedona grabbed his arm and convincingly smiled up into his face. "Besides there's all of that food left upstairs. With Mitch gone, and Austin and I leaving soon, most of it will have to be thrown away. So, why don't you stay for dinner and let me wrap up some for you to take home."

Sedona, noticing him glance up the beach, pushed aside his concern of Austin not wanting to see him. "I wouldn't worry about Austin. There's no telling when he's coming back. Plus, don't you want to say goodbye?" she added.

What could he say? The thought of sharing supper with the rather attractive ingenuous woman was far more appealing than going back to his empty apartment. "Ok, ok you've got me. But I'm staying only if you promise that you won't force me to eat anyone's casserole, identifiable or otherwise."

From the leftovers, they were able to lay out quite a spread. As she sat and listened to Michael talk about his job on the oilrig and his volunteer work at the hospital, it was difficult to imagine the man to be anything but loving and conscientious. Unable to keep a lid on her curiosity, she asked the obvious. "No offense, but what happened to you over the years? I mean, what changed you from the reprobate that Austin describes you as being, to the man that you seem to be now?"

Not offended by her directness, Michael laughed. "The Lord Jesus Christ – pure and simple." Never embarrassed to speak of his conversion, he witnessed how the Lord changed his life as if it had happened only yesterday. "I gave the Lord my life right there in Harland's bar, fifteen years ago, on April the thirteenth. Sure did."

"Harland's *bar*?" repeated Sedona. Not sure that she had heard the man correctly. "You got saved in a bar?"

Laughing at her reaction, Michael's sad eyes twinkled. "I know, I always get that reaction. But you have to understand old Harland. You've met him, he was here at the house last night."

Immediately the small, cheerful man came to mind. "So what happened?"

"Oh, I was just drunk out of my mind, as usual. Around that

time, I stayed on the bottle. It was my company keeper, it didn't ask questions or make me feel guilty." As he settled back in his chair, Michael all in one motion, relaxed his shoulders, crossed his long legs and stuffed his hands in his pockets. The mannerism reminded Sedona so much of Austin. "I had just come around from the Goodly's, they had mentioned that Austin was coming to town to see Stephanie graduate from grad school. She had just earned her master degree in education. So I had the bright idea of getting myself cleaned up and joining them. I thought that maybe I could put things right between all of us. So I got my suit cleaned, got washed up and dropped by the house."

"But Mrs. Goodly, bless her heart, when she opened that door and saw me standing there – me and my drunken self, standing there like I had done something grand; she called me out. She let me know that I was the most selfish man that she ever knew. She said wearing a clean suit didn't fool anyone, least of all my drunken cold heart. She said that the best thing that I could do for the kids was to stay away. They were getting along just fine without me," she said. "Probably even better."

"Ouch," flinched Sedona shaking her head. "That had to hurt."

"It did. But it was the truth. If I didn't know it when she said it, I believed it when I stood over in the yard; across from the house and watched them all leave for the ceremony. No one missed me, gave a second thought of my not being there. So, I did what I always did. I went and got my company keeper."

Sedona, thoroughly wrapped up in his story, sat forward in her chair and tried to imagine the affable man sitting across from her as a drunk. "So how did you meet up with Harland?"

"Well, I used to like to take my habit on over to a pier down at the beach. That night was no exception. The only thing though, I was at my rope's end, ready to call it "kaput". So I laid out at the beach's edge and begged God to wash me out with the surf. But do you know what I got for an answer?"

Shaking her head, she took a stab. "Harland?"

"Ol' Harland and a rain storm." Chuckling at the memory, he laid back his head and stretched out his arms. "You should've seen me. Sprawled out on the sand, still in my suit, in the middle of a thunderstorm. When that last cold wave hit me, I just knew that I was on my way to see my maker – even felt him tugging at my sleeve. When I opened my eyes to see, I liked to jump out my skin. There was this face, as black as the night sky staring down at me. *C'mon, get up. It's time to go,* he said. Oh Lord, I cried. You didn't send an angel, you've sent Satan himself."

Laughing, she tried to imagine anyone getting Harland – that sweet little old man, confused with Satan. "You must've been stoned out of your head."

"That I was. But it didn't help much that he was wearing that long black rain slicker of his and a red hat. I tell you, a man that dark has got no business wearing a red cap. Well, ol' Harland, pulled me up out of the water and helped me on up into his bar. Dried me up and preached. Told me that God had something better for me. That I was throwing away a life that had been given to me. But that's all right he said. It's all right because God has a way for me to get a second chance, to start all over. And that way was Jesus. When I think back to how much I wanted to hear those words, *needed* to believe those words, it makes me . . ." Momentarily closing his eyes he gave up a quiet word of praise. "He was my answer."

Emotionally right there with him, Sedona reached over and patted his arm; she felt his joy. "Praise God is right. That was your Damascus experience. So from that point on, your life was changed?"

"From that point on. Now, I don't want to mislead you. The road hasn't always been easy. You know, Satan likes to throw in a few bumps and snags along the way. But God has always seen me through, and I have never turned back to the bottle."

Truly touched by his testimony, she rubbed her arms. "Wow, just hearing the love and excitement in your voice is raising the hairs on my arms. But, I'm just curious, what happened in the first place to make you so . . . so . . ."

"Unkind, irresponsible, unwilling to be a good husband and father?"

"Yeah."

He didn't mind the question, in answering though, he just had to be sure to do right by the truth, so he took his time and walked over to the photograph of him and his wife and picked it up. While lovingly stroking her face, he attempted to explain. "Sedona, some would argue that doing the right thing isn't always the best thing. But I've come to realize in this long life of mine, that it's not that it isn't the best thing, it's just that sometimes it is not the easiest thing."

"We got married, and Carissa got pregnant. I loved her, but I had my dreams." Placing the frame gently on the table, he took a seat at the wet bar. "Believe it or not, I wanted to be a pharmacist. A broke black man with a wife and kid on the way, wanting to be a pharmacist in Texas, in the 1950's. Imagine that. I had a plan, was going to a Negro college up in Austin, Houston-Tillotson, then on to Meharry Medical College in Nashville. But a plan is mighty hard to pull off without resolve, money, and no one willing to help you out. So, I eventually gave up – it's that simple."

"Carissa, she was good at dreaming with me. She even named Austin after the city that we were headed for, to remind us . . . she said. She understood how desperately I wanted to get out, but unfortunately understanding doesn't pay the bills when a man can't find work. So to help make ends meet, she took on domestic work, worked in a cafeteria for a little while, and to her credit, for a while there, we were able to set some aside. But then comes along my little Stephanie – I tell you, she was a pretty little baby."

Michael, at the memory of his baby girl, eyes lit up. "But you know, with kids come more bills. That's when we moved in with the Goodly's. She watched Austin and Stephanie while Carissa and I went out to work. Except most times, it was Carissa who did the working. After a little while she got on with the Monk's – a wealthy family that used to run things here around town. They liked her because she ironed so well. Hmph, isn't that a kick of a reason to want someone around."

"You know, it's hard for a man to watch his wife work at something so menial. You can't feel like a man. During that time, I felt like I was getting it from all sides. She never complained, but it use to tear at me not being able to say, honey, stay home and forget about them. I tell you, it is a bitch being poor – excuse my language."

Sedona, so drawn to his story, sympathized with his frustration completely. Taking in her compassionate expression, Michael, sad eyes softly smiled as she came to sit closer to where he was standing.

"The more Carissa dreamed, the more I felt like I was the butt of some cruel joke. It just beat me down. Then one day, it seemed as if she just stopped dreaming about me becoming a pharmacist, and she started dreaming about her and the kids taking a trip – away from me. At least that's the way I saw it. They were going to leave me behind and move out to Arizona. So, I got angry. At the time, I saw them as being the reason that I was stuck here on this sand trap, so how dare they have the nerve to leave me. So I left. I took the little money that they had saved, and left. I know that it sounds petty and childish, even cruel, but that's what I did."

"So what made you come back?"

Once again picking up the photo, he stared into his wife's eyes. "I received word that Carissa had taken ill, the cancer had taken a hold of her. By the time that I had gotten back, it had pretty much consumed her." Even though he had long made peace with the memory, the pain was still very real, and it was very much in evidence in his expression as he walked over to the window that overlooked the water. "The kids needed somebody to look after them, and family wasn't much to speak of. So, I hunted around and got on as a laborer out on the shipping channels. Hard work, but it paid decent enough. Made enough to pay the Goodly's to care for the kids, with enough left over for liquor. At the time, I thought that I was doing okay, the kids were eating, had clothes, a place to stay. As far as I was concerned, they had everything that they needed."

"Except you," sadly whispered Sedona.

"You're right," he nodded as he turned towards her, "except me."

"After a little while, Austin joined the navy, went off to medical school, you don't know how proud that made me. Stephanie became a teacher, married Mitch. For a long time there, neither one of them were speaking to me. Heck, the last time I even spoke to Austin was on his 18th birthday when I showed up at his graduation ceremony drunk. Did you know he was valedictorian? I was proud, but I let the jealousy get a hold of me. I started dwelling on what happened to all of my hopes and dreams."

"Right there at the school, he told me to stay away, said he would take care of Stephanie, that he had had enough. I've got to hand it to him; he kept his word, better than I ever did. Just thinking about him used to make me feel like a failure. I mean he worked, put himself through school, cared for his mother, looked out after his sister, all without help from me. I resented him for figuring out how to make all of the pieces in life work. When the liquor had a hold of me, I used to think that the only reason he became a doctor was to get back at me, to rub my nose in it."

"Well, it didn't help that he was named after the town that you were trying to get to for school. Every time you either said or heard his name, you were reminded," quipped Sedona.

Heartily chuckling at her observation, he found a spot across from her on the arm of the sofa and reached over to tweak her nose. "I never thought about it quite that way, I suppose that you're right though."

With a shrug, he crossed his arms and concluded, "That pretty much sums it up. I stayed out of their lives until I found Christ. Harland made me see that if God could forgive me, then I could forgive me. I had a new life, I felt good about myself. So I sought out Stephanie and asked her to forgive me, to give me another chance. She did. Then I mustered up the courage and wrote Austin, I even drove out to see him, but he didn't want anything to do with me. Can't say that I much blame him. He was just tired of all of the 'I'm sorrys'. I thought that maybe, hoped that we could come to some kinda understanding about the whole thing. But, I pretty much gave up on that wish after I read a couple of Carissa's old diaries that Stephanie had come across."

"Why? What did they say?"

"Quite a bit actually. They offered a running account of all the disappointments and sorrow that I had caused. All the broken promises, forgotten birthdays, missed programs at school and church. She even wrote of my drunken tirades, how they use to frighten the kids. Just reading about the misery, the hell that I caused, things that I can't remember because of my drunkenness, made me realize how difficult it would be for Austin to ever forgive me."

Sedona, knowing Austin as she did, had to agree. "It will be hard, but remember, Stephanie did."

"Yeah, but keep in mind that Stephanie was a bit younger than Austin. Plus, she looked at me through the eyes of a daughter. Steph was just like her mother. Always willing to give me the benefit of the doubt, trying to understand. That was her mother up and down. Those old diaries reminded me just how much she cared for me. Carissa knew my burden as well as I did. Oh, the tears she must've cried."

"But she loved you," gently inserted Sedona.

"That she did . . . and never stopped believing in us, trusting in our love. "

Sedona, all at once sad, thoughts turned towards the man who held her heart. "Your wife was so unlike Austin, she wasn't afraid to love. But with Austin, just the mention of the word and he's rendered speechless. To me, it doesn't make sense. When he has someone who loves him. Someone who has never given him reason to doubt, he can't trust enough to love in return."

"There is no fear in love, but perfect love casts out fear. For fear has to do with punishment, and he who fears is not perfected in love. We love, because He first loved us. I John 4:18-19. Those verses hold the key to unlock that mystery."

Not making the connection, Sedona shook her head. "You've lost me, I don't understand."

"Look at it this way. Austin can't quite believe, can't quite comprehend that you love him simply because you do. He's afraid that loving you is just too risky. There are no guarantees, I taught him that. In the past, what has he gotten out of loving?" Michael leaned forward and used his fingers to tick off the list, "A no count father, a mother that left him as a child, a wife that didn't know how to be patient . . ."

"And now Stephanie," finished Sedona.

"Exactly. Sedona, I sincerely believe that he wants to love you, he needs to love you, but he's afraid. Look at it this way; we love God because He first loved us. It didn't happen the other way around. Well, it's the same way when people fall in love. There is always someone who loves first, and that love – that assurance is what draws the other near. But they have got to feel safe enough to trust it, to rest in it. Austin just hasn't gotten there yet."

While understanding the correlation, she also understood its reality. "Austin may never get there."

"You're right. But prayerfully he'll find a bit of peace and in the process, do some forgiving and then trusting."

Feeling somewhat better, she sighed. Michael's perspective had put everything in a clearer light. "So what am I suppose to do until then, just sit around and wait? "

"I can't answer that question for you. It all depends on your needs, what you want, and how patient you are willing to be . . . can be for that matter. No, Sedona, I can't answer that question."

"But . . ." Ring, ring!

While Michael answered the phone, Sedona mulled over the advice that she had just received and wondered if she had that kind of patience. It all made sense, but did she have the strength?

"Sedona, the phone."

Assuming that it was Mazey checking on her, she was more than a little surprised to hear Gary's easy voice.

"Hey beautiful, how are you doing?"

"Gary?"

"Yeah, it's me. I've been thinking about you. Mazey let me in on what's been going on there. Pretty heavy stuff. I just called to see if you're okay."

Not sure what to make of the phone call or the man on the other end, Sedona hesitated before answering, "I'm fine. Thanks."

"Austin's treating you okay?"

Conscious of Michael standing close by, Sedona shrugged. "Yeah. Why would you ask? How did you get this phone number?"

Gary, ignoring the last question simply laughed. "My cousin, your best friend is worried sick over you. Say, I know that you have company and can't talk, but just remember that whatever problem Austin's got, it's not about you. You're alright. Alright? Call if you need anything," and with that, he hung up.

"Now that was odd," remarked Sedona as she replaced the receiver. "I wonder what that was about?"

"Anything wrong?" asked Michael, both a little curious and concerned.

"No," Sedona explained, "Nothing's wrong. That was just my ex. He called to see how I was doing. He and Mazey are cousins, I guess when she got back, she shared a little of what's been going on here. I just don't get him though, he wasn't this concerned or protective when we were married."

"Maybe he's still interested."

"Na!" Sedona laughed, waving aside the thought. "It's nothing like that. For some reason he's just leery of Austin."

"Well, I guess he knows how men can be. You become pretty good at assessing people, when you've been guilty of doing a good bit of hurting yourself. So, the two of you must've separated on good terms. I've always thought that if a couple had to part company, that's how it should be."

"At the time when we separated, that was hardly the case. The traits I admired at the start of our relationship, were the very ones I hated at the end. You have to know Gary. He has always been fun loving and easy going. When I met him, we were in France studying in Giverny. He is an exceptional architect, very talented. But despite what people think, being talented and rich carries with it baggage just like if you're poor. Gary has always been frustrated with something to prove."

"Ok," Michael chuckled as he leaned against the counter, "seeing how this has become true confession time, I have to ask. What broke you two up?"

"Well, best I can figure is that I just didn't make him happy. I couldn't keep the banjoes strumming. In Europe, we were inseparable. Our life was like one big postcard. If we weren't painting in the meadows, or walking along the River Seine, we were enjoying the gardens. Together we discovered and explored museums and romantic haunts, talked about our hopes and dreams. He wanted to make it on his own, so bad, without any help from his father. In France, for the first time, he felt as he was calling his own shots, establishing a reputation amongst his professors, no one was pulling strings. But once we settled in New Orleans, we couldn't figure out how to keep the magic going. While he was dissatisfied, I was in awe. Coming from a small Nebraska college town, I was doing good just to keep up. But not Gary, he was in his milieu. He was always chasing the fastest crowd, the biggest client, and the prettiest woman. He thrives on the challenge of proving that he can get."

"I see; he was a womanizer."

"In a word, yes. While I was focused on trying to live up to his expectations, his parents high hopes of having a daughter-in-law who could corral their wild son, and a calendar of social engagements, he was out getting."

Michael found it hard to imagine any man not being happy and content with the attractive and bright woman standing before him.

185

"What made you put up with all of his nonsense"

Sedona, thinking back on that time, shrugged. "He always had a plausible explanation for everything. That's Gary's style. He's a good talker. Even when you catch him in a bold face lie, he can make you doubt your mind. And I guess that I fell for him for the same reason why a lot of women fall for the wrong type of men. He made me feel loved – like I was someone special." Laughing aloud at the illogicality of her statement, she apologized. "I'm sorry, but just the thought of a philandering husband who makes his wife feel loved and special is just too funny. Someone should've taken me to have my head examined." Almost too embarrassed to look over at Michael, Sedona drummed her fingers on her knee, "You must think that I have more than a few buttons missing."

With a smile, Michael prayed that his son would do right by this charming woman. "On the contrary. I am curious though, what was the straw that broke the camel's back?"

Upon hearing the question, Sedona's broad smile faded, "Losing Lilie. I was about three weeks short of my due date when Gary invited me to fly down to Cabo San Lucas; he had to oversee a major hotel renovation project. Of course he knew that I couldn't go, his asking was just a cover to throw me off the track. Right after he left for the airport, I noticed that he had left his portfolio that held all of his plans. So being the dutiful wife, I decided to drive out to the airport to bring them to him. When I didn't see him at the gate, I decided to give up and head back home, but first I had to go to the ladies room. You know pregnant women and the bathroom. Well, on the way out, who do I see at the bar all hugged up on the wife of one of his clients?"

"Did he see you?"

"Yeah, what do you think? Can you imagine me walking away quietly? Me and my mouth?"

Michael let out a quiet chuckle. "So I guess you confronted him."

"Big time. Of course, he was furious at me for causing a scene, and embarrassed that everyone around heard how he was cheating on his very pregnant wife. But in typical Gary style, he simply called me delusional, forgave my jealousy, blamed my highly emotional state on the pregnancy, arranged for airport security to drive me to my car and boarded the plane as if it was all a part of a normal day's work. Well, that night, I went into labor."

Angry with Gary, a man he had never met, Michael took her hand. "The baby, died at birth?"

Sedona nodded, "She was still born. The doctors were baffled, Gary was devastated, and I filed for divorce. Another black mark for love."

"So what got you through?"

"Prayer and Mazey. She allowed me to cry for a couple of weeks, even to feel sorry for myself. But one morning, she drew back the curtains and said enough with the pity party. I could either permanently check out and always be on the run from heartache and disappointment, or I could swallow hard and see things through. It was my choice. So I chose to . . ."

"Give love and life another shot," finished Michael. "That's what it's all about." Reminded of the time by glancing out the window at the tide, he held onto her hand, "Well my dear, it looks like it's about that time . . ."

Interrupted by the sound of a key in the front door, Sedona and Michael turned to face a somber looking Austin. The younger man, taking in both his father and Sedona with a sweeping glance raised a brow, "I hope that I'm not interrupting anything."

Making no move to release Sedona, Michael smiled over at the woman. "No, I was just telling your girl friend goodbye."

187

Affectionately patting her hand, he asked her not to forget their conversation. "Just remember what we talked about."

In response, Sedona reached up and gave him a warm hug, "Michael, I am so glad that we had a chance to talk. You've given me a lot to think about."

Before he drew away, he softly whispered in her ear, "Remember, love will have its way."

"I won't forget."

"Well, Austin . . ." Michael turned towards his son and placed a weathered hand on his arm, "It's been wonderful seeing you, but I'm not going to fool myself into thinking that you want me to hang around. I don't want to be guilty of treading too long on your kindness. You've handled things like a man . . . always like a man, and for that I've got to give you your due and say thank you."

Sedona could have cut the silence with a knife. Even though Austin glanced down at his father's hand, he made no attempt to move it, but neither did he immediately look his father in the face.

Undaunted by his son's reaction, Michael continued, bent on saying his piece. "I've already said my little speech about the past. I know how you feel about it, about me. I can't do nothing about it; I can't change it. But I can say that I love you." After self-consciously patting his eyes with his handkerchief, Michael cleared his throat. "Now you take care and treat this wonderful woman square."

It was all that Sedona could do to keep from crying herself when Austin momentarily sought strength in her eyes before returning them to his father. "Um, dad, you take care too. I just need a little time." Helplessly shrugging while including both his father and Sedona in his glance, he continued. "I can't make any promises. I . . . I can't say what I know I should be able to say. I just can't; at least not right now."

With a strong loving embrace, Michael made it clear that he

understood. Encircled in the arms of his father, Austin once again sought Sedona's face. Taking in his eyes, Sedona realized that their resigned sadness, matched his father's. In that same instance, she also realized that he was speaking to her as well as to his father. He was explaining his goodbye to her as well.

Refusing to accept the reality of their relationship, she quietly watched as Michael quickly kissed his son on the cheek. As he prepared to head for the door, Sedona forced down the lump that had risen in her throat and reminded the older man of the food that he was to take home. Packing the leftovers in a paper bag, she explained to Austin that Mitch had decided to pay his aunt and uncle a visit in Seattle. Anyone who knew her could tell from her rambling explanation that she was on the verge of tears. "Michael, could you give me your phone number and address? I've written mine down, along with my e-mail address. I'll like to keep in touch."

As he wrote down the requested information, Michael guessed at the reason that she was asking for the information instead of getting it from Austin later. Torn between offering his son his opinion on Sedona, and keeping quiet, he wisely chose the latter.

"You'd like to stay in touch? You better stay in touch," Michael teased. "Here, I'll give you my e-mail address too. Even though I'm a bit old, I've kept up with technology. I even bought myself one of those laptops." Handing the info back to Sedona, he gave her a final hug and kiss goodbye. "Remember what we talked about. You hang in here."

She should've seen the writing on the wall when they had their

189

very first falling out back at the airport in New Orleans; it was raining on that day as well. Now here she was miserable and rejected, looking at Austin for perhaps the very last time. Lorraine couldn't have called it any better. With him so close, right next to her, it was hard to accept that there was the distinct possibility that she would never see him again. Still clutching the handkerchief that he offered the night before when he explained his decision to return to California, she willed herself not to cry. There was nothing left to say or to do that would encourage him to change his mind.

"Listen, like I explained on the way over here, this isn't the last time that I will see you. I just need some time." Austin, wanting nothing more than to bolt from the terminal and run out to hot sun for air, instead took her hand. "You've got to understand, this whole thing with Stephanie, my dad, it's . . ."

Not wanting to hear any more cowardly explanations, she quickly withdrew her hand and clipped, "Austin, you've got to do what you've got to do. There's no point on going on about it. You know how I feel about you, so there's nothing more to be said. Nothing more." When she heard a ground attendant explain over the terminal intercom that her flight would be delayed for another half hour, Sedona sighed. *Prolonged agony.* "Listen, it's getting late. There is no point of you missing your flight because of me." *Missing anything for that matter.* "When I get back, I'll send the rest of your things on to San Diego. So, *please*, just go."

"Sedona, don't do this. There is no reason to make this any harder than it need be." Despite her taciturn expression, he took a chance and leaned over to offer a kiss that went unreturned. "Okay, it's going to be like that," he clenched his jaw as he rose. "Well Sedona, have a safe trip and I'll keep in touch," and with that he was gone.

When she could no longer see his figure down the terminal hall, she put her head in her lap and cried. Not caring of those around who stared but offered no consolation, she sobbed with heartbroken abandon. When all of her tears were spent, she reached for her sunglasses and walked down the terminal to the ticket counter and handed the agent a credit card. "When is your next flight to Lincoln, Nebraska please?"

"Hmm . . . I hope that you have some time, there is a flight departing in about an hour and a half, but it is not direct. You'll have to fly to Dallas, layover for about an hour, from there fly into St. Louis, wait another hour and then fly into Lincoln. And, you're in luck; we have seats open on all three flights. Would you like for me to book you?"

Nothing else in her life ever went smoothly, why should this be in different, so she shrugged and adjusted her shoulder bag. "I'll take it. Could you have my bags removed from Flight #3621 leaving for New Orleans?"

"What a difference a day makes."

CHAPTER ELEVEN

"Dad? Mom?"

Dead quiet. . "Okay, what else is new?" There was no point in being disappointed; she had half expected them to be gone. They were always gone. When neither one of them returned her call from the airport, she knew that she was taking a chance flying home. Spring semester had already ended, so they could quite literally be anywhere on the face of the planet. *Sedona girl, you better ditch that dream of coming home to the smell of fresh baked cookies and daddy sitting by the fire waiting for a visit from his little girl. It never has happened, and unless they become stricken and rendered totally housebound, there's serious doubt if it ever will happen.* Obviously, there was no point of wasting energy on sighing, wishing and hoping. So with a shrug, she dragged her things up to her bedroom.

Along with the other consistencies of her parent's home, her room was the same as the day she moved out on her own. The same sun bleached stuffed animals, the same dusty LP's and 45's, the same 70's mod wallpaper, and the same faded bulletin board. The bulletin board, done up in her sorority colors of pink and green, albeit faded, still had the snap shots taken from the last college party that she attended. Despite the fact that she visited at least two to three times a year, she ignored her mother's suggestion to update the furnishings. There was a comfort coming back to its familiarity. The room was one of two spots in the entire universe where she had ever felt as if she truly belonged, the other was the huge oak tree outside her window.

"How many times have I climbed up that tree and cried?" she wondered as she walked over to the window and looked out. Immediately thinking of Austin and his tree back in Galveston, she frowned. Despite the tiresome robe of pity that he had chosen to cloak himself in, he and his had not cornered the market on familial disenchantment and dysfunction.

True, she never had to worry about finances, or ever doubt if she would be able to go on to college and fulfill her dreams. But like Austin, she too had spent a whole lifetime being lonely; wondering where she fit; who was there to love her; and if she should disappear, who would miss her company. With a sigh, she flopped back onto the pillows and closed her eyes. Well Austin, at least you have a reason for your father's emotional neglect and distance, whereas with my mother, I don't even have a clue.

Sure, when pressed, her mother said the right words and showed up when appropriate, but her eyes and remoteness always belied the truth. Never had she known the comfort of her mother's arms or the protectiveness of her loving rules. As tears threatened to fall from her eyes, she shut them back hard. No, she had not come home for a pity party – she had left that to Austin. The purpose of her return was to confront the two who had brought her into the world. She had to find out why she wasn't good enough to be loved.

Slowly rousing to the shadowy stillness that surrounded her, she looked over at the bedside clock – 6:30! Had she really slept that long? As she turned on the lamp, her eyes caught her bedraggled reflection in the bureau mirror. "You look like crap," she told herself as she rearranged the collar of her blouse and smoothed down her hair. From the looks of the circles under her eyes, the last few days had definitely taken their toll

Curious if anyone was home, she slid on her shoes and headed down the staircase. When she heard the soft clicking of a computer keyboard as she neared the bottom stair, she broke into a smile and followed the sound into her mother's study.

"Hey Mom," greeted Sedona as she gave her mother a kiss that was met with a quick pat on the cheek.

The attractive woman looked up over her bifocals and returned a faint smile, "Hello dear, so you're finally up. What time did you get in?"

"Oh, around 3:30. Is dad here?"

"No, he had a departmental meeting. You know how those run on, he'll be in soon enough." With a dismissive turn back to her computer screen, Ms. Tinney effectively put an end to any small talk that her daughter may have had in mind.

For want of nothing else better to do, Sedona leaned over her mother's shoulder to take a look at what she was working on. "Is this another paper?"

Annoyed with the interruption, Ms. Tinney abruptly stopped typing and impatiently placed her hands in her lap. "Dear, this is not a paper, but a funding proposal. We're wanting to take a team into western Cameroon next winter."

"What's there?"

Her mother, wanting nothing more than to finish her task, sighed as she brusquely explained. "Rain forests . . . very dense . . . very wet rain forests. Listen, I don't have time to go into the details. If I don't finish this portion up tonight, it'll mean more work tomorrow."

Stepping back as if she had been slapped, Sedona studied her mother's flawless complexion. Just like her bedroom upstairs, nothing had changed.

"If you're hungry, dinner is waiting in the kitchen."

"I'll wait to eat with you and dad," murmured Sedona, still holding fast to her warm cozy family dream. After all, she reasoned, she had flown almost a thousand miles to be with her parents.

If the woman had shared even a remote desire to converse with her daughter, it wasn't apparent. "No, you go on and eat. I warmed up my plate when I got in, and your dad has more than likely grabbed a bite on campus. So, go on back to the kitchen, there's a casserole in the oven."

When Sedona didn't immediately make a move to leave, her mom irritatingly pursed her lips. "Are you on vacation? I mean, your phone call this morning was quite out of the blue.

Instinctively translating her question to mean, 'Why are you here?' Sedona shrugged. "Actually, my plans were last minute. School let out a little over a month ago. Remember, I asked about you all's summer plans?"

"Sedona," Mrs. Tinney began as she studied her daughter, "You probably talked to your father. I would have told you that there is just way too much going on right now for this to be a good time for a visit." And with that, she returned her attention to the computer.

All of eighteen again, and more depressed than when she'd arrived; Sedona quietly left the room and headed towards the kitchen. The tears that she held back on the plane now streamed down unchecked. Even though she knew what to expect when she decided to make the trip home, she had prayed that things would be a bit different. Talking to herself once again, Sedona whispered, "Don't let her push your buttons. Let it go."

After almost a week of eating unidentifiable casseroles at Mitch and Stephanie's, the thought of forcing down yet another one, did little for her appetite other than to stir a wave of nausea. But determined to give her mother's creation a half of a chance, she lifted the lid to the casserole pan. Words could not do justice to what greeted her. It's unidentifiable contents looked and smelled like something her mother had shipped home from one of her digs.

Oh well, might as well get out the bologna and bread. Despite being starved, a sandwich, chips and a coke sounded much more appealing than her mother's casserole surprise. Seated at the massive hand hewn table, she looked around the kitchen. Like the rest of the house, it was old and dark. Though heavy antique furnishings filled the spacious rooms flatteringly, home always reminded her of one of her mother's archeological tombs. She wasn't quite sure if the analogy was due to the artifacts and relics that dressed the walls and tabletops, or just her prevailing impression of home. Always disliking the decor, she felt as though it gave guests the false impression that her family cherished their earthy familial ties.

This was definitely not what I had in mind, she thought as she munched her sandwich; I could have saved myself a couple hundred bucks and had this kind of company at home. With nowhere else for her thoughts to roam, she wondered what Austin was doing at that exact moment. It was impossible not to wish that he was thinking about her. "Don't do this to yourself," she whispered aloud as she toyed with the spindle of a pepper mill that sat close by. But despite all of her *best* efforts, she found herself humming a Bonnie Raitt ballad, *"I can't make you love me if you won't."* Ugh! Get over it!

Again in the hallway, she paused at her mother's doorway and wished that she could go in and ask for a hug. The mere thought was almost as far fetched as the possibility of it ever happening, so Sedona settled for the next best thing – her father's recliner.

"Donne?"

"Daddy," Sedona jumped at the sound of her father's elated voice. In one motion, she stood and threw her arms about his neck and gave him an affectionate kiss.

"Hey sweetie, my you're a pleasant surprise, " Sidney Tinney gently touched her, as if he couldn't quite believe that she was really there. "What a treat. This is just great. Believe it or not, I was talking to Ms. Sanchez about you; it couldn't have been no more than an hour ago. You remember her don't you?"

"Ms. Sanchez?" murmured Sedona, not quite placing a face with the name.

"Yeah, you remember her. Tall, a long face, keen but pretty. She's gone out with your mom a couple of times. In fact, right before you left to go to Europe, she was the linguist on that dig your mother set up to . . . to . . . some dessert or jungle or the other down in South America. Hell, she's gone so much, I can't keep track of where all she's been."

Sedona, still stinging from her mother's cool welcome home, agreed. "She does stay gone a lot; and when she is here, she's so wrapped up in getting away to somewhere else that she barely takes the time to say hello. After you all's trip this summer, isn't she commandeering a bush taxi into the Cameroon? How do you stand it?"

Sidney, well familiar with his daughter's animosity, rounded the desk to sit in his chair. "I see that you two have been at it again. You go away, come back, go away and you've found that nothing's changed. I teach this every semester to my freshman class – you are who you are. In other words, your mother is never going to change, Sedona. How many times have we gone over this?"

"Too many for me to be still getting my feelings hurt. I guess that I am still clinging to wishful thinking."

Softly chuckling, Sidney smoothly eased the conversation down what he hoped was a less troublesome path. "So, tell me, what's been going on with you? The last time we spoke, you were talking about plans for the summer."

With a shrug and a sigh, Sedona sat on the edge of the desk and crossed her arms. "There's nothing new to tell, just the same ol' same ol', the usual heartache and loneliness."

Not even conscious of what she was doing, Sedona proved her father's point regarding the behavior of people. "Sedona, you still know how to tire me out. No matter what you say, you and your mom do have one thing in common – you're both consistent."

"Meaning?" Sedona frowned.

"You're still the little dramatist." With no hint of compassion, he continued, "Let me guess, some guy dumped you."

"Yeah, some guy dumped me," she whispered. Toying with a pencil that she had taken off the desk, she silently wondered why she even bothered about coming home. "It's a man that I love very much . . ." Embarrassed over the tears that were now slowly rolling down her face, she quickly wiped them with the back of her hand. "The one caveat is that he . . . he doesn't quite love me in the same way."

Despite his heart breaking over her tears, Sidney wished that she had confided in her mother. "Come over here," he stood as he drew her close. Not knowing quite what to say, he clumsily patted her on the back and glanced over at the door, silently calling for his wife. As he handed Sedona his handkerchief, he looked down at her and spoke far more brusquely than he intended. "Here, stop all of this nonsense. Use your words and stop crying like a child. It can't be all that bad."

As he waited for her to regain her composure, he was reminded of the day she came to him crying because Ed Samson up the street backed out of escorting her to the junior prom. He felt as much at a loss then as now.

"Ok, now that the tears are gone, just *whom* are we talking about?"

"Lt. Commander Austin Edmund James, MC," Sedona mockingly replied.

"Lt. Commander Austin Edmund James, MC, my that's a mouth full."

"Please don't be impressed. He's not as together as he sounds. Remember, Austin is the doctor friend that I went out to visit in San Diego last fall."

Suddenly recalling the man that she was referring to, Sidney reminded her of the advice that he given her back in October. Waving a finger, he shook his head, "I hate to say that I told you so, but I warned you about those navy men. They're so transient . . ."

"I know, I know," Sedona interrupted.

"Well, you live and you learn. Sedona, honey, I don't know what to tell you except . . ."

Sedona, desperately wanting to talk the whole affair over with someone, again interrupted what she knew was going to be his usual detached formulaic advice. "I just don't know what went wrong. Over the last year, we had gotten so close. I know that it wasn't just my imagination. He opened up; we talked, and shared so much. I mean, I really felt as if we were working on something permanent. But, then poof! I fell in love and he couldn't, at least not in the way that I needed for him to."

Neither addressing nor ignoring his daughter's torment, Sidney picked up a journal from his desk and placed it in a nearby bookcase. "Sweetheart, once again you've been duped by that disarming aberration called love. I guess that Sophocles didn't have a clue. Welcome to the club my dear."

Very well used to her father's antics, Sedona rolled her eyes. No arms to cry into here. Without considering his point, she retorted, "What does Sophocles have to do with any of this?"

Impatiently frowning at the question, Sidney Tinney shook his head as he prayed for a quick end to the conversation. "Come on Sedona, please don't tell me that sending you to college was for naught."

Just once she wished that her parents would break through their intellectual reserves and show just a semblance of empathy and understanding. "Daddy, I did not come home for a discussion on Sophocles."

Sidney continued undeterred, "Sophocles wrote, *'One word frees us all of the weight and pain in life. That word is love.'*"

"Either Sophocles is wrong or I've *never* been blessed to experience love from *anyone* in *any* form."

Uncharacteristically at a loss for words, Sidney studied his daughters face. "Oh Sedona, you sound like a spoiled child. You're just feeling sorry for yourself."

Wanting with all of her heart to disagree, to bare her weight of loneliness and the pain of unacknowledged love, she instead sighed.

Once again taking in her sad face, Sidney attempted to lighten her spirits in a typical fatherly fashion. "Donne, you're too pretty and smart to be down in the dumps over something like this. Why don't the two of us walk on over to the East Campus Diary Store? If we hurry we can make it before they close."

"Ice cream, your solution for everything."

"Well, it used to work when you were a little girl."

Jim Anderson of "Father's Knows Best" he was not. Accepting the fact that in terms of an emotional foothold, that this was the best that she was going to get, she reached over and gave her father a peck on the cheek.

As they made their way into the kitchen towards the back door, Sidney whispered, "There's no need to bother your mom. When she gets going with that writing, nothing else matters. Besides, she'll just bug me about that damn casserole."

"More consistent behavior, " laughed Sedona.

Walking across campus, Sedona found solace along the familiar path. Despite the cropping up of some newer buildings, the old halls helped to remind her of her true self. "How many times have I walked this way to class?"

"And for ice cream," teased her dad, remembering their frequent walks over to the Agriculture Department's diary store.

"Yeah, the only difference is that this evening it's because of a man. Back then it was usually due to a fight with mom." Walking a bit in silence, Sedona heard herself ask, "So what is it with her any-way?"

With an amused laugh, Sidney experienced a sudden sense of déjà vu. "How do you mean?"

"You know what I mean? Why do I bug her so? Take tonight for instance, I traveled a thousand miles to come home, she hasn't seen me in almost a year, and she barely says hello."

"You know your mother."

"Yeah, that's just it. I really believe that she resents me."

"She probably does." The admission slipped out before he had a chance to consider his words. Not sure whether it was the clear evening, the unexpected surprise of his daughter, or the combination thereof, he had no idea why he provided credence for Sedona's fears.

Not so much surprised at his words, but his admitting it, Sedona suddenly felt a bit chilled.

Sidney, recognizing her silence for hurt, quickly jumped in. "That came out all wrong. Sedona, your mother loves you, don't ever doubt that. But you have to understand, she carries a lot of baggage."

While being extraordinarily curious as to the contents of the bags, Sedona wasn't quite sure if she wanted to hear the truth about her mother.

Just wanting to be through with it all, Sidney did his best to explain in the only way that he knew how – straight and to the point. "You have to remember, at the time that you were born, abortion – that type of thing, really wasn't acceptable. You made your mistakes, you took your lumps."

That's dad. Always straight to the point. "So . . . what you are saying is that I wasn't planned."

"*I* wasn't planned," corrected Sidney. "Your mother, when we first met, in so many ways was just like you. A free spirit, happy and bent on following her dreams. Quite honestly, marriage and children just weren't in her plans. She wanted to travel, study abroad, and explore ruins. But when she found out she was pregnant, her idea of herself vaporized. There she was, the modern woman, caught by the age-old snare – pregnancy."

"So she resents me because she didn't want me."

"Maybe at the beginning, but I think that it wound up being she envies you."

"Envies me?" retorted Sedona, surprised at even the notion.

"Yeah, your lifestyle, your personality, your independence, your talent, your freedom. I dare imagine that quite a few envy you."

In silence they walked, allowing the words to settle. Even though the truth provided answers, it hurt like hell.

"How did you feel about . . ."

"Having you?" finished Sidney.

Sedona, putting her hands in her pockets, quickly nodded.

"Oh, I was up for the challenge."

"Did you love mom?"

"As much as I could at the time. You know, love is a type of energy that's constantly changing, growing, developing."

Both, instinctively knowing what the next question was going to be, braced themselves.

"Did you love me?" she asked.

"I didn't know you to love you."

Nope, that wasn't quite what she wanted to hear. But it was honest, and for that she could be appreciative. Knowing her father, she knew that any other answer would have been a lie.

Oblivious of the tears that were threatening to once again fall from his daughter's eyes, he continued softly, almost to himself, "But it didn't take long. Donne, after I picked you up and held you, looked in those soft brown eyes of yours, you had me hook, line and sinker."

Instantly putting her hand in his jacket pocket, she grabbed a hold of his hand.

"Daddy, maybe Sophocles wasn't too far off."

The next morning, her parents were up and out before she even had one eye open. Not feeling quite her old self, she forced down a slice of dry toast to settle her stomach.

Desperate to keep her mind off of Austin, she decided to walk to a nearby bookstore to buy a novel written by one of her favorite authors. In the store, while browsing though the magazine rack, the cover of a gourmet cooking publication grabbed her attention. Instantly craving the black bean and tomatillo soup featured on its cover, she decided to prepare the recipe, along with a wonderfully decadent dark chocolate brownie cake for dinner.

Lost in the kitchen, her mind drifted to other things beside Austin. Before she realized it, the afternoon was half over. With a sense of accomplishment, just as her mother walked through the door, she pulled the rich dessert from the oven.

"Well, I see you've been busy," lifting the lid of the soup pot she smiled approvingly. "I can't quite make out what it is, but it smells good." After helping herself to a spoonful of the soup, she slowly chewed and inquired about the ingredients. "I recognize the black beans, tomatillos, cilantro and coriander, what else is in it?"

Sedona, as she ran through the list of ingredients, inwardly beamed. She had finally done something right.

Halfway through the recitation of the recipe, Helena frowned, "Why did you mess up a perfectly healthy dish by adding sour cream?"

"Well . . . I didn't know that I was messing it up. It wasn't that much really, only a half cup."

"Hmm, it all adds up, Sedona. The sour cream along with the chocolate cake is going to wipe out my fat allowance for the week. Besides, your father is trying to watch his cholesterol. I thought that I mentioned that."

As her mother, self absorbed and critical turned to leave, Sedona's patience snapped, "Listen, if you don't want it, don't do me any favors by eating it. I didn't cook it for you anyway, it was something that I wanted."

Her mom, seemingly unfazed by the sudden display of temper, turned to study her daughter's face. Speaking as if she was addressing a spoiled child, she humored rather than apologized. "Sedona, the soup tastes just fine. Good Lord, I didn't mean to offend you. Why you are so overly sensitive, I don't know. I would think that you would have outgrown it by now. You are definitely still your father's spoiled little girl."

Her sense of peace, now faded, Sedona refused to be spoken to as if she was an adolescent. Unconsciously stinging at the confirming knowledge that she had never been especially wanted, she wickedly tried a few buttons of her own. "Maybe it's that charmed life of mine that you're always referring to that has me so spoiled," sarcastically murmured Sedona under her breath, just loud enough for her mother to hear.

At the doorway, her mom turned and their eyes locked.

"Sedona, I am not going to stand here and allow you to pick an argument. Unlike you, I have better things to do with my time."

Not sure if it was the tension filled air, jangled nerves, or the strong aroma drifting from the soup, Sedona suddenly felt her stomach rise and the room spin.

Sedona, rousing to the coolness of the stone floor beneath her, and the damp cloth that her mother gently pressed against her face, she slowly opened her eyes.

Satisfied that her daughter was awake, Helena sat back on her heels and quietly asked, "Sedona, are you pregnant?"

All at once, not wanting to entertain the thought, but forced to acknowledge the possibility, Sedona vigorously shook her head. "Oh God, no. Why would you automatically jump to that conclusion?"

"I haven't jumped to any conclusions, I'm simply asking. I heard you in the bathroom last night, sick to your stomach."

"Well, I'm not pregnant. I haven't even been intimate with anyone until a little over a month ago."

"Both you and I know how many times don't matter. Any time when you're not prepared for the consequences is one time too many."

Embarrassed, Sedona quickly waved aside her mother's reprimand as she used the table to pull herself up. "I know, I know, you don't have to lecture."

Not put off so easily, Helena persistently pressed the subject. "Well, then I know that you know to use protection. After all, in this day and age . . ."

Still feeling a bit nauseous, Sedona slowly sat down. "Why won't you leave this alone? I am 37 years old, have been married and divorced, and you're still talking to me like I'm a teenager."

"I'm talking to you like a mother." Placing the back of her hand against her daughter's forehead, Helena frowned. "You don't have a fever, but you are clammy. Maybe, to be on the safe side, you should go on over to the campus infirmary."

Once again abruptly interrupted, but this time by her daughter rushing pass her into the guest bathroom, Helena shook her head and followed.

Pregnant. Replacing the receiver, she slowly sank into her father's chair and tried to comprehend the news. Helena, hearing the phone ring, walked into the study, already certain of the verdict.

"I can't be. I just can't be." With her head on the desk, she broke down and cried as her mother calmly soothed the nape of her neck."

Fully relating to her despair, Ms. Tinney pulled her daughter close and held her tight, the first time either ever remembered her doing so. "Well honey, you just got caught. Don't beat yourself up about it. It happens to the best of us."

Quite use to her mom's frankness, Sedona shrugged. "So much for my charmed life."

Helena, biting her lower lip, the only outward sign that she was upset at the news, replied, "Well, unlike when I was young, you have choices. You can keep the baby or . . ."

"There is no or," Sedona pulled away. I've already been through the pain of losing a baby – it's an experience that you never quite get over."

Propping herself on the desk, the mother studied her daughter's tense face. "Well, despite what you're feeling right now, don't allow the baby to rush you into something that you're ill prepared to handle. *That* would be the experience that you will never quite get over."

"Is that what happened to you?" Sedona blurted out the question before she could think.

Looking directly into her daughter's eyes, Ms. Tinney did not hesitate. "Yes. So I know of what I speak."

Aware that her mother was referring to her, Sedona felt those demon tears slide down her cheeks.

Unmoved, Ms. Tinney calmly handed her a tissue. "Don't cry when you ask a question and don't get the answer that you want to hear. Whether or not you choose to believe it, this issue is not a question of love."

As if debating on whether or not to continue, Helena thought-fully eyed her daughter before explaining. "Last night, your father told me about you two's conversation. So, if you're wondering if I love both you and your father, the answer is yes. I love you two dearly, more than I have ever loved anyone on the face of this earth. But that love isn't some magical spell that can change who I am, my basic makeup. My personality today is the same as it was the day that I was born, and it will be the same on the day that I die. Love can't change that, at least not the human kind. You keep that in mind as you envision the happily ever after future of your baby with you and the father."

Accepting a brusque but loving hug from her mother, Sedona closed her eyes and allowed her mother's words to sink in. In a matter of minutes, her mother explained 37 years of distance. "So it has never really been about me?"

"No, never. It's been about me seeing myself as something else other than Sidney's wife or Sedona's mother. Your father was supposed to be one of many stepping-stones along the path to where I thought I was going. Not my final resting place. But because of a night of passion, that is what he became."

"And because of me, your life changed forever."

"That it did. But it turned out ok, and in retrospect, I have few complaints." Looking into her daughter's face, she smoothed down her hair. "So, tell me about the father of your little bambino. Your dad mentioned that he is a doctor in the Navy, living in San Diego."

Unaware of the sudden light that lit her eyes, Sedona filled her mother in on Austin. "You and dad would like him. He's quite smart, a bit reserved but a good conversationalist. He is a photography buff, plus he's rather attractive, almost as good-looking as dad. He's gone through a bad patch lately though. Last week, his sister committed suicide, and he was the one who found her body washed up on the beach."

"The beach?"

Yeah, down in Galveston. That's where I flew in from; he was visiting in New Orleans when we got word that his sister was missing."

"So after the funeral, he returned to San Diego? Since you're on summer break, why did you come here and not go with him on out to California?"

Swallowing hard, Sedona turned away and fidgeted with the desk blotter, "I suggested it, but he didn't want me to. It seems as if his sister's death, his estranged father's presence at the funeral, along with the history of a failed marriage have made him a bit skittish when it comes to matters of the heart. He's been in this perpetual phase where he is constantly questioning the meaning of love, both his definition and mine. Even though he claims that he loves me, he still feels as if he needs a bit of time to sort things through."

"Hmm, I can understand that. It goes back to what I was talking about before – love is not the magic potion that songs and poems make it out to be." Helena, patting her daughter on the arm, remarked, "He sounds very prudent. I know that ruminating is not very romantic, but it is better to be certain than sorry." After a moment of silence, she asked, "So, how and when are you going to break the news to him about the baby?"

Truly not having a clue, Sedona shrugged her shoulders. "I don't know."

"Well, I know that I speak for your father when I say that if it would make things easier for you, you can stay here. There's plenty of room."

Touched by the offer, as well as a third hug offered by her mother, Sedona joked, "Wow! Three hugs in one day? That's a record."

Helena, not put off in the least by her daughter's comment, chuckled and added with more than a note of truth, "Well, you better savor them while you can. You know better than anyone that I am not exactly the huggy-feely type."

"Life is funny, it took us 37 years to finally have something in common."

Aware that Sedona was referring to her pregnancy predicament, Helena grimaced, "I think they call it irony"

Telling her father about the baby proved to be easier than she had expected. Midway through their dinner – black bean soup for daughter and dad, citrus salad for mom, Helena ceremoniously rang her fork against her water glass. "Well, Sidney, it looks like we have some news. We are going to be blessed with a baby."

Not blinking an eye, Sidney dryly remarked, "I thought that you had that taken care of 37 years ago."

"I'm not the one, silly, it's Sedona. She's pregnant"

If he was fazed by the announcement, Sidney didn't let on, instead he looked over at his daughter, "Life sure has a way of coming around full circle, it bites you in the behind every time."

"Yeah, and this time I'm the one who got bit," Sedona rejoined, at ease with her parents odd sense of humor.

"So when are you going to break the news to his commander-ship?" quipped Sidney.

"I don't know," replied Sedona, not evasively, simply not having an answer.

Never allowing a question to go unanswered, her father persisted,

"He is the type to do what is right isn't he?"

"You mean marry me? Probably. But just because he is, doesn't mean that it's necessarily the right thing."

Stressing his point, Sidney pushed his bowl to one side. "I married your mother when we found ourselves in the same pickle."

"That may be true, but like I said, it doesn't mean that it is the right thing."

Fully aware of the point that her husband was trying to make, Helena cut to the chase and went straight to the heart of Sidney's poorly expressed concerns. "You're pretty set in terms of money aren't you?"

Quickly losing her appetite, Sedona twiddled with her fork and murmured. "Yeah, Gary's settlement was quite generous. And I have the house, plus the teaching and my business."

"Good," her father nodded as he returned to his meal, "And with this Austin being in the military, collecting child support won't be a problem. Then, whether he does right by you or not, it doesn't much matter. It sounds like all you have to do is have the baby."

Despite being well familiar with her parents' bluntness, Sedona found it impossible to continue the conversation. "Oh really, Dad? What happened to your quote of the week, *'One word frees us all of the weight and pain in life. That word is love.'* I can't take anymore of this conversation, I am going upstairs." Weary and irritable, she excused herself and retreated to her bedroom.

"It must be her whacked out hormones," Sidney reasoned, as both he and his wife flabbergasted, watched her storm up the staircase.

Tired of crying and desperately needing someone sane to talk to, Sedona could think of nothing else to do except to call Mazey. But instead of her best friend picking up the phone as expected, Gary came on the line.

"Gary, what are you doing answering the phone?" complained Sedona in a tight voice.

"Oh, I don't know, it rang and I picked it up."

Not up for another tiresome conversation, she sniped, "I'm really not in the mood. Where's Mazey?"

Even over the phone line, he could make out the tiredness in her voice, so he held back the urge to tease and instead explained, "Mazey and Miles are out at some symphony 'thingamajig'. Their usual babysitter canceled, so they called in the reserves – me. What's up?"

Unable to find the words, Sedona, feeling like an emotional basket case audibly caught back her tears.

"Sedona, what's wrong?" her ex asked, truly concerned. "Where are you? If you tell me, I can come get you."

"I wish. I'm home, here at my parents."

"Well, that's enough to make anyone cry," drolly commented Gary, quite familiar with the Tinney persona. "Why don't you come on back to New Orleans, or is Doctor Casey with you."

"No, no Austin's back in San Diego."

"Is that why you're are crying? Because he went on without you?" asked Gary, beginning to put together the puzzle.

"Well, that's a part of it," she sniffed.

"You know that you are too good for him. Now, you said that was only a part of it, what else is wrong?"

"I'm . . . I'm pregnant."

Caught off guard, Gary let out an expressive, "Ouch! That bastard, he left after you told him."

"No, no," Sedona quickly corrected. "He doesn't know yet. I just found out this afternoon."

"So shouldn't you be calling him instead of Mazey? Or are you not going to tell him?"

Just wanting her life simple again, Sedona tiredly explained, "I don't know what I am going to do, or when. I haven't put together a plan. I haven't had time to think straight. My parents are driving me nuts, the baby is bringing up all kinds of emotions, I can't stop crying, and I feel sick. In other words, I am losing my mind."

"I tell you what, why don't you come on back to New Orleans. You've got people down here who care about you, who are normal, and who . . . who love you. We can help get things sorted out, perhaps even keep you from hitting your head against that brick wall called Austin."

Touched by the uncharacteristic sincere tone in his voice, Sedona quietly diverted the subject. "Speaking of brick walls, my mother told me that she loved me today. I mean she said it to me first . . . usually I have to say it. That was the first time that I ever remembered *her* telling *me* that she loved me."

After a moment of silence, Gary, unsure of quite what to say, cleared his throat, "Sedona, I'm happy for you. Now maybe you're finally free. It's been what you've been needing to hear all of your life."

Wiping at her tears, she agreed. "You're right."

"So when are you coming home, either Mazey or I can pick you up at the airport."

"Probably day after tomorrow, in the evening sometime."

"Fine, one of us will be there. Just call me back with the time and flight number."

Ring . . . ring . . . ring . . . *You have reached* . . ."Damn!" Slamming the receiver down, Austin paced across the floor. How long was she going to avoid picking up the phone? Debating on whether or not to call Mazey, he looked at his watch and decided to wait a little while longer before drawing someone else into his mess. It had only been three days since he had last seen Sedona, but it felt like a lifetime. Even before landing in San Diego, he was missing her.

As soon as he had gotten back to his condo, he had called, but the only response he received was her answering machine – for three days, her answering machine. He had even tried e-mail, but no luck. He knew that she was angry, but refusing to hash out problems was so unlike Sedona. Usually she was the one who initiated, facilitated and ended most arguments. *Let's get it all out in the open* was her mantra.

If he ever got a hold of her, he would reassure her that he loved her. Somehow make her understand that he just wanted to be sure that he was ready for the risk of a forever relationship. Sedona had to realize that the past few weeks contained more emotion, more drama than the total of his entire life. How could he rationally discuss love and long-term commitment when he had to also deal with Stephanie's death, finding her body, planning the funeral, facing his father, and haranguing with his ex-wife? Good Lord, when was he supposed to have sorted through his feelings regarding marriage, his father and sister, not to mention God and his faith.

Turning on his computer, he quickly went on online and searched his e-mail. The only thing of particular interest was a message from Mitch and another from his father. After reading Mitch's apology for leaving without personally telling him goodbye, Austin remembered the harsh words that they had exchanged. Later, he would have to send his own apology, when his mind was a bit clearer. As he rubbed his brow, he opened his father's message.

The letter was brief, but poignant. In the past, he would have deleted it as soon as he had read the name of the sender, but since their parting in Galveston, he so desperately wanted – no, needed to make sense out of things. After re-reading Michael's urgings not to give up on love, and his assurances that a belief in God's love, faith and courage would provide the key to overcoming his trials and uncertainties, Austin fought back an unfamiliar desire to give his father a call.

The message brought forth the memory of his father's last hug. It was hard not to wonder how different things would be if he had expressed his forgiveness, spoken of his feelings, and accepted and returned the love offered by both his dad and Sedona. If only he knew what was holding him back, keeping happiness at bay?

He didn't have to pose the question, to know the answer. Not liking the truth, he quickly turned off the computer and headed out to the beach and walked. Closing his ears to the surf, he prayed. Prayed for courage to ask Sedona to marry him, prayed for forgiveness, and then prayed for the compassion to forgive his father and the ability to trust. Lastly, he prayed for the courage to face the truth.

In response, God's spirit laid it out for him plain. All that was holding him back was himself.

CHAPTER TWELVE

Gary! I thought that Mazey was meeting me?"

With a warm kiss on the cheek, he pulled his ex protectively out of the stream of passengers disembarking from the plane. "Carly cajoled her into chaperoning a museum lock-in with her Brownie troop. So, I was given a choice, either fill in as surrogate parent or pick up the lady fair."

"You mean more like the lady spent." Truly feeling the toll of the last several days, Sedona tiredly smoothed back a few stray tendrils as she longingly thought of her bed and its cool cotton sheets.

Picking up on her body language, Gary quickly relieved her of her carry-on tote. "Here, let's hurry and collect your bags so we can get you home. Better yet, give me your claim ticket and you sit here until . . ."

"Gary . . . please," chuckled Sedona. "I'm just a little tired, that's all. You sound like a mother hen. What's gotten into you?"

"Nothing. I was just thinking about you and . . . and the baby. I mean, I wouldn't want anything to happen . . ."

Sedona, genuinely touched, reached over and gave him a hug. "You know, when you want to be, you can be downright sweet. Don't worry, the baby and I are just fine."

Appreciatively sliding in between the sheets, Sedona immediately remembered the last time she had slept in her bed. Austin warmed the empty spot next to her. Even late into the night, while he lay sleeping and she laid praying that he would awaken and whisper, *I love you*, she had never imagined that he would leave so quickly.

Neither had she ever imagined that she would be carrying his child. As she ran her hands along her belly, she smiled and then frowned as she, not for the first time, pondered her – their predicament. Her mother was right when she advised against getting her hopes up that somehow Austin would change, would miraculously embrace the notion of love and long-term commitment. Baby or not, him finally saying I love you would do nothing to change his basic makeup.

How does a woman break the news to an unsuspecting lover that she is pregnant? Does she simply call and say, *hey guess what?* Or is it done via an apologetic letter or impersonal e-mail? Maybe she should have asked her dad to break the news, that's what they used to do in the old days. No matter how he would broach the subject, it was certain to be logical, blunt and direct. Laughing out loud at the picture of her father spelling out the contractual and financial obligations, she imagined her mother in the background, pounding away on her computer keyboard – oblivious to the proceedings. "Don't hold your grandparents against me," she whispered to the baby. "No one has been able to explain them. They aren't, as Gary puts it, normal."

The ringing phone breaking into her thoughts, Sedona reached over and picked up the receiver. Instantly smiling, she settled back against the pillows. "Hey, I was just thinking about you."

"Of course," the familiar voice smoothly replied. "It's late, you're in bed, who else would you be thinking about?"

"My, aren't we a bit full of ourselves. Tell me, why is the great paramour spending the night talking on the phone and not out making love to a sexy unsuspecting damsel?"

"The answer is simple, I'm talking to her."

Despite the teasing nature of their exchange, Sedona didn't miss the serious shading in her ex-husband's tone. At a loss for words, she waited for him to continue.

Gary, well aware of her discomfiture softly inquired, "So beautiful, how are you doing?"

Flattered by his seductive attentiveness, she giggled, "Gary, have you been drinking? You've seen me no less than one hour ago."

"I am truly offended. Here, I call to inquire about your well-being, and you accuse me of being inebriated. I thought that we were on much friendlier terms."

"It's just that . . . that sometimes I just don't how to take you. You . . ."

"*You* think too hard. It looks like we are going to have to work with you on going with the flow."

"That's what got me in trouble, going with my heart and not with my head," she quipped with a rueful smirk.

"No, what got you in trouble was a sea *dog* named Austin. Your heart is just fine. Has Ben Casey given you a call?"

"Not that I am aware of; a few minutes ago, I checked my answering machine and remembered that I had turned it off before we left for the cabin. So as far as I know, he is still out somewhere walking a rut into the beach assessing his feelings. I've decided not to rush and tell him about the baby until he has made a decision on his own, without pressure. And even then, if he asks me to marry him, who knows."

"So your feelings for him have started to change?"

"Maybe, I don't know . . ."

After a moment or two of silence, Gary changed the subject. "Are you up to taking a drive out with me to Lafourch Parish? I've got a contract to redo a little chapel in Thibodaux. Not a big job, but a worthwhile one. If it was just a simple redo, I would delegate it to an associate, but the congregation, mostly poor black folk, needs some assistance in restoring it. They say that the church is over one hundred years old."

"What happened to it?"

"Some arsonists vandalized and then torched it a couple of years ago. It's taken them this long to raise enough money for building materials."

Curious at Gary's involvement, but not necessarily surprised, she asked, "So how did they find you?"

"A fraternity brother of mine stopped by the office. He's donating the equipment and labor, and asked if I would be willing to draw up the plans and oversee the restoration. The reason that I'm asking you to drive down is because a section of the stained glass window was miraculously salvaged. I thought that it would be kinda nice to incorporate it into a new piece."

"It sounds like a fun project but . . ."

Quickly assuaging what he assumed to be her main concern, he cut in, "Of course, the firm will pay you for your work. I'm not asking that you donate your time or anything."

"No, no it's not the money. It's just that I still have the last project that you commissioned left to finish, and now with the baby and not knowing how things are going to work out with Austin, I would hate to commit to something that I might not be able to finish."

Already ahead of her, Gary's voice loss its usual lightheartedness and took on a more steady tone. "Listen, I've been thinking about you and your situation. I was going to suggest this tomorrow, but now that we're talking about work and the baby, I might as well throw you my idea. As you know, the first window won't be needed for another five to six months. But, I have several more projects that you might be interested in working on – with a couple of them being pretty substantial. So I've decided, if you're interested mind you, to work it into the budget for you to hire one or two assistants. That way, you can focus your attention on the design work, and the help can do the labor. Like I said, the firm already has more requests for your work than you have time. The way I see it, with the baby coming, it makes the most sense."

Not knowing quite what to make out of his generous offer, she hesitantly asked, "How do you mean? I know that it makes sense for you and the firm, but how does it benefit me? Are you talking about me giving up teaching? If you are, there's a lot to consider; like for instance, there's my medical benefits."

"Well, the firm can cover you and the baby. As far as I am concerned, that's a non-issue there. And if you think about it, by working this way, not only will you be able to take things slow until the baby comes; after your maternity leave is over, you won't be forced to go back to the class room." Mindful of the fact that she always felt that he thought little of her profession, he quickly added, "I know how much you love your job, it is important and fulfilling – there's no doubt about that; but I also remember how you felt when we were expecting Lilie. You wanted to be at home with her at least until she got into school."

Both touched and surprised by the extent of his concern, Sedona felt her eyes tear as she took in the sincerity of his voice. "Gary, I really don't know what to say. You've seemed to have given this whole situation a lot of thought; and the baby isn't even your responsibility."

"Not in the way that you think," he murmured, almost too soft for her to hear.

"I don't understand?"

"Don't worry about it, all that you need to know Sedona is that there is a part of my heart that will always love you. I have no problem telling you that."

Not hearing her ex-husband speak so open and earnest in more years than she could remember, Sedona quietly wiped away tears.

"So, what do you say? Are you up to a drive in the morning?"

Once again listening to her heart, she smiled, "What time?"

With a wave goodbye, Mazey closed the shop door behind her cousin, turned and quizzically scanned Sedona's face, "Wait a minute, am I in the twilight zone or what?"

Aware of the impetus behind the remark, Sedona shrugged as she poured herself a cup of herbal tea. "What you just witnessed, has been Gary all day. Just as sweet as he could want to be, almost fawning even.

Mazey, looking out the window at her departing cousin, placed her hands on her hips and shook her head. "If I didn't know any better, I would be willing to swear that we have gone back in time almost fifteen years." Walking over to the counter, she stuck out her arm, "Pinch me."

"Someone needs to pinch me. I feel as if I'm caught in a bizarre comedy of errors. Think about it. I'm pregnant by a man, who becomes lost in an abyss of confusion while on his trek to gain the courage to say I love you. My ex-husband, who while during our marriage, lived in an abyss of confusion regarding the meaning of I love you, has now inexplicably made it his mission to comfort and care for me."

As she explained Gary's business proposition, Sedona furrowed her brow. "The thing is, his proposal makes perfect sense. In fact, it couldn't be more perfect. Not only will it provide a very tidy little income, but it will allow me to stay home with the baby."

"Yeah, but how about Austin? How will he feel about you working so close with Gary?"

"At this point, I'm not even figuring Austin into the picture. I don't want him marrying me just because I'm pregnant. If I learned nothing else from Austin's father and my parents, it's that a baby can't change the basic anatomy of a person's personality, hang-ups or idiosyncrasies. If anything they only solidify. And love definitely has nothing to do with any of it."

"I would have thought that Gary taught you that little lesson," Mazey frowned.

Sedona, not caring for her friend's aside, found herself growing defensive and irritated.

Either unmindful or simply not caring, Mazey continued. "Listen, make your own decision. But while you're doing it, don't forget, it took Gary over fifteen years to come to terms with what loving someone really means. And in my mind, even though he's family, the jury is still out. So, out of fairness and love for him, yourself and that baby, give Austin his time."

"Listen, I'm going to tell you just what I told Gary, the ball is in Austin's court. If he calls, he calls. We can talk and *maybe* work something out. If not, I . . . ," touching her stomach she corrected herself, "we will just have to move on and deal with it."

"So when are you going to tell him about the baby?" Mazey asked, clearly of the opinion that Austin should be informed as soon as possible.

"I have not a clue. When the time is right, I hope that I know."

"So he hasn't e-mailed you?"

Not considering that he may have, Sedona shrugged her shoulders while purposefully swallowing down any notion of hope. "Honestly, I don't know. I really haven't had time to check. When I got home yesterday, Gary stayed and fixed dinner. We ate; I unpacked, showered and went to bed. This morning, I got up just in time to get dressed to drive down with him to Lafourche Parish.

More than just a little curious at the rekindled interest that her cousin now seemingly had in his ex-wife, Mazey interrogated, "So, you spent the whole day with Gary?"

"Yeah, I told you about the church . . ."

"You could have been there and back way before three. He didn't drop you off here until close to seven."

"So?" replied Sedona, clueless as to why her friend was finding her itinerary so interesting.

"So what did you two do all day?"

With a sigh, she retraced the last ten hours and obliged Mazey with a run down. "Let's see, Gary picked me up about 9:30. When he found out that I hadn't eaten breakfast, he insisted that we stop for a light meal. You should have heard him, he was so cute going on and on about eating healthy, taking the right vitamins, old wives' and voodoo tales. Then we finished the drive and took a look at the site, met with a couple of members from the congregation – which was useful, because I was able to get some historical information to incorporate into the window. The pastor showed us some photographs of the building going as far back as the turn of the century. Since we had missed lunch, the pastor's wife insisted that we stay for supper. She cooked up some catfish and hushpuppies. The baby must've not liked the grease because on the way back home, I got sick."

"Sick?"

"Yeah, a full blown case of morning sickness." Shaking her head, she remembered how Gary quickly pulled off the road when she warned him that she was about the ruin the inside of his Navigator.

"Knowing how much Gary loves that fancy Jeep of his, I bet that made his day?"

"No, actually he was quite sweet about it. He wet his handkerchief with some of my bottled water and held it against my forehead until I felt better. He even reminded me that when I was pregnant with Lilie, I got sick in the late afternoon as well. He called it my evening malaise."

As she thoughtfully studied the soft smile on her friend's face, Mazey's intuitive nature formed more than a couple of questions to pose to her *dear sweet* cousin.

Another night alone. Stepping into the dark foyer, she flipped on the light switch as she waved goodbye to Mazey. Long used to coming home to an empty house, she reset the alarm and slowly made her way up the staircase. *Mazey was one to talk, what did she know about coming home at night with no one to share the quiet darkness. It's always easy to give someone advice when you aren't the one living with the consequences.* After turning on the television, she tossed the remote onto the bed and checked her messages. Sales calls, several hang-ups, a message from Gary with a time to stop by the firm to meet with the insurance coordinator, several more hang-ups and Austin.

Austin! With her heart racing at the sound of his easy baritone, she determinedly quelled her feelings of eagerness, and replayed his message.

"Tinney, listen. I need to talk with you, not leave messages. I take it that you're still angry because you're not picking up the phone or returning my e-mail. I've been trying to get a hold of you ever since I got back from Galveston. It was important that I talked with you today, but after trying at least a half a dozen times, I give up. You're upset; I understand that. When you get around to it, try reading your e-mail. You know how to get in touch."

Not believing the arrogance of what she had just heard, she replayed the tape. "Don't you have some nerve?" she muttered as she changed out of her clothes. "Like I'm suppose to be sitting by the phone waiting for you to call. It wasn't my idea for you to run back to San Diego. Now you see how it feels to be disregarded and ignored. You give up? Well, I beat you to the punch. I gave up when I said goodbye." Still baffled at his audacity, she looked over at the machine, "You don't leave messages, you need to talk, since when? Please! You have my cell phone number." Her thoughts turning to her cell phone, she reached for her purse to retrieve it. She hadn't thought about the phone since she boarded the plane to Nebraska. It was turned off. Before she even turned it on, she knew that there would be voice mail messages. Her fears were confirmed, Austin had tried to call, not once or twice, but repeatedly. *"Oh baby, I'm sorry."*

Even though it was late in New Orleans, it was only 8:30 in San Diego, so she grabbed up the phone and hoped that he was home. At the end of the last ring, she twisted her mouth when she realized that the answering machine had picked up. "Austin, Sedona. Listen, I just received your messages. I've been gone to my parents' all week, so my cell phone has been turned off. Call me, I'm at home." Damn!" she muttered as she replaced the receiver. "What kind of cloud am I living under?"

Why was all of this so hard, so complicated? Some people date, fall in love, marry and go on living without skipping a beat. But for her, love was always analogous with drama. With nothing left to do but take a shower, she willed herself away from the depression that was threatening her spirit. After all, she reasoned, nothing has changed. Just because Austin wants to talk, doesn't mean that he's ready for a commitment. She could not allow her mood to be yo-yoed about. Her focus had to be on the baby and their plans for the future. After her shower, she would calmly send him an e-mail message explaining the past week, and wait patiently for a reply.

More in control, more like her old self, she sat at her laptop and checked her e-mail messages. In the time that she was gone, her mailbox had accumulated over 70 messages. A lot of junk, forwarded stories that friends thought important to pass on, and FYI letters from friends. Purposely taking her time to read and respond to the one's that demanded her attention, including a reply to Michael, she saved Austin's e-mail for last. The first letter was sent on the same day that he arrived back to San Diego.

Date: Thu, June 17 2002 14:00:14 -0700 (PDT)

Sedona . . . As you are well aware, I have phoned you several times, with no luck. First, just let me say that I am sorry that you are having difficulty understanding my position. By now, it should be rather plain how I feel about you. I am not a hearts and flowers kinda guy, what can I say. But yes, I do love you. Trust me when I tell you this. Do I want you to leave me? No. Do we have a future? In all likelihood, yes. Give me a call in order for us to possibly work this out.

Best, Austin

Nope, somehow that just didn't do it. Gary has displayed more emotion. *Do we have a future? In all likelihood, yes . . . possibly we can work this out.* What kind of crap was that? Agitated, she tapped her fingertips along the edge of the desk and re-read the message. There weren't even any lines to read in-between. No one was asking him for hearts and flowers, she could buy her own damn heart and flowers. No, all that she wanted was something more than just lukewarm affection and feel good platitudes.

Despite her earlier vow, the familiar feelings of loneliness and depression soon cloaked her as they had done so many times in the past. Why, in every area of her life, was she predestined to feel as if she was little more than someone's token love?

As she scrolled down the screen further, she noticed a second, more recent message that had been sent several hours before she arrived home.

Date: Thu, June 17 2001 14:00:14 -0700 (PDT)

Sedona . . . Obviously I got neither the sentiment nor the words correct. I know that you want to hear more. I want to be able to tell you more – to be able to take that step and ask you to marry me; but I can't. Not that I won't, but I simply can't. And believe it or not, it is tearing me apart.

I asked you once before to be patient with me, to give me a little more time. It wasn't to stall, or to put off the inevitable. I just need time to get some things straight in my mind.

I will stay in touch as often as I can. I've temporarily been reassigned to another carrier and by this time, already on deployment to the Gulf. It was an assignment I requested. I expect to be gone until mid November. I hope that your silence is not goodbye. Until my return, you can e-mail me at the address above.

AML

Austin

Not yet believing what she had just read, Sedona re-read the last paragraph several times. He had left for six months. In the midst of things being as unsettled as they were, he had volunteered to leave the country for a half of a year. Anger hardly did justice to what she felt, and it did nothing to stop the flow of tears as she cried herself to sleep.

Every time Sedona walked into the building, she silently gave her kudos to Gary. Starting up his own firm, separate from the family business, was the best thing that he could have possibly done. Not only had it proven to be a good business move financially, but also on a personal level, it gave him possession of something that he had rightfully earned.

Upon entering the benefits office, she was pleasantly greeted by its coordinator. "Hello, you must be Ms. Tinney."

Returning the smile, Sedona accepted the proffered hand and shook it.

"When I arrived this morning, I found a note on my desk that Gary . . . I mean Mr. Chandler called to say that you were stopping by. Do you mind if I call you Sedona? " Still smiling, the bubbly young woman continued without giving Sedona a chance to respond. "My name is Hillary . . . Hillary Wellborn. If you would, please follow me into the conference room. There's a brief presentation that I go through that explains the various benefit packages and salary deduct . . ." Ms. Wellborn stopped mid sentence.

Curious as to why the woman stopped speaking, Sedona, who had obediently taken a seat, glanced up from fishing an ink pen from the bottom of her handbag. Not having missed Ms. Wellborn's earlier faux pas of addressing the boss by his first name, Sedona perceptively took in her soft features, French manicured nails, pale lavender suit and sandals, and light brown sugar complexion. Pretty and prissy.

Yup, Gary would definitely find her appealing. Slyly scanning her left hand for either a wedding band or engagement ring, Sedona asked, "Is there anything wrong?"

"No . . . I was going to give you info on salary deductions. But it states here that Gary . . . Mr. Chandler says that there are to be no deductions taken out for your benefits. Even though you are on special contract, that just doesn't make sense. During the time that I have been here, insurance premiums have always been deducted. Maybe I should call . . ."

"By all means do, but it probably has something to do with the fact that I'm his ex-wife," casually explained Sedona. With a bit of perverse pleasure that even she couldn't explain, she innocently added, "We're still on very good terms, intimate friends you can almost say."

Noticing how "Ms. Hillary" quickly assessed her with a sweeping gaze, Sedona smiled sweetly when their eyes met. "I might as well tell you, I mean you'll find out soon enough any way, I'm pregnant."

Never losing her smile, the younger woman flatly offered her congratulations. Certain that she had been correct in guessing that either Ms. Wellborn was in the midst of an office affair or had recently indulged in a little hanky-panky with the boss, Sedona guilelessly smiled a thank you.

This time in a tone markedly less chipper, the young woman shuffled her presentation notes back into her binder. "Well, with that being the case, it's just a simple matter of you selecting the package that suits you and the . . . the baby. There's no point in me reading out loud what you can read for yourself." Without making eye contact, she pushed a folder and several forms across the table. "If you need anything, I'll be right outside." And with that, Ms. Wellborn quickly left, allowing the door to noisily close behind her.

Mean spirited she typically was not, but softly chuckling to herself, Sedona got a rise out of making the young woman uncomfortable. Tip-toeing to the door, she listened for what she was sure to follow – an emotional phone call either to an office pal or if they were still seeing one another, Gary. After a pat on the back when her hunch proved to be correct, Sedona forced her attention back to the insurance forms.

After about a half hour of muddling through an array of HMOs, PPOs, dental and vision plans, Sedona marked her choices and repeatedly duplicated name, birth date and social security number onto the necessary documents. Setting her pen down, she stretched and shuffled the papers back into the folder. Appreciatively taking in the conference room's high styled avant-garde furnishings and appointments, she ran her hand along the wooden arm of the chair. It was obvious, as usual; Gary left no detail unintended. Walls coordinated with floor coverings, floors with furniture and the furniture with clocks, bookends and even desk accessories. Ordinarily, she would have found the blond wood and silver color scheme a bit cold and too austere for her taste. But somehow, he managed to soften the modern lines by infusing the area with natural light and color via strategically placed sunroofs, mini garden atriums and fountains. It felt as if he brought the warmth of nature indoors.

Walking over to the Hillary Wellborn's desk, Sedona innocently handed over her papers. "I hope that everything is in order. I have a prenatal appointment tomorrow morning."

"How far along are you?" asked the coordinator.

Sedona, so tempted to ask if she posed the question in order to figure out if she's been two-timed, instead smiled sweetly. "About a month. I don't mind telling you that the baby wasn't planned." But that's how life goes. We all get caught sooner or later, don't we?"

Unclear as to how she should respond, Hillary busied herself with the insurance forms.

Feeling delightfully evil, Sedona was about to continue her little charade until she saw Gary enter the office.

"Well, hello beautiful."

Neither quite sure as to who he was addressing, both hesitated. But only having eyes for his ex-wife, Gary gave her a friendly kiss and placed an arm around her waist. "Did Hillary here take good care of you?"

No longer offended by his shameless flirting, Sedona's soft brown eyes smiled warmly into his face. It felt good being the preference of choice for a change. "Oh yeah, Ms. Wellborn – Hillary was very helpful. So what brings you in here?"

Gary, perched himself on the corner of the desk and winked as he possessively drew her towards him, "I was hoping to take you to lunch. You don't have plans do you?"

"No, not a one." Quite flattered by his outward display of affection, Sedona did not question his motivation or why it had become so important to her that she was the center of his attention. She basked in it. She had won – finally finished first place. It had been a long time since she had been made to feel as if she was the most important person in the room. Without a doubt, no matter what the outcome, it felt damn good.

"Well Sedona, barring any complications, it looks like you will be a mom sometime between the end of January and Valentine's Day."

Dr. Mayra Tomlinson had been her OB/GYN since the beginning of her first pregnancy. She was one of the few doctors whom she enjoyed seeing. No matter how insignificant the question or concern, she always addressed the issue with gravity and patience. It was also refreshing to speak with a doctor who knew how to be forthright without being arrogant or judgmental.

Still not quite used to the reality of it all, Sedona placed a hand over stomach and focused on keeping her voice modulated. "So it's official," she weakly smiled with a bit of humor.

Dr. Tomlinson, very well familiar with Sedona's background, nodded. "Sedona, this really isn't any of my business, but I'm going to ask anyway. Are you and the baby's father currently together?"

"No," she softly replied. Even though she expected the question, she still wasn't prepared for how foolish it would make her feel. After all, she wasn't an impulsive teen, but a 37-year-old-woman who should've known how not to get herself in such a predicament.

With no evidence of censure, Dr. Tomlinson left from behind her desk and took a seat in the empty chair next to her patient. "Now listen, don't beat yourself up, you aren't the first woman who has found herself in this situation, and you won't be the last. This is surmountable. Don't take offense at what I am about to say, but I feel that I must go over all of your options." Taking in the tears that threatened to spill from Sedona's eyes, Dr. Tomlinson handed her a tissue. "Sedona, I'm sure that you know that if you don't want to keep the baby, you can either put it up for adoption or terminate the pregnancy. Right?"

In her heart, already knowing her decision, Sedona wiped at her eyes and nodded.

"This is a very personal decision that only you and perhaps the father can make. From the looks of things, you are a little over four weeks pregnant. So if . . ."

"There are no ifs," quietly interrupted Sedona. I've thought this through and I want to keep the baby. I really can't see it any other way, especially after the way we lost Lilie."

"Okay," Dr. Tomlinson patted her on the knee and then followed with a sincere hug. "Sometimes we do get second chances, don't we? I'm going to write you a prescription for some vitamins. You remember those, don't you?" She smiled, as she took the prescription pad from the pocket of her lab jacket. "At this point, everything looks fine, which should help to alleviate any anxieties that you may have. In order to monitor both you and the baby's development, for the next couple of months, I would like to see you every three to four weeks. You'll also need to make an appointment with my nurse to go over diet and any general questions that you may think of once you get home. If you think of any questions between now and then though, you call me."

"So, you don't anticipate any complications? I know it's too early to tell but . . ."

"But you're thinking about your last pregnancy," finished Dr. Tomlinson.

"Yeah."

"Well, when you lost Lilie, to be frank, it threw us all for a loop – it was totally unexpected. It was one of those one-in-a-million births that leaves us stumped. But, what I can tell you right now is that physically, you are okay. You've taken great care of yourself; your lifestyle and diet are already healthy. On your side, there is no family history of medical problems. Just to give us some added assurance, it would be helpful, if you can, to get the father's family history. Sedona, at this point, all I can say is that we expect this to be an uneventful pregnancy, that we will keep our eyes open for any complications, and address them if they should arise. Okay?"

All that Sedona could do was to nod. Nod and wait. "I understand. It's just that I don't know if I could handle it if . . . if anything happens to this baby."

"Well put such thoughts out of your mind, and focus on staying happy and free of stress. If or when you do decide to contact the father, tell him that I would be more than willing to sit down and talk with you both. Who knows, he may have some questions or concerns."

"Even if he knew, he wouldn't be coming in anytime soon," tiredly laughed Sedona. "He's a medical doctor in the Navy and his ship is on deployment for the next six months."

With this enlightening bit of information, Dr. Tomlinson wondered aloud about her patient's emotional support, "I know that your folks still live in Nebraska, do you have any close friends or family here?"

"I have friends, no family – but plenty of friends. Don't worry, believe me, I'll be fine." *I have no other choice but to be,* she silently added as she headed out of the door. "Well, I've taken up enough of your time, you have a waiting room full of patients. So I'll see you next month."

Despite the brave front, Dr. Tomlinson was not convinced, so she stopped her patient as she rose to leave for the appointment desk. "Sedona, remember you can call me if you need anything. Okay? Even if it is just to talk."

As Sedona walked out of the office, she never felt so alone. What she wouldn't give to have an eager husband sitting in the waiting room, or a soul-mate anxious to hear confirmation of the good news. *Baby, joy-of-mine, the only thing that is eagerly awaiting us right now is this elevator. Even if your daddy knew about you, he couldn't be here; he has seen to it. It is just the two of us, so we will have to deal with what we got and make the best of it.*

Just as she reached her car, the cell phone rang. "Hello?"

"Hey baby!"

"Gary?"

"The one and only. How was your appointment? Does everything look in order?"

"Everything is fine. I'm fine, the baby is developing as she should."

"She? Do I denote a bit of wishful thinking?"

"Gary," Sedona chuckled as she felt her spirit brighten, "no wishful thinking. I just want a healthy baby; you know that. It's just kinda awkward saying he or she."

"This baby has made you think of Lilie a lot. I know that it has me."

Before she could reply, Gary softened his voice, "You're on my mind a lot lately Sedona, both you and the baby. When we out yesterday, I started to offer to go along with you to see Dr. Tomlinson, but I didn't want to overstep, you know – make you feel uncomfortable or anything. "

Touched by his thoughtfulness, Sedona didn't know quite what to say. "Gary . . . I . . . thank you."

"Listen, I should be the one thanking you. You never have had a problem with giving out second chances." As the words settled, Gary once again changed the tone of the conversation. "So, what's on your agenda for dinner tonight? You don't have a date or anything do you?"

"Not hardly," she laughed. "Are you asking me out?"

"Sure, we have reasons to celebrate. You're doing fine, the baby is healthy, and I am happy. How does around 7 P. M. sound?"

Spirits high, she cast aside all of her 'feeling-sorry-for-herself' emotions and took a hold of the day. There was plenty to do, sketches to work up for the church, her ongoing glass project to complete, an assistant to hire, and a letter to write to Michael. What she was going to tell him, she had no idea, but she had to inquire about his family history. There was no way around it, she would have to tell him about the baby, which would certainly bring the conversation back around to Austin and the reality that he would have to be told – sooner rather than later. Even though it would make her life a whole lot easier to keep her pregnancy a secret and not tell Austin about it until after the baby was born; a perverse part of her screamed that it would serve him right to know that she was carrying his child, but not be invited to share in either the development or the birth.

From her tasks, she tackled the most difficult one first, writing Michael. Once logged onto the Internet, she felt her heart rate quicken as she scanned the mail that sat in her incoming mailbox. As she suspected, there were none from Austin, but to her delight, Mitchell had sent along a letter.

Subject: I'm Here!

Sedona, I made it to Washington safely and am doing okay. Life is so lonely without Stephanie; I suspect that it will always be. You would think that I would want to stay as far away from the water as possible, but in an odd way, I find comfort in looking out at the ocean. It is where Steph found her solace and surprisingly, it has been where I have found mine. In the sounds of the waves, I hear her voice speaking to me. It is the oddest thing; every evening I go out and we talk. Her favorite time of the day was the evening time-out on the water. You and Austin – the two of you, if you aren't already, need to be together. He loves you, and I know that you love him – it is so obvious. Remind him that life is much too short to allow the insignificant and the surmountable to get in the way and rob you of a lifetime of happiness. I can honestly say that Steph and I had no regrets because we knew how to love and enjoy one another.

In any case, don't be a stranger!

Stay in touch.

Mitch

He was right, life is way too short; but you can't make 'grown folk' do what 'grown folk' don't want to do. I could love Austin until the birds in the sky fly backwards, shout it from the hills even, but it wouldn't force Austin to love me back in the way that I need to be loved. With a sigh, she responded to his e-mail as positively as she could.

Subject: Re: I'm Here!

Mitch: I'm glad that that you made it safe and sound. How was the drive? I hope that it was uneventful. With any luck, the change of scenery will do you good. I have never been to Washington, but I hear that it is beautiful. Michael and I have become friends, and we have promised to stay in touch. He is really a nice man, a true testament to prayer and a changed heart. Austin doesn't know what he is missing out on.

Before we left Galveston, Michael tried to patch things up with Austin, but you know Austin. He managed to separate himself from both his father and me. Right now, he is out on the Pacific somewhere, spyglass in hand in search of a fresh beach to rut out. When I returned home, he had sent an e-mail message that stated that he volunteered for deployment, so he won't be back in the States for six months. Typical Austin, right? Oh well, what can I do?

Listen you, don't be a stranger and stay in touch.

Sedona

It was amazing how easy it was to pretend that her situation with Austin wasn't tying her up in knots; that she was so nonchalant and laid back about it all, so in control of her emotions. She wished that she had even half as much control as her letter portrayed. As things stood now, at any given time she could easily let go a faucet of tears. With a deep breath she tackled the more difficult letter, the one she had to write to Austin's dad.

Subject: Just curious . . .

Michael: Sorry this has taken so long. I hadn't forgotten about you, it's just that I decided at the last minute to visit my parents up in Nebraska. After Austin and I parted at the airport, I felt compelled to go home in search of some of my own answers. And I found them. Not all were to my liking, but they cleared up some concerns that I had been carrying around with me for a very long time. My parents are still my parents, as aloof and distant as ever, but I understand them a bit better, and that is what counts.

I have received some surprising news, unexpected but wonderful. It is difficult to explain in an e-mail, I would much rather relay it to you in person; it's not exactly the kind of news that you would write in an e-mail message. I also have a few questions for you . . .

At this last sentence she stopped typing and instead, gazed at the computer screen. No matter how she worded her request, it wouldn't make sense. How does one go on about inquiring about someone else's family medical history and noted maladies without explaining why? After several failed attempts, she gave up and grabbed the telephone. She had to call him, there were no other way around it, besides, he'll find out the news sooner or later. After several rings, she was greeted with his hearty hello. "Um . . . Michael . . . this is Sedona."

"Sedona! How's my girl? What are you up to?"

"I'm fine. You sound rather chipper this morning. I take it that life is treating you okay?"

"I can't complain, can't complain. I'm blessed; proof of that is this phone call. You know that you've been on my mind quite a bit, don't you? Both you and Austin. He e-mailed to tell me that he's volunteered for some sort of deployment or the other. Even though he did it to help out a friend, I was a bit surprised. I thought that the two of you would've . . ."

"You and me both," cut in Sedona. "But you know Austin. Love and attention don't affect him like most people."

Michael, with a chuckle, agreed. "Being busy like he stays, keeps him from his thoughts. We all have our own way of coping I suppose, I used to do mine with the whiskey bottle."

"I guess," despite the logic, somehow his explanation didn't make her feel any better about the situation.

"So you two didn't get to spend some time together in New Orleans? What a shame."

"I was disappointed." *Pissed* was a more apt description, but Sedona kept that thought to herself. "Austin flew on to California, and I flew up to Nebraska to see my folks. It was a nice visit, something that I needed to do." Tempted to rattle on about her parents and her newly revised understanding of why her childhood had been so miserable, she instead got straight to the point of her call. "So, Michael, have you ever wanted to be a grandfather?"

The pause was deafening. "Michael?"

"You don't beat around the bush, do you? Wow, the cat doesn't usually get my tongue . . . so you're pregnant? How far along?"

"About a month. I found out last week while I was home with my parents. I was just about as surprised as you are right now."

If Michael was dismayed, he covered it well, for he simply followed with the next expected question. "Does Austin know?"

"No. I haven't told him yet. Don't know how, or even if I want to or should." Even to her own ears she sounded contrary and bitter. No matter how she ought to have wanted to do the 'right' and mature thing, at this point, her emotions ruled.

"Why wouldn't you?" Michael, calm as always, kept his voice modulated as he employed reason. "He needs to know Sedona, you know that don't you? Besides, what would not telling him accomplish?"

She wanted to go with her first thought and say that it would make her feel better, but even she knew how nonsensical it would sound. But logic wasn't the mode that she wanted to operate under, so the best that she could muster was, "I guess, he should know. But I don't see what knowing at this point will accomplish, if anything, it'll just stress him out more."

"Sedona, listen to yourself." Michael, even before they spoke, knew that Sedona had to be hurt over Austin's actions. She truly loved his son, there was no doubt in his mind, so he patiently reasoned, "I am sure that it will stress him out. It would, even if the timing was perfect and you two were together. That is what expecting babies tend to do. Austin and I may not be close, but I do know a thing or two about his values. He'll want to do right by you."

Then he needs to tell me that he loves me, like he means it, she silently screamed. "But that is not what I want, I don't want anyone to step up to the plate because they're supposed to or even have to, I just want . . ."

"Romance, flowers, violins and all of that. Most women do. But Sedona, this is the real world. I am a living testimony to the fact that for most of us, life doesn't naturally go that way. Now, if you can get two people on the same page, you make it that way – or at least, give it a good try."

What could she say? Not one damn word. After a moment of clock-ticking silence, she murmured, "So how do I tell him? I mean, it's not like I can simply pick up the phone and call him. All that I have is the e-mail and the post office. Sometimes he calls while out, if he can, but those conversations are usually pretty short."

"That I can't tell you, you'll find the words. You always do," he added with a loving chuckle. "If you send him the news via an e-mail, you know that he'll call, and that's the whole point, right?"

"Right."

"You said that you were at home when you found out that you were pregnant. How did your parents take the news?"

As she recalled the scene at her parent's dinner table, she could think of no words to do them justice. "You have to know my mom and dad, nothing but nothing that I or anyone else could say or do would ever rattle them. They live in their own world, separate and apart from us regular folk. They are as Gary so eloquently stated the other night, not normal." *Sorta reminds you of Austin,* she added to herself.

"Gary, your ex-husband, right?"

"The one and the same."

"You two see each other often?" He hated to pry, but he was curious. In this day and age, it wasn't uncommon for divorced couples to stay friends, in fact it was great when it happened, but such friendships always left room for speculation.

"Well, up until this past week, only for business reasons. Remember, I do contract work for him?"

"Oh yeah, the stained glass windows. So what happened to change things this past week?"

Sedona, so wrapped up in her emotional swirl, gave no thought as to why Michael would be curious as to the 'friendliness" of her relationship with Gary. "Well, he's been such a dear, a God-send even. I mean, get this, when I told him about the baby, he came up with a business proposition that I couldn't resist, it was so perfect." After filling Michael in on Gary's proposal, Sedona softly added, "I just don't know what I would do without him. He has been so kind, so loving."

"You're right, his offer is mighty generous. What brought it on? I mean, if I remember what you have told me about him, this . . . this new and improved changed side of him is a bit out of character."

"It is, yes and no. Gary, back when we first married, was just the sweetest man. Maybe he is maturing with age."

"Umph," Michael cleared his throat without comment. "I don't know the man, but I do know that aside from when we get a helping slap upside the head from God, people don't change overnight; especially a man who's been used to the fancies of women. You just go careful."

"You sound like his cousin, now," Sedona laughed. "I'll tell you just what I told Mazey, I just want to focus on having a healthy baby, and raising her to be happy. If Gary's offer can help me do that, then all I am going to say is thank you. Which leads me to my next point, your family medical history."

As Sedona explained the doctor's request, Michael's thoughts stayed on Gary. He recognized guilt when he saw it, it was written all over the man's actions. And Sedona was vulnerable enough, thanks to his son, to mistake his generosity for love. Maybe it was offered in love, he didn't know the man, so he couldn't say if it was or not. But if he were still a gambling man, he would hazard to guess no. Sedona more than likely will find herself hurt and emotionally, in worst shape than she was in now. Once told, his son better decisively make his move before someone else claimed his sweetheart.

Upon their goodbyes, Sedona promised to e-mail Austin straightaway. As she started the letter, she wondered how one went about breaking such news.

Subject: Still Preferring the Ocean . . .

Dear Austin, How have you been? I have a bit of news that you might find interesting. I am pregnant . . .

Aught! This was akin to writing a 'Dear John' letter – even worse. Walking away from the computer and then back again, she pulled up her chair and made several more attempts. No matter how she started the letter off, the wording was clumsy. *Maybe I'm just trying too hard.* So she decided to answer the many e-mail messages that had accumulated during the time that she was gone. Finally, after every letter was either answered or trashed, she took another stab at her letter to Austin.

Subject: Still Preferring the Ocean . . .

Dear Austin– I hope that this letter finds you well. Upon my return, I received your e-mail and phone messages. Sorry for just now responding, but I changed my plans after you left me at the airport. Instead of heading back to New Orleans, I decided to go home and pay a visit to my parents. After I boarded the plane, I turned my cell phone off and forgot to turn it back on until last night. So I missed all of your messages. When I did finally hear them, I tried calling. But, needless to say, I was too late, you had already left . . . seems to be the story of our lives.

You will be gone for six months, so what is this suppose to accomplish? Hmm, consider this thought – if you can't order and categorize your life in that space of time, maybe it's set. I wish that I could say that I understand, but I don't. I mean, how can anyone not handle being told that they are loved, needed, cherished and wanted? You are probably offended by the tone of this question, but I'm sorry, there are just way too many of us who wish that someone would tell us that we are loved and cherished, and actually mean it.

You know, my mother just told me for the first time in 37 years that's she loves me. In fact, last week was the first time since grammar school that I can remember her giving me a hug. At the time, it felt so good, so very good. But looking back on it now, I know that the only reason that she could bring herself to pull me close was because I have landed myself in the same boat that ruined her life – I'm pregnant. Ironic, isn't it?

Sedona.

And with that, she addressed and sent it. No proof reading, no retraction. She was angry and she was mad and she didn't care. She was tired of caring for everyone else's feelings over her own. She was tired of being the 'little fool', the understanding one, the one who always managed to take the 'high road' and do what was right. Just so tired of smiling when all she wanted to do was cry.

All that she had been doing for the past several weeks was crying. Even though her eyes constantly watered, there were no tears left to spill. Besides, even if they were, what good would they bring? Simply because in terms of Austin, there wasn't much else left for her do, Sedona grabbed up her sketch pad and worked until it was time to change for dinner. When she was done, she looked down at the pad and sat back in her chair. There was no way to describe what she felt, the sketch evoked no new emotion and didn't register in her mind as being either good or bad, for it was simply an extension of what she was feeling in her heart. All of the unhappiness, frustration, and heaviness had seeped out of her soul, into her pastels and onto the paper. She had no control over the hanging outcomes; they were left up to someone far wiser than she.

Ready?

As she picked up her purse, Gary made a study of her face.

Despite her brave front, it was obvious that she was tired; he knew her way too well not to see it. Just thinking about the needless changes that Austin was putting her through, made him angry. Not patting himself on the back for having treated her any better, he had little empathy for the man. With the benefit of twenty/twenty vision, he was aware of his mistakes and in this moment and time, would give anything in the world to go back and change things, at the very least, to make amends.

"So, what do you have a taste for; or is that a question I should ask the baby?" Gary smiled.

Sedona, truly not craving anything in particular, shrugged.

"Hmmm . . . let's see." Without quite knowing why, he immediately thought of 'Poppies', a quaint French bistro that he and Sedona used to frequent while married.

"I haven't thought about that place in ages," Sedona voice brightened. "Do you think that it's still opened?"

"Well, there's one way to fine out." Picking up the receiver to the phone, he quickly dialed directory assistance and then the phone number given. "Yup, they're still there."

"Okay," Sedona gently smiled as she allowed the suggestion to settle. "It'll be fun, almost like old times."

As Gary handed his keys to the valet, Sedona took in the restaurant's unpretentious and slightly worn front, everything still looked the same. With very little effort, she was transported back in time to when she and Gary took special delight in discovering colorful reminders of France to remind them of their studies in Europe.

The meal, Salmon Mousse with Capers, followed by Pork Filet Mignon and Gratin Dauphinois was fabulous. And before she knew it, much of Sedona's usual warmth and humor had returned. The meal and conversation harkened her back to when she first found out that she was pregnant with Lily. During those early months of her pregnancy, she and Gary would sit and talk about the baby and their future together. If she allowed, she could almost convince herself that Austin and all of the craziness of Gary's infidelities and ensuing divorce was just a dream, a very bad dream. Without realizing it, and despite knowing better, she found herself doing just that.

She listened as Gary talked about his projects and future plans for his firm. She offered her opinions and shared ideas that he seemed to accept. They even talked about the baby, her nursery, and all of the wonderful things that she should experience. Dinner was enjoyed and the check presented much too soon, so they decided to drive over to another old favorite haunt, Harry's Ice Cream. After the cold treat, they took a stroll along Riverfront Park. As they walked, they talked a bit more before allowing the conversation to lapse into a comfortable quiet. In the car, each lost in thought, they silently mulled over the evening and appreciated the friendship of the other.

"Well, it looks like we're home," Gary glanced up at the house and remembered when it really was his home. "If you don't mind, I'll walk you in."

"No, I don't mind at all. In fact if you'd like, I'll make us a pot of tea." She knew that Gary could care less about a cup of tea, but used it as a good excuse not to allow the evening to end

Gary, just as Sedona, was caught up in the warm coziness of the mood, and accepted the offer. They both had chosen to forget the drama that evaded their relationship during their "other life". It was so much easier to remember the warm and cozy, rather than the lying and cheating.

In the kitchen, watching Sedona fill the kettle with water, Gary wanted nothing more in the world than to take her into his arms. Not quite sure as to how she would respond, he patiently bided his time.

"Say, Sedona, after all of that walking, you have got to be tired. Why don't you go and prop your feet up while I put on the tea? Better yet, go on up and change for bed, as soon as the chamomile is ready, I'll bring it along, and tuck you in."

"Tuck me in?" Sedona giggled at the thought. "I don't remember the last time anyone tucked me in."

"No?" Gary winked.

"Un-uh."

'Well, I tell you what. You go on and get in bed, and I might even treat you to a good night story." Gary's tone had lowered to a teasing drawl, that Sedona, despite common sense, found intriguing.

As she waited in bed for Gary, Sedona reflected on the evening. They really enjoyed one another; the night was perfect. She couldn't have written it any better. Gary was attentive, concerned, loving even. The perfect date – just what she needed. Settling back against the pillows, she looked across the room, and her eyes fell upon her computer, and instantly she felt her spirits falter and then suddenly fall. Just whom was she kidding? The evening was due for a major rewrite. Austin was the one that she loved, and his was the baby that she was carrying. Not Gary. Why couldn't it be Austin downstairs preparing her a cup of tea? His arms were the ones that she wanted to pull her close.

Upon knocking, Gary entered the room, and placed her cup of tea on the nightstand alongside her bed. "Ready for your bedtime . .
"

As he took in her face, the question froze in mid air. "Sedona, Sedona honey, what's wrong?"

Embarrassed, Sedona vainly brushed aside her tears. "Just hold me," she whispered.

Obliging, Gary kicked off his shoes, and sat alongside her as he pulled her into his arms. Not needing to ask the source of her tears, he held her and talked about the first thing that entered his head, a documentary on Prairie School architecture that he had recently caught on cable. Before he knew it, they were both fast asleep.

CHAPTER THIRTEEN

"Good morning beautiful," Gary kissed her forehead as she roused.

"Morning . . . ," she murmured as she pulled herself back against the pillows with her elbows. "What time is it? It feels like I just went to sleep."

"Where's my morning glory? You used to beat the sun up?"

"That was many, many, many moons ago," she smiled as she rubbed his arm. "You know, despite the tears, I really enjoyed last night. Dinner could not have been better, the walk along Riverfront Park, it reminded me so much of when we were back in France. Even . . . well, just thank you," she murmured as she wrapped herself in his gaze.

Gary, totally smitten, lowered his head towards hers and kissed her gently on the lips.

Although unexpected, she sensed the kiss before their lips actually touched. Allowing her body to respond, she moaned as his tongue found hers. It was impossible to deny that he felt good. Her nipples had hardened and the base of her stomach lifted as he leaned in towards her. Gary could feel the betrayal of her body through the thin silky fabric of her nightgown. Careful not to say or do anything that would stir her resolve, he focused his desire on the folds of their tongues. It was only when he couldn't bear the hard pricked nipples against his chest, did he dare move to caress them. He knew that they would be his "open sesame."

Hmmm . . . his hands felt so good on her breasts. *God, this is so crazy,* her brain screamed. With each grazing brush, she lifted her lower back in order to meet his hard warmth. *He would have to remember how to turn her on.* As her legs involuntarily opened to invite him in, she heard herself moan, "Austin, stop . . ." It was out before she realized. Just as she had anticipated the kiss, she anticipated the stillness that followed. Instead, she heard his chuckle.

"Irony is a bitch. I guess that I had that one coming."

"You did!"

"It's cool, it's all good. Are you hungry? I tell you what," he proposed, already out of the door, "while you're getting dressed, I'll rustle us up some breakfast." And with that, he was gone.

On the way to the bathroom, the framed photo of Austin that sat on the dresser-top caught her eye. "What are you laughing it?" she sneered as she grabbed it up and threw the photograph against the wall.

"How's your appetite?" Gary inquired as she sat down at kitchen counter.

"Gary, listen, we have got to talk. Upstairs, a little while ago . . ."

"Like I said, I'm cool. There is no need to explain. It happens to the best of us, trust me I know."

"What?"

"You know, the name thing." Gary chuckled.

Sedona struck by the humorous truth that laid in his comment, laughed as well. "I guess you do know at that. You have been guilty of the very same crime, how could I have forgotten."

Back on leveled playing field, Sedona smiled as he placed before her a plate of scrambled eggs, bacon and toast. Fixated on his hands, she watched as he prepared his plate. He still put jam on his toast before the butter, and sprinkled way too much salt on his eggs. His habits were the same. He was still Gary – the man who had put her through hell and back. But somehow, in that time and space, he wasn't so bad.

"Anything wrong?"

"No, it's just that I . . ." There was no way for her to explain what she was feeling, at least in a way that made sense. "It's just that I was thinking that I could get used to this."

"Why shouldn't you get used to being looked after and loved? Don't you deserve it?" He knew that the questions weren't fair ones. They were impossible for her to answer, considering her predicament. He knew it, but he didn't care because he wanted to be the one that she turned to, sought comfort from, to make things right. Just to know that he fulfilled that role was like redemption. After all, he was the reason why they had lost Lilie. It was all of the stress that he had put her through while she was carrying their baby. No one had to tell him, he could see it written in everyone's faces. Even his own eyes condemned him every morning when he stood before the mirror to shave, and at night when he had to face his reflection when readying for bed. How he had prayed to be able to put things right.

"Gary . . ." Before she could complete her thought, she felt a wave of nausea make its way from the pit of her stomach, slowly up her chest. "God, I'm going to be sick!" And with that, she took off for the bathroom.

"It's the baby telling you that she can't stand my cooking! Already she's a critic," Gary teased as Sedona retreated down the hall.

251

Ring! Ring! Ring!

"I'll get it," he yelled. "Hello."

"Hello?" After a moment, the caller continued. "I think that I may have dialed the wrong number, I'm trying to reach Sedona Tinney."

Gary, recognizing the voice to be Austin's chuckled, "Naw, man, you have the number right. So how's the sea been treating you? Say, I'm sorry to hear about what happened to your sister and all . . . an unfortunate break."

"Is Sedona in?" Austin was in no mood for small talk or pleasantries. He had just read his e-mail; Sedona was the only voice that he wanted to hear.

"She's in, but it seems that the baby doesn't like my cooking."

"Your cooking?" It was obvious from Austin's tone that he didn't quite know what to make of Gary's statement.

"Yeah, I was the first one up, so I decided to make breakfast. Besides, if it were left up to Sedona, she would just make do with dry toast and a bit of juice. Even though the nausea is kicking her butt, I'm telling her that she has got to eat. Check this out; the woman has morning sickness, afternoon sickness, *and* evening sickness. Last night was okay though, she was able to keep dinner down."

"Last night?"

Gary, without missing a beat replied, "I told her that I am here for her, 24/7. I'm not leaving her high and dry, nope not me."

"You're there for her, I see." After a rather lengthy pause, Austin continued, "Just tell her that I called." And with that, he hung up.

"Who was that?" Sedona asked, as she rounded the corner.

"Just, Austin. I told him that you were dealing with a bit of morning sickness."

"Just Austin? Did he a leave message?" Her disappointment

apparent, not only in the tone of her voice, but in the way that she ran her hand over the receiver. "Is he going to call back? I don't have a number."

"No, no message." The sorrowful look on Sedona's face now made him wish that he had kept Austin on the line. "Listen, I'm sure that he'll call back. He seemed concerned. The man wanted to talk to you."

"You're right, I don't know what is wrong with me. If he calls, he calls. How much is a phone call is going to change things anyway? I'll still be here, and he'll still be a million miles away. Besides, if he had anything new to add to what he has already made clear, he would have stayed on the line a little longer. I'm tired, I'm through!"

Gary, feeling guiltier by the minute, was desperate to change the subject. "Say, last night, before you fell asleep on me, you mentioned that you drew up some ideas for the church window. While I'm stacking the dishwasher, why don't you go get the sketches?"

As soon as she had left the room, he let out a slow silent whistle. He was heading into some pretty deep waters, was he ready for the swim? The thing about it, Sedona wasn't waving the red flag begging to be rescued. She had long since turned her back on that notion. As far as she was concerned, Austin, her rescuer of preference, wasn't making the swim. He had proven that he had solid feet of clay that sunk like a rock. As Gary placed the last glass onto the rack, he raised a brow as he thought of the phone conversation. No, it really wasn't necessary for him to have yanked the seaman's line; Austin had already snagged himself up just fine. But who could fault him for wanting to even up the odds. If he was going to make the swim, he had to be sure that the waters were clear and still.

"Okay, be honest and tell me what you think."

So lost in his thoughts, Gary hadn't heard Sedona return, "Honest

. . . okay, let's see."

As Sedona laid out the sketches, one for each of the five panels of glass that she planned on designing, she explained her intent. "The theme is, 'Despite troubles, God brings hope'. In all five panels, I have depicted God as a bird, brilliant and ubiquitous."

Gary, even without Sedona's explanation, understood the message of the first panel. The brilliant bird was wrapped in a blaze of blinding light. It's beam dove in and out of the dark tides of an ocean that rolled below. The bird's unrelenting ray of light searched and found souls, both lost and in hiding.

"In this second panel, I have the bird winging away from the ocean, flying across the sky towards a new sun."

"I like how you have its halo shining brighter than the rising sun. The effect is powerful," commented Gary, quite taken by the emotion of the color.

"Well, I wanted to convey the thought that hope comes with the start of each new day."

"You did that, I mean, the message is unmistakable. Now in this third panel, you have the bird flying across a sun that is high in the sky. I gather that you're depicting the noon-day."

"Um-hum, it is," she nodded. "Its presence is letting the people who are tending the fields below know that God is always close by. He is a constant and unchanging."

"Wow, the story you paint with pictures."

"I can't take any of the credit. The ideas just come, I can't explain it . . . you know how it is," Sedona smiled as she met Gary's eyes. The connection was so tangible; in terms of understanding the creative process, they were kindred spirits. "In this fourth panel, you'll notice that the sky is washed in the colors of the evening. Even though twilight means a setting sun and rest . . ."

"There is still work to be done," supplied Gary. "I guessed that from the way that you have the tools propped up against the door. They aren't put away, very clever."

"There's always more work to be done, that's life; but you know, it's all right. That's what I want the panels to suggest – that it is all right. I mean, look at the bird in this last panel; with its halo shining bright, it's singing with the nightingales. Their song is one of joy, and full of the promise that with the coming morning there will be hope that is renewing."

"Sedona, I'm just at a loss for words. I don't know what to say." Gary brought the rendering closer to his face as he read the passage intertwined in an arbor of fig trees and vines ripe with grapes, ". . . the time of the singing of birds is come, Solomon 2:12." Not expecting the sudden rush of emotion that filled his heart, Gary sat the panel down and pulled the woman close. "You are a true gift. One that I never want to be foolish enough to overlook again."

Not making a move to pull away, Sedona allowed herself to enjoy his affection. After all, it felt good to be appreciated and wanted. She could tell by the strength of his embrace that his emotions were very close to the surface. "Sedona, I love you."

Before she could respond, he had her hips pulled toward his and his tongue searching for hers. Just as earlier, she found that she wanted his touch, the warmth of his body against hers. It lit her mind in that it made her feel desirable, sexy and beautiful, all the traits that Austin found so easy to ignore. It was all about vanity, she knew it; but it was also about feeling that she was acceptable to someone, wanted by someone and desired. Would Gary cherish her as he had suggested earlier? She hadn't a clue. Would he pledge unflagging love? Maybe, but she knew that she couldn't count on it for a lifetime.

As Gary ran his hands across her butt, and up her spine, he took his time as he slipped under her t-shirt. Her skin was warm, and he could feel the vibration of her heart as he fanned his fingers along her breastbone. Not satisfied until he had found the center of the soft hollow between her breasts, he lingered. He had always loved to hear her moan when he visited this spot, a long ago favorite of his. It was obvious from her ragged breathing that she was desperately clinging to control. Gary knew what Sedona was waiting for and he obliged; he traveled his thumbs out wider and brushed his fingertips across her nipples. First he caressed them, ever so gently; and then he gave each one a pleasant tweak. Not too hard, but with just enough pressure to make her mew like a kitten. This time, when she whispered a name, he wanted it to be his.

"Gary . . . Gary, stop!"

With his mind bent on having his way, he grabbed her by the waist and lifted her onto the counter. "Gary," she heard her voice protest, which even to her own ears, was not convincing enough. The tile felt cool along the back of her thighs. It could have been years before, when they used to make love wherever and whenever the mood hit them. Spreading her legs apart with his torso, he scooted her to the edge and ground in deep.

"Hmm . . . baby, you want me, I can tell. Talk to me, tell me what you want me to do to you."

"Gary, listen . . . listen, you have got to stop. I want you to stop . . . right now!" This time there was firmness in her voice. True, there was a part of her that wanted to urge him on with a wicked plea to make love to her, to enjoy her thoroughly and completely. But she knew that the urge, the desire was purely physical. All that she would be using Gary for was to ease her desire for Austin, at least for a little while. But this wasn't the way.

"Gary, I want you to . . ."

"Ring! Ring! Ring!"

"Ignore it!" he hissed. "It's just you and me, baby."

"Ring! Ring! Ring"

"Gary, I can't. It might be Austin"

"Damn . . . What is it about that man?" Gary banged his hand against the tile in exasperation.

"Ring . . ."

"Hello . . . Austin?" There was no mistaking the lift in her voice. "I'm fine, and you?"

"As well as can be expected considering the news that I've just read." Monotone and flat was his voice, no hint of enthusiasm or joy. "So, you're pregnant? When did you find this out?"

"When I was back home. I mentioned in my e-mail that I flew up to see my parents. I . . ."

"How far along are you?" he cut her off, seemingly not interested in the details.

Not knowing what she should have expected, Sedona became defensive. Certainly he was going to muster up more than a series of detached questions. "A little over a month, don't worry, the baby is yours. If you need proof . . ."

"Sedona, don't talk crazy. Even though that ex of yours would like for me to think otherwise, I'm sure that . . ."

"What that ex of mine would like for you think?" It was Sedona's turn to interrupt; she couldn't believe the man's nerve. "Where do you get off insinuating anything about Gary? He's been nothing but nice. There is no need to put him down for being concerned, especially when you've chosen to be elsewhere."

"Listen, Sedona, you know that you are not being fair. When I took this assignment, I had no idea that you were pregnant."

"My being pregnant should not have made a bit of difference, and you know *that*," she stressed the last word with more than just a little attitude. "If Gary is here for me, it is because he wants to be, and the emphasis is on the word – want. There was no begging, no twisting of the arm, and no tears shed in order to stir guilt. And guess what, he didn't even have to go walking along the beach to figure out that I needed someone."

"Truly the man of the hour, my God, your tune sure has changed. I thought better of you Sedona, I thought that you had more backbone, a little bit more strength than to run to the first man who promised you a . . . forget it, just forget it."

"No, go ahead and say it. Promise me what, Austin? Reciprocation of emotion, some level of intimacy?"

"That's not what I was going to say."

"I guess you wouldn't. You don't know the definitions of those terms. How could I forget, I am dealing with a . . . a . . ."

"Try Vulcan," Gary laughed aloud, struck by the humor of his comparison of Austin to the unemotional and detached Star Trek character.

"I want a relationship that I can count on getting as good as I give, because I know what I offer is worth receiving. You want a relationship that you get to control the balance of the scale. You want the attention, the love, the affection when you want it, and you don't want to be bothered with it any other time. Well, baby or not, those terms are not going to work."

"Where do you get off telling me how I should respond to your affection? That's your problem, Sedona. You think that just because you would respond in a certain way, that I should as well. It doesn't work that way. Sometimes, I just don't feel like being bothered, I just don't feel like talking. Sometimes it is just that simple. Just because you need to go on like a magpie every time a disappointment or event goes on in your life, doesn't mean that I need to. There are times when all I want to do is just think, to mull things over and get them figured out."

"A magpie?" That was all that she heard, the insult. Sedona didn't hear any of the read 'in-between-the-line' messages that Austin was offering. So focused was she on her feelings, that she missed the opportunity to gain insight into how his mind worked. "So the ostrich sees me as a magpie? My question is, how are you able to see anything? If you're not walking in the sand, then your head is buried in it."

"Okay, fine . . . just fine, Sedona. I didn't call to pick an argument. Why don't we try this another time?" and with that he hung up.

Gary, who had thoroughly enjoyed his front row seat, clapped as Sedona slammed down the receiver. "Wow! You're good, real good. Your tongue just cuts to the quick. Crack! Snap! Pop!" Gary imitated the sound of a whip. "It's worst than twenty lashings. After that whuppin', I know that the brother is in need of some serious first aid. How does your brain work that fast?"

Far from flattered, Sedona became remorseful, "I didn't sound that bad, did I?"

"All that I know is that my baby has got skill. Listen," Gary took hold of her hand as he headed towards the front door, "I have meetings this morning and afternoon, but my evening schedule is cleared, just for you. What do you have going?"

Not forgetting what had just transpired in the kitchen, Sedona frowned, "Why? You're planning round three of 'Let's Seduce Easy Needy Sedona'?

Gary, seemingly not hearing, pinched her nose. "Why don't I meet you over at Mazey's around 8:00; she's working late. Maybe the three of us can go over to Copeland's for desert after she closes.

"Whatever."

Gary, choosing to miss the fact that she was just as irritated with him as with Austin, attempted to restore her good mood. "Say, don't beat yourself up over the phone call; Austin's a big boy, and he had it coming. Okay? If you need anything, I'll have my cell on, see you tonight."

Mazey didn't know what to make of this latest chapter. The Austin and Sedona romance had turned into a saga of complicated proportion. "I've never met two people who went out of their way to make being in love so hard."

"I'm not making anything hard," Sedona straightened a display of bookmarks. "If anything, I'm trying to keep life simple. After Gary gave me a hard time about the way I spoke to Austin over the phone, I had made up my mind to send an e-mail apologizing for my tone. But before I could, Austin sends me this nasty message insinuating once again, that the baby is Gary's." In a lowered pitch, Sedona mimicked Austin's clipped tone, "*You're right, maybe my head has been buried in the sand!* Please, if he had hung around for more than a half a minute, he would be the one sharing in this pregnancy. It was his choice to go away, so why drag Gary into it?"

"Maybe he sees that Gary has placed himself in the middle of someone else's mess," Mazey reasoned.

"I am going to tell you, like I wrote to Austin, Gary is only thinking about the baby. He wants this baby as much me. Neither one of us is going to allow anyone or anything to cheat us out of having this baby, not this time."

All at once, things made sense to Mazey – Gary's renewed interest in Sedona, his concern for the baby and Sedona's attachment to her ex. They both were trying to make up for the loss of Lilie. "This baby isn't Gary's, you can't make up for Lilie." Mazey had to say it; she couldn't keep quiet on this one.

"Who said anything about making up for Lilie?"

"You just said that neither one of us is going to allow anyone or anything to cheat us out of having this baby, not this time. Cheat *us*? Come on Sedona, what does that sound like to you?"

Sedona couldn't ignore her friend's question, "I . . . I," she struggled to explain her feelings, ". . . I'm not trying to bring back Lilie, not even subconsciously. If you ask me if I fear losing this baby, or if I'm on constant pins and needles wondering if things are going to turn out okay, then I would have to answer yes. Am I so scared at the thought of going through this alone, that I am guilty of clinging to Gary?" Sedona, with all of the weight of her worries, sat heavily in a nearby chair. "Mazey, all that I can tell you is that he is keeping me from losing my mind. With Austin taking off as he has, these last few weeks would have just been simply unbearable. Gary keeps me feeling up and positive, he reminds me that there is light at the end of tunnel. He has a way about him that makes everything seem doable."

"That's because everything is doable, but you've have just got to give Austin half a chance."

"I've given Austin more than his fair share of chances, I've smiled while he has ignored me, walked over me, leaned on me, vented, and exorcised his demons. How much is enough? I have my self-respect, some days that's all I have, so if you are wanting me to beg him to love me or to plead with him to accept the baby, I can't – I'm not."

"No one is asking you to beg or plead. I'm just suggesting that perhaps you should cool things down a bit with Gary . . . to keep things in proper perspective."

"How do you keep a spontaneous kiss from someone who has told you, has shown you that he loves you in perspective . . ." before Mazey could respond, Sedona continued, "especially when the man that you want to love you with all of his heart, can't even express it? God Mazey, do you know how good it feels to finally be held after you've spent weeks longing for someone to pull you close?"

"Sedona," even though Mazey empathized with her friend, she was determined to make her point, "believe it or not, I can relate, I really can. But don't you see, you're just feeling vulnerable right now. After all, you're pregnant, Austin is thousands of miles away, and . . ."

"I know, I know, I know." She was tired, so tired of having to explain, to justify why she was no longer able to bury her feelings and pretend that emotionally everything was alright. All through her childhood she had done it, as well as through most of her adult life. She couldn't much blame Mazey for expecting more of the same; after all, she had handled the loss of a child and divorce without anyone's assistance, why should things now be any different?

"I know that you want to feel loved and cherished, and all of that other good stuff. But, Gary is Gary; he hasn't changed. Sure, he loves you, but hasn't he always? He holds you because you feel good in his arms. And he wants to be a part of you having this baby because he feels that he owes it to you. But, does his love and actions come from that place in his heart that it needs to come from in order for him to be true? I won't deny that you need someone, especially now, but Gary isn't the one."

At the end of her rope, Sedona retorted, "Gary isn't the one, Austin doesn't want me; so what do you propose Mazey? Suck it up, stuff it down, go it alone? Been there, done that, and am sick and tired of it."

Mazey, despite empathizing with her friend, remained determined. "I want you to be careful, I don't want to see you get hurt by settling for Gary. Think about it, Austin has just lost his sister, that in it self is devastating, not to mention that he was the one who found her dead body washed up on the beach. Then to top it all off, his *born again* dad is back on the scene after God only knows how many years. Imagine what that must be doing to his equilibrium. It's impossible for me to understand why all of a sudden, you are now having such a hard time giving the man a break. If you ask me, you're being just a little self-centered."

"Self-centered?" That was the last thing that Sedona wanted to hear. "Let me see if I'm getting this right, you're telling me that Austin's feelings and his emotional 'trauma'/garbage/baggage is more stressful than my finding out that I'm pregnant by a man who unprompted, has never told me that he loves me, who prefers solitude to my company, and in order to find peace of mind, he finds it necessary to go half way around the world. In all of this, I am living on my own and by myself; no family, no nothing. I can't even claim the support of a best friend."

Sedona couldn't have hurt Mazey's feelings more than if she had tried. If she was aware of the sting of her words, Sedona did not let on. Instead, she turned her attention to cleaning up the counter area where Mazey served her customers tea.

"Lock the door after the last customer, would you? I'll be in the store room if you need anything," Mazey snapped. As usual, she had managed to say way too much. Usually, she didn't have to worry about offending Sedona with her frank style of speaking. They were close enough friends to know the intentions of the other, but not this time around. Not only had she angered Sedona, but she managed to get her feelings hurt in the process – which was rare.

It's not personal, it's not personal, Mazey reminded herself as she readied at shipment of books to be set out in the morning. After cutting open several boxes, she felt better. If only she could cut into Austin's brain and make him see what he was setting himself up to lose. Just as she was ready to slice into another box, she got an idea. Why couldn't she cut into Austin's brain? All that she had to do was to contact him and let him know what was really going on between Sedona and Gary. Sedona sure as hell wasn't going to do it. With a plan turning itself over in her mind, she turned off the storeroom light and headed towards the voices coming from the front of the store.

"Gary, how long have you been here?" She kissed her cousin as she grabbed up her handbag.

"Oh, about five minutes or so. Are you coming with us for dessert?"

"I don't know, I wasn't invited," smiled Mazey as she looked towards Sedona.

"Didn't I mention it?" Sedona knew that she hadn't extended an invitation. When she first arrived at the shop, she had every intentions of inviting her friend along, but as their conversation progressed and became more heated, all desire left. But her mood had lifted, and she wanted them to work their way back to friendlier terms.

"Nope, not a word."

"I'm sorry, Gary thought that it might be fun if we stopped by Copeland's on the way home. I really want you to come. So what do you say?" With a smile that she hoped would convince Mazey that her invitation was sincere, Sedona added, "maybe we can share a slice of Turtle Pie."

Upon the mentioning of the dessert, Mazey knew that Sedona was extending an olive branch. "I don't see why not, give me a minute to call Miles."

Located several blocks from Mazey's shop, in the area where Canal

Street meets the river, the eatery's renowned soul food, and down-to-earth ambience attracted tourists, conventioneers, and locals alike. No matter what time of the day or night, they kept the place jumping. Gary, spotting an empty corner, beckoned to the approaching hostess that he was going to grab the table. "I'm here so often with clients, this place feels like home."

"Well, here comes one of your sisters now," teased Mazey as an attractive waitress beamed her way over to their table.

"Gary! Back so soon? I could have sworn that you were just in here."

Sedona couldn't help but notice how the waitress leaned in towards her ex as she handed each of them a menu. Mazey and Sedona ordered a slice of Turtle Pie to share, while Gary took his time to peruse the selection of desserts.

"And 'Gar', what would you like?" the waitress sugared her tone as she called him by her own pet name.

"Now that's a dangerous question," Gary teased as he looked up at the waitress.

"Well, you know everything is good." Innocent words, out of anyone else's mouth, but from the way the sexy waitress smiled and took a hold of the man's gaze, it was obvious that much more lay behind the remark.

"No doubt," flirted Gary, "no doubt. Just serve me up my usual, and I'll be happy."

"I know that's right." With a soft chuckle, the waitress collected the menus. "How do you girls stand him?"

"Up against a wall, readied to be whipped," smirked Mazey.

Gary, unfazed by the remark, laughed out loud, "Gloria, this is my always witty cousin Mazey and my ex-wife, but very dear friend, Sedona – she's my sweetheart."

If Sedona had any questions regarding Gary and the waitress, she still had them. What she was witnessing was Gary's 'M. O.' – modus operandi. He had a knack for making everyone feel loved and special, so much so, it was impossible to tell whom he was messing around with and whom he wasn't.

After Gloria left with their order, Mazey quickly glanced over at Sedona before raising a brow in her cousin's direction, "She's cute; have you two done the do?"

"Mazey, Mazey, Mazey, you definitely have sex on the mind, girl. What's going on, Miles isn't taking care of his honey?"

"His honey is being taken care of just fine, thank you. Like you, he's been busy as a bee. In fact, Sedona tells me that . . ."

Certain of the path that Mazey was attempting to guide the conversation, Sedona cut in, "that you've been working on a church over in Thibodeaux. Let me tell you about the windows . . ."

By the end of the evening, Sedona was exhausted, both mentally and physically. If she wasn't refereeing the sparring going on between Mazey and Gary or waylaying Mazey's efforts to talk about Gary's interest in the baby, she was finding herself increasingly conscious of Gary flirtatious behavior. On the drive home, Mazey's comments regarding Gary kept coming to mind. Nothing about him had changed too much. She definitely owed her friend an apology. Just as Austin had absconded with her heart, if allowed, Gary could erode her self-esteem and confidence, and send her right back to the place where she had left years ago. Hmm . . . men, what were they good for? Absolutely nothing!

CHAPTER FOURTEEN

A brand new day. Her night's sleep had been peaceful and dream-free. Sedona had been so tired when her head hit the pillow that checking her e-mail for a message from Austin barely crossed her mind. When it had, she found it impossible to rustle herself out of bed to turn on the computer.

Not giving in to her first inclination to put off her shower until after she had checked her e-mail, Sedona forced Austin out of her mind. He was not going to control her – not her moods, not her thoughts, nor her actions. She was the one in charge.

Ring! Ring! Ring!

"Good morning, beautiful. Any dreams of me?"

"Gary," she chuckled. "No, I didn't have any dreams of you, at least none that I care to remember. What's up?"

"Nothing, it's 6:00 and I figured that if you weren't already up and dressed working on that window project, you would be heading for the shower."

"Oh, you think that you know me so well."

"Was I wrong?" It was obvious from the way that he posed the question that he was certain of his answer.

"No," laughed Sedona. "You were right. I can't wait to get start-ed."

"Would you mind if I fax you a couple of resumes that have come across my desk? You know, you really need to get going on hiring an assistant. I can tell you right now, you are going to have a challenge in finding someone who even comes close to your level of talent, not to mention skill. But who knows, one of these may work out for you."

"Go ahead and fax them over. So much has been going on, I haven't even thought about qualifications, hours, let alone salary."

"Well, when you're ready, you can use one of the offices over here for interviews. Umm . . . Austin hasn't called or anything has he?" Gary didn't quite know what possessed him to ask the question.

"As far as I know, he hasn't. Why? Are you worried about him?" Sedona teased.

"Why would I be worried about him? I just don't want him harassing you, that's all. Being under unnecessary stress won't do either you or the baby any good." Gary, tuning into his emotions as he spoke them continued, "Instead of faxing you the resumes, why don't I meet you for an early lunch, let's say around 11:00?"

"Gary, you are going to have me weighing more than a ton. That's all we've been doing is eating. I know that I'm eating for two, but I can't afford to eat out everyday. No one is going to want me after I have this baby."

"I don't think that is going to be a problem, do you Sedona?" His tone was much more serious than even he had intended, but surely, she knew how he felt about her.

"Gary, thanks for the offer, but not today. I really do want to get started on that project. Plus, I still need to finish up the window for the first project." She didn't want to hurt his feelings, but after her conversation with Mazey, she didn't want to give him any ideas, at least not until she was certain in her own mind as to what she wanted.

It was best not to press, he reasoned, so he lifted the mood by changing the subject. "Tomorrow, I'm meeting John Baronne and his wife at their home up in St. Francisville. They've hired me to design a resort out in the Caribbean. I thought that you might want to come along, there could be some work in it for you."

The opportunity was obvious, as was Gary. But, I'm a big girl, Sedona reasoned. I just won't let the conversation go beyond business. After making the vow, Sedona asked, "Sure, what time are you leaving?"

"Let's see, the appointment is at 1:30 . . . Ginny is making us a late lunch . . . let's say that we pull out of your place around 12:00."

"Noon it is, maybe on the ride over, you can tell me something about you all's plans thus far." After several more minutes of light chitchat, they said their goodbyes. "Gary," Sedona stopped him before hanging up, "thank you." Despite all of his faults, he definitely was proving to be a friend.

In the shower she focused on her day and laid out an agenda. Besides the studio work, there were errands to run that included a visit to one of her suppliers. As she pulled on a pair of jeans and a t-shirt, she reached over and switched on the computer. Try as she might, it would be pointless to go through the day pretending that Austin wasn't on her mind. Mixed in with all of the junk mail messages advertising quick weight loss sites and work at home schemes, was a letter from Austin.

Subject: Working with lead

Sedona,

I don't know what to say, I really should learn not to write while I'm angry. I think that after we've had a chance to talk, we'll be able to get this situation resolved. Expect a call from me some time today. I wish that I could tell you when, but at this point I am at the mercy of the LAN.

LOL . . . Austin

P. S. If you haven't already, I strongly recommend that you stop work-

ing with and around lead while pregnant – copper for that matter. The fumes are highly toxic and will cause harm to the baby.

Sedona, determined to draw every nuance of emotion and sentiment from out his message, read and reread the few short lines. All that she knew for certain was that he was sorry for losing his temper, he was going to call, and that there was concern over her soldering her stained glass pieces. Everything else was supposition on her part. She would like to think that his, "we will be able to get this situation resolved," was the suggestion that perhaps there would be a happy-ending to her 'situation'. But, she knew nothing for sure.

God, I can't live my life like this, Sedona mentally screamed, as she pushed back from the computer. She could stay rooted near the phone and computer, or she could get on with life. Those were her choices, plain and simple. After all, life before Austin had been full and enjoyable and there were no reason why it couldn't return to some sense of normality. With enhanced resolve, she ate a quick breakfast and headed towards her studio.

It had been weeks since she had spent any meaningful length of time in the space that had come to mean the most to her. The supplies and the glass project that sat forlorn waiting for her attention were her trusted friends. They offered her a way back into her much needed routine.

Before she could begin work, she had to first re-acquaint herself with her project – play catch-up if you will. To establish the mood, she put on the music of her Muse and lit an incense cone of his favorite scent – sandalwood. She learned a long time ago to go with his flow – whatever he wanted to hear, is what she played. Experience had taught her that in order to create, she had to not only invite him in, but also make him feel comfortable. This morning he whispered in her ear, "Fill the room with the seductive strands of 'Aria'. So she did, and immediately lost herself in its entrancing vibe. "Pace, pace, mio Dio!" filled the room. The Italian translated into English meant "Peace, peace, my God!" Verdi's *La Forza Del Destino* fused magically with the jazz arrangement. So swept by the music, the irony that Austin had first introduced her to the CD did not weigh her spirits. Instead, she ran her hands along the glass pane and in her head, and sat alongside her Muse.

Without further conscious thought, she unfurled the full sized drawing of the window. Always in love with Marc Chagall's stained glass work, Sedona tended towards the same rich jeweled colors. Unlike Chagall, who had a cadre of French glassmakers at his disposal, Sedona, in order to achieve the same effect, had to utilize a different technique. She cut all of her glass in clear and sifted colored powered glass mixed with a binder onto the panes. The panes were then fired in her kiln. This method of fusing, gave the same dense coloring found in the master's work.

After placing the clear glass over the cutline of her drawing, with confidence she picked up her oil cutter and placed it perpendicular to the surface. As the wheel scored the glass, Sedona listened. The slight scratching sound confirmed that she was applying just the right amount of downward pressure. Then with care, she gently squeezed the handles of the cut running pliers and broke the glass along the cutlines.

The monotony of the activity was perfect for her frame of mind. Ordinarily, she found this part of a project to be the most tedious. The real creativity and challenge came from mixing and fusing the glass to just the right density of color. Sometimes she would have to fire the glass three or four times. This morning though, Sedona relished the groove of focusing while allowing the music to heightened her creativity. With every turn of the wheel and musical overture of love and seduction her mind elevated to a plane occupied by only the sensuous Muse and her subconscious. There were no trip wires to blast her back to reality, impediments to cause her to stumble, raise doubts and ask why, or tow lines to keep her from drifting a field. She took on the aura of her Muse – a perfect balance of sensuality and strength. In that place and time, everything was not only plausible, but also possible. Sedona knew where she was going. She had a plan, a conveyor and a brightly burning star already picked out. Austin, Gary, and all of the dilemmas that they represented were of no consequence.

The morning had been productive and quickly passed. Despite the fact that she had worked nonstop, there was still much to be done. Gary was correct in reminding her that she really needed to hire an assistant. If she was to finish the current project, as well as the panes for the church over in Lafourch Parrish by deadline, not to mention take on other new projects, she had better step up production. If she managed to cut all of the glass by the week's end, she still had to fuse, foil and solder the panes, none of which, because of her pregnancy, she alone could do. There was no way around it, she had to hire an assistant, and soon.

Even though a mask would filter out the metals contained in the powdered glass, she didn't want to take any chances with the baby's health. So, she cut until she felt the strain of it across her shoulders and back. Rising to stretch, she decided to give her muscles a break and work on hiring an assistant.

Gary, true to his word, had faxed over several resumes. Out of a half a dozen, only one looked promising; a personal friend of his, a Ms. Brenda Berry. According to her resume and Gary's glowing recommendation, she possessed substantial experience in stained glass using both lead and copper foil techniques. Sedona, although interested, remembered the resume, a friend Sandra Petain, the owner of

Lavender & Hops, had passed on to her several days before. Just as she recalled, it too bore some consideration. The young man, Joseph Toussaint, a recent college graduate with an art degree, portfolio consisted of highly creative pieces of stained and blown glass. According to his resume, his specialty was fused glass and glass blowing. Sedona, deciding to interview them both, picked up the phone and set up afternoon appointments.

The interviews were to take place in the same conference room that Hillary Wellborn had discovered that she no longer was, if ever, Gary's one and only. As she walked into the office, Sedona offered the coordinator a sincere smile, "Hillary, how are you?"

"Mrs. Chandler . . ."

"Tinney, I'm divorced, remember?" softly reminded Sedona. "I hoped that Gary called to let you know that I'll be interviewing for an assistant this afternoon."

"His secretary informed me right after your call," the woman replied in a tone more polite than cordial. "I've set up the conference room for you."

As Sedona followed the petite woman into the room, she surmised that she and Gary were no longer intimate. The main clue was Hillary's mention that Gary's secretary, Myra, had called to let her know of the interviews. "Hillary, I'm expecting two applicants, Brenda Berry and Joseph Toussaint. Brenda is scheduled to come in first, Mr. Toussaint about an hour later."

"Would you like for them to complete an application?"

"To be honest I hadn't thought about it," Sedona admitted. "I guess that . . ."

Hillary, more than happy to take advantage of what she considered to be a rather obvious faux pas, stepped in, "Don't worry about it, I work with you creative types all day long; I'll take care of it. Oh, by the way, has Gary mentioned how much he wants you to offer Brenda?"

"Hold up, wait a minute. I think that you're making some assumptions that you don't need to make. For one, you don't know me well enough to know what type I am. And secondly, I run my business, not Mr. Chandler."

"Excuse me," the younger woman smirked, "I only assumed that Brenda would be the one that you would hire because she's been slinking around with Gary ever since . . ."

"You and he broke up?" finished Sedona. She knew the tune line, verse and melody even before it was sung.

Hillary with a facial expression that answered Sedona's question, elaborated. "Brenda works here, but doesn't. You know, sorta like you. Gary uses her for 'special projects' and takes her on business trips. I saw the two of them together this morning, so I just put two and two together."

"Your math is probably correct." Sedona wasn't angry with the woman, couldn't be, after all, she knew Gary just as well as Hillary, better for that matter. "Listen, I appreciate what you're telling me, I really do, and I'm sorry that I snapped. The last time that I was here, I figured out that you and Gary had a relationship that was a bit more personal than business." With her mind racing, Sedona shook her head. It was no coincidence that Brenda Berry's resume stood out from the others. He intentionally fixed it that way. And to think, he almost pulled it off. *When am I going to stop being such a fool?*

Hillary, reading her mind, empathized. "Say, don't beat yourself up. Gary's smooth, he wakes up planning on how to cheat."

"Oh, you best believe that I already know that." Sedona, so fed up with all of the drama – first from Austin, now being imposed on her life by Gary, quickly made a decision. "Hillary, if you don't mind, please call Miss Berry and explain to her that I've decided to hire someone else. In order to catch her before she arrives, you probably need to reach her on her cell phone. I have her cell number here on her . . ."

"I have her number," wickedly smiled Hillary. "Brenda and I have had several long talks. This time around though, I'm looking forward to making the call."

Sedona, figuring that she would, added, "When Mr. Toussaint arrives have him fill out an application and then show him in. Unless his portfolio falls flat, he has the job."

Since she had an hour before Mr. Toussaint's arrival, she decided to pay her ex a surprise visit. Luck was on her side in that his secretary, Myra, was away from her desk. As she walked into his office, she was washed with an unsettling sense of *deja vu*. It could have been years before.

Gary, seated behind the sleek teak desk of his magazine picture perfect office, looked every bit the king of the castle. So much so, she wished to high heaven that she could have knocked him off of his black leather throne.

"Sedona, hey baby, what's up?"

"Hey baby?" she mimicked as she slammed shut the door behind her. "Don't hey baby me. I've had enough, do you hear me, enough."

The man, thoroughly surprised, stood and made his way over to the furious woman. "Calm down, you're going to make yourself sick." As he attempted to touch her, Sedona pulled away.

"Don't you touch me, don't you ever touch me again!" If her words didn't convince him, the palatable heat that emanated from her anger warned him to stay away. "To think that I trusted you, that I allowed you back into my heart. Gary, you've treated me no better than Austin."

Uncertain of what was prompting her accusation, Gary attempted to feel her out. "Sedona, I've got to tell you, I'm at a loss here. What have I done?"

With a grimace, Sedona stared him down. "I couldn't even begin to answer that question, Gary. Your crap is so deep, you probably don't even have a clue. My concern is what you would've done if I had given you the chance. Am I some kind of bizarre challenge to you? Do you figure that if you can't get me one way, then you'll get me another?"

Still totally in the dark, Gary locked onto her soft brown eyes and unconsciously murmured, "I love you." What he received as a response was far from what he expected, far from what Sedona expected for that matter. She didn't remember raising her hand, and was only aware of the fact that she had when she felt it meet the side of his face with a stinging blow.

"Don't you ever tell me that again; we don't share the same definition of the word. So just save your empty sentiments for Brenda."

It was now clear. Sedona somehow figured out his relationship with Brenda. "Listen, Sedona, Brenda doesn't mean anything to me, she's just a friend – have been for years. I just thought that if I could hook the two of you up, it would help your business out and . . ."

"Just save it, you don't give a damn about my business. You just got a kick out of the thought of sleeping with me while *fucking* Brenda. The perfect fantasy right? Like I said before, nothing about you has changed. The only difference is that you're not going to have the chance to cheat me out of happiness or my baby, not this time. The only good that you can possibly bring into my life is to keep business, business, is that clear? I am hiring an assistant this afternoon, and you will pay him as we have agreed. Gary, from this point on, we are business partners and nothing more. If you want to be a part of my life, or the baby's life, then you are going to have to earn your way back in on my terms. Do I make myself clear?"

Gary couldn't quarrel with her demands. He was wrong, he was at fault, and he knew it. "Listen, Sedona, for what it's worth, I'm sorry. I . . ."

"Save it for our trip up to St. Francisville in the morning." And with that, she was gone.

Joseph Toussaint proved to be just as promising as his resume. Sedona's first clue was the smile on Hillary's face when she announced his arrival to the interview. As with many recent college graduates, he had enthusiasm and zeal for his work. Sedona found his excitement refreshing, as well as his appearance and quiet manner. He was such an 'artist', from the black scarf he wore over his well cared for dread-locks to his pressed but comfortable denim shirt and jeans. He had earned brownie points in her book when he showed up for the inter-view wearing what she would soon discover to be his prerequisite scarf. The scarf, fashioned over his dreads in a cross between an old fashioned 'in the hood' do-rag and a high seas pirate's skull, added wonderful style to his tall ebony brown frame.

Mr. Toussaint's portfolio proved to be as equally stylish as his per-sona. Despite his age, he had a very creative and mature body of work. As they went through the film slides of his pieces, she gave him time to explain the significance of his works of art. One piece in particular, a stained glass window he titled, 'Clock Without Numbers', gave her more than a moment of pause. Toussaint based it upon Ecclesiastes 3:1-8, the familiar time for everything passage. She knew it from memory, and often thought of it during the trying periods of her life.

Joseph's unhurried voice had a healing affect on her senses. It's calm drifted her thoughts first to Gary and his antics, and then onto Austin and how they first connected while he was on deployment. As she so often thought, maybe she was meant to be in his life only for a season. On her way to convincing herself that she had overstayed her welcome in his life, Joseph commented that life had a way of playing itself out.

"You know, there is no clock with an alarm programmed to go off at a preset time. If people learned to live and enjoy life with that thought in mind, they and the world would be a much happier place."

He was so right, so undeniably right. Her only problem was a lack of patience. Austin wasn't a problem, Gary wasn't a problem, and the baby certainly wasn't a problem. There was no need to press, to obsess. If she stayed in her zone and lived and worked with passion, with zeal, life would evolve as it was meant. Good Lord, she herself had drawn out this truth in her rendering for the five panels for Lafourch church window. She had worked on them pane by pane.

"Joseph, I can tell you right now, without even viewing the rest of your portfolio, the job is yours." Without further discussion, she offered him a salary doubled what she originally had in mind and preceded to explain the working arrangement.

Without any mistake, the young man was excited by the offer. Within an hour, they worked out an arrangement where he would be able to work from his studio when possible, using the kiln on his premises. This would address the health concerns that the baby posed, as well as free Sedona's schedule in order to meet with clients and work up renderings. Sedona promised to incorporate his ideas into the pieces that they jointly crafted. Satisfied, she suggested that if he didn't have a significant other in his life, that he ask Hillary out for a celebratory dinner.

As soon as she reached her car, the cell phone rang. It was Austin.

"Sedona, you have a little time to talk?"

"Austin?"

"Um . . . Mazey called and told me about Gary's antics. I'm . . ."

"I love you."

"I love you too."

"I know."

Silence, "Listen, if I could go back in time and change things, I would."

"But you can't, and that's okay. There is no alarm clock that says time's up."

The void between them was filled in those few precious seconds. It didn't matter that he was thousands a miles away; he couldn't have felt any closer to her. He could think of nothing else better to say that could convey the depths of his feelings, his emotions. "Tinney?"

"Hmm?" she murmured quietly.

"I love you."

"I know."

Like a lark on the wing.

AUTHOR BIOGRAPHY

Born in Chicago, IL, Phyllis Hamilton received for Bachelor of Journalism at the University of Nebraska in 1983. She is a freelance writer and is associated with a Dallas, Texas area law office as a mediator. Read more about Phyllis on her website, www.phyllishamilton.com.

Other titles by Phyllis Hamilton:
Cypress Whisperings

Excerpt from

ANGEL'S PARADISE

BY JANICE ANGELIQUE

Release Date: October 2003

Ashley woke at exactly eleven, took a shower, applied moisturizer to her feet and hands then got dressed in white slacks and a red silk blouse. Sitting on the stool in front of the mirror, she applied moisturizer to her face and a thin layer of lipstick to her full, beautiful lips. She passed the comb through her hair, placed a clip to the side then decided not to wear it. She threw the clip on her dresser, passed the comb through her hair once more allowing it to frame her face. She pushed her feet into red sandals, picked up her purse and was out the door. As she reached the street, she remembered that she had not returned her sister's call. She shrugged her shoulders and wrote an imaginary note on her forehead. "Call pain in the ass when you get home."

Mr. Hastings hailed a cab for her and she was on her way to Soho to meet Robert who was waiting for her in front of the small Italian Bistro where they'd decided to have lunch. And as she got out of the cab and paid the driver, she asked. "Have you been waiting long?"

"Just a few minutes," he said, smiling as they walked into the half empty restaurant and were immediately shown to their table. The waiter took their drink order of two white wines then left them with the lunch menu.

"So, are you going to see this Evan person when you go to Jamaica?"

Ashley laughed. "Why. Are you jealous?"

He didn't answer, and she looked up from her menu and squinted.

"I just don't want anyone to hurt you, that's all."

"Robert, you know more than anyone else that I'm not romantically involved with anyone. Evan and I were once romantically involved, but that was a very long time ago, now we are just very good friends." She was silent for a minute as she remembered that she had almost married Evan until she found out that he was a womanizer. And although he promised her that he would change, she was not willing to take the risk of having him break her heart.

The waiter came back with their wine, took their lunch order for two seafood salads and left.

"I don't intend to become romantically involved with anyone for a very long time, Robert."

"I know how busy you are. We're both busy, but we still have time for a life, and as you said, you and Evan were once romantically involved, so there's no reason why he can't sweep you off your feet again."

"Robert, what's gotten into you today? I don't ever remember you being this serious about my personal life. You know Evan; you've met him. And you know me. I am not that easily swept off my feet. We're just friends. Good friends."

"Yeah, I've met him. When he was here last month, he didn't look at you as just friends."

Something was definitely bothering Robert and she wondered if their friendship was keeping him from a romantic life of his own. "You're allowing your imagination to run away with you, Rob. Maybe we need to curtail our relationship out of the office, although I would really miss our lunches and walks." She watched his reaction to her suggestion with amusement, and when he gazed into her smiling eyes and twisted his mouth in surrender, she shook her head.

"No, that's not necessary. I just feel that it's my duty to protect you from all the wolves out there." He smiled at her with dimpled cheeks, and as his brown eyes lit up, she knew everything was all right again. She loved Robert, but in no way wanted to complicate both their lives with romance. Sometimes she wondered if she really had a heart. Why didn't she want to fall in love and have children like other normal women? Maybe I'm not normal. Maybe I need to see a shrink. Then she'd recover. Nah, I'm fine.

Their salad came and they ate in silence.

At the end of the meal when the waiter brought the check to their table, Ashley reached into her bag for her wallet only to look up and see a scowl on Robert's face.

"What?" she asked.

He shook his head. "Can't you just give me this one little pleasure? This is my treat. I invited you to lunch. I'll pay for it."

She shrugged, glanced at the bill, took the tip from her purse and placed it on the table.

"You're too independent," he complained taking his American Express out of his wallet, but she just looked at him and said, "Deal with it."

2003 Publication Schedule

January	Twist of Fate	Ebony Butterfly II
	Beverly Clark	Delilah Dawson
	1-58571-084-9	1-58571-086-5
February	Fragment in the Sand	Fate
	Annetta P. Lee	Pamela Leigh Starr
	1-58571-097-0	1-58571-115-2
March	One Day At A Time	Unbreak my Heart
	Bella McFarland	Dar Tomlinson
	1-58571-099-7	1-58571-101-2
April	At Last	Brown Sugar Diaries & Other Sexy Tales
	Lisa G. Riley	Delores Bundy & Cole Riley
	1-58571-093-8	1-58571-091-1
May	Three Wishes	Acquisitions
	Seressia Glass	Kimberley White
	1-58571-092-X	1-58571-095-4
June	When Dreams A Float	Revelations
	Dorothy Elizabeth Love	Cheris F. Hodges
	1-58571-104-7	1-58571-085-7
July	The Color of Trouble	Someone To Love
	Dyanne Davis	Alicia Wiggins
	1-58571-096-2	1-58571-098-9
August	Object Of His Desire	Hart & Soul
	A. C. Arthur	Angie Daniels
	1-58571-094-6	1-58571-087-3
September	Erotic Anthology	A Lark on the Wing
	Assorted	Phyliss Hamilton
	1-58571-113-6	1-58571-105-5

October	Angel's Paradise	I'll be your Shelter
	Janice Angelique	Giselle Carmichael
	1-58571-107-1	1-58571-108-X
November	A Dangerous Obsession	Just An Affair
	J.M. Jeffries	Eugenia O'Neal
	1-58571-109-8	1-58571-111-X
December	Shades of Brown	By Design
	Denise Becker	Barbara Keaton
	1-58571-110-1	1-58571-088-1

Other Genesis Press, Inc. Titles

Gentle Yearning	Rochelle Alers	$10.95
Glory of Love	Sinclair LeBeau	$10.95
Heartbeat	Stephanie Bedwell-Grime	$8.95
Illusions	Pamela Leigh Starr	$8.95
Indiscretions	Donna Hill	$8.95
Interlude	Donna Hill	$8.95
Intimate Intentions	Angie Daniels	$8.95
Kiss or Keep	Debra Phillips	$8.95
Love Always	Mildred E. Riley	$10.95
Love Unveiled	Gloria Greene	$10.95
Love's Deception	Charlene Berry	$10.95
Mae's Promise	Melody Walcott	$8.95
Meant to Be	Jeanne Sumerix	$8.95
Midnight Clear	Leslie Esdaile	$10.95
(Anthology)	Gwynne Forster	
	Carmen Green	
	Monica Jackson	
Midnight Magic	Gwynne Forster	$8.95
Midnight Peril	Vicki Andrews	$10.95
My Buffalo Soldier	Barbara B. K. Reeves	$8.95
Naked Soul	Gwynne Forster	$8.95
No Regrets	Mildred E. Riley	$8.95
Nowhere to Run	Gay G. Gunn	$10.95
Passion	T.T. Henderson	$10.95
Past Promises	Jahmel West	$8.95
Path of Fire	T.T. Henderson	$8.95
Picture Perfect	Reon Carter	$8.95
Pride & Joi	Gay G. Gunn	$8.95
Quiet Storm	Donna Hill	$8.95
Reckless Surrender	Rochelle Alers	$8.95
Rendezvous with Fate	Jeanne Sumerix	$8.95

Rivers of the Soul	Leslie Esdaile	$8.95
Rooms of the Heart	Donna Hill	$8.95
Shades of Desire	Monica White	$8.95
Sin	Crystal Rhodes	$8.95
So Amazing	Sinclair LeBeau	$8.95
Somebody's Someone	Sinclair LeBeau	$8.95
Soul to Soul	Donna Hill	$8.95
Still Waters Run Deep	Leslie Esdaile	$8.95
Subtle Secrets	Wanda Y. Thomas	$8.95
Sweet Tomorrows	Kimberly White	$8.95
The Price of Love	Sinclair LeBeau	$8.95
The Reluctant Captive	Joyce Jackson	$8.95
The Missing Link	Charlyne Dickerson	$8.95
Tomorrow's Promise	Leslie Esdaile	$8.95
Truly Inseperable	Wanda Y. Thomas	$8.95
Unconditional Love	Alicia Wiggins	$8.95
Whispers in the Night	Dorothy Elizabeth Love	$8.95
Whispers in the Sand	LaFlorya Gauthier	$10.95
Yesterday is Gone	Beverly Clark	$8.95
Yesterday's Dreams, Tomorrow's Promises	Reon Laudat	$8.95
Your Precious Love	Sinclair LeBeau	$8.95

About Genesis Press

Founded in 1993, Genesis Press, Inc. has become the largest wholly owned African American book publisher in the United States. Striving for rare and premium quality in each and every publication, Genesis Press has received countless blessings in the form of tremendously talented authors and editors, loyal and intelligent readers, and a widespread family of supporters. Our goal continues to be bringing high quality novels to the market that encourage a positive self-image and inspire self-reflection in Black and Multi-cultural communities. We are grateful for all support and ask that you visit us online at www.genesis-press.com. Any advice, inspiration, or comment is welcome and should be e-mailed to: comments@genesis-press.com.

Grab one of our Indigo Series Novels . . .

Indigo

The Indigo imprint presents elegantly woven love stories surrounding central female characters of African-American descent. Intriguing plots intertwine with nuances of African-American culture while remaining true to the essence of traditional romance novels. Indigo brings to light the fantasy of true romance with characters of depth, intrigue and seduction. Indigo is the eldest imprint of Genesis Press. The first Indigo novel entered the market in 1995, introducing the pioneer in African-American romance series.

Indigo Love Spectrum

With the growing number of cross-cultural couples and families in the United States, Genesis Press' groundbreaking Indigo Love Spectrum imprint talks to the romantic of diverse love. This unique collection of romance novels offers a fictional look into the real life experiences and emotions of cross-cultural lovers that have been largely absent from the literary scene for years. Indigo Love Spectrum titles delicately exhibit issues facing interracial couples, while creating beautifully woven tales of love, romance, and seduction, highlighting the splendor of cross-cultural romance while straddling the boundaries of possibility within each reader, regardless of race, color or religion.

Indigo After Dark

Indigo After Dark is a line of sensuous and stimulating love stories that offer a thrilling plunge into the vibrant and mysterious world of erotica. Steamy, tantalizing narratives push the buttons from love to unbridled lust. This adult erotica imprint presents readers the ability to delve into the sensual fantasies of women beyond their hearts, while striking a soulful chord of familiarity somewhere deep within. Tasteful, fun, and artistic . . . these stirring novels make a great read for lonely moments or with a companion. Indigo After Dark is a quarterly release for the late night crowd looking to take romance to a new level of ecstasy.

Order Form

Mail to: Genesis Press, Inc.

1213 Hwy 45 N
Columbus, MS 39705

Name _____

Address _____

City/State _____ Zip _____

Telephone _____

Ship to (if different from above)

Name _____

Address _____

City/State _____ Zip _____

Telephone _____

Qty.	Author	Title	Price	Total

Use this order form, or call 1-888-INDIGO-1

Total for books	_____
Shipping and handling: $5 first two books, $1 each additional book	_____
Total S & H	_____
Total amount enclosed	_____
Mississippi residents add 7% sales tax	

Order Form

Mail to: Genesis Press, Inc.

1213 Hwy 45 N
Columbus, MS 39705

Name _____

Address _____

City/State _____ Zip _____

Telephone _____

Ship to (if different from above)

Name _____

Address _____

City/State _____ Zip _____

Telephone _____

Qty.	Author	Title	Price	Total

Use this order
form, or call
1-888-INDIGO-1

Total for books	_____
Shipping and handling: $5 first two books, $1 each additional book	_____
Total S & H	_____
Total amount enclosed	_____

Mississippi residents add 7% sales tax

Order Form

Mail to: Genesis Press, Inc.

1213 Hwy 45 N
Columbus, MS 39705

Name _____

Address _____

City/State _____ Zip _____

Telephone _____

Ship to (if different from above)

Name _____

Address _____

City/State _____ Zip _____

Telephone _____

Qty.	Author	Title	Price	Total

Use this order form, or call 1-888-INDIGO-1	Total for books _____
	Shipping and handling: $5 first two books, $1 each additional book _____
	Total S & H _____
	Total amount enclosed _____
	Mississippi residents add 7% sales tax

Order Form

Mail to: Genesis Press, Inc.

1213 Hwy 45 N
Columbus, MS 39705

Name _____

Address _____

City/State _____ Zip _____

Telephone _____

Ship to (if different from above)

Name _____

Address _____

City/State _____ Zip _____

Telephone _____

Qty.	Author	Title	Price	Total

Use this order
form, or call
1-888-INDIGO-1

Total for books _____

Shipping and handling:
$5 first two books, $1 each
additional book _____

Total S & H _____

Total amount enclosed _____

Mississippi residents add 7% sales tax